ESCAPING YESTERDAY

Nowak

GALE
CENGAGE Learning®

LIBRARY OF CONGRESS CATALOGING-IN-PUBLICATION DATA

Nowak, Pamela.
    Escaping yesterday / Pamela Nowak. — First edition.
      pages ; cm
      ISBN 978-1-4328-3104-2 (hardcover) — ISBN 1-4328-3104-6
    (hardcover) — ISBN 978-1-4328-3103-5 (ebook) — ISBN 1-4328-
    3103-8 (ebook)
      1. Single mothers—Fiction. 2. Man-woman relationships—
    Fiction. I. Title.
    PS3614.O964E83 2015
    813'.6—dc23   2015008355

First Edition. First Printing: September 2015
Find us on Facebook– https://www.facebook.com/FiveStarCengage
Visit our website– http://www.gale.cengage.com/fivestar/
Contact Five Star™ Publishing at FiveStar@cengage.com

Printed in the United States of America
1 2 3 4 5 6 7 19 18 17 16 15

ESCAPING YESTERDAY

PAMELA NOWAK

FIVE STAR
A part of Gale, Cengage Learning

GALE
CENGAGE Learning·

Farmington Hills, Mich • San Francisco • New York • Waterville, Maine
Meriden, Conn • Mason, Ohio • Chicago

For Ken . . .
my love, my life, my joy.

ACKNOWLEDGMENTS

This story has been alive in my thoughts from the first moment it took root, but it would not have made it to the page without the support of many others.

My critique group (Janet, Robin, Kay, Peggy, Steven, Denee, Thea, Carla, Jessica, and Cate) gave me much needed guidance on character depth, general craft, plot issues that helped build this story from its initial germ to all it has become. Janet and Heidi lent writing encouragement at our weekly soup days. And, my beta readers (Liz, Sharon, Janet, and Heidi) made sure everything worked in the final versions. Finally, appreciation goes to my editors: Tiffany for her constant support and Hazel for her steadfast insistence that the manuscript be improved despite my reluctance. Thank you all—you are the essence of what makes a writer successful!

I am also indebted to the staff at the Kit Carson County Carousel Museum for their research assistance, for patiently answering questions and allowing me to take endless photographs, and for the carousel ride! I also am appreciative to Rocky Mountain PBS for all the information I found in their documentary on Elitch Gardens. The Denver Public Library and the Colorado Historical Society were fountains of information, as always. I also extend appreciation to those incest/abuse and PTSD victims who were willing to share with me—I know how hard it was for you and I hope you know how valuable I found it.

Acknowledgments

My family members hold a special place in my heart for all their encouragement. Katrina and Shane (who may spot something of themselves in Lottie and Caleb) and Asher thank you for your support. Mom; Judy and Dave; Mike and Brenda; Ilka and Edgar, Luca, Enzo, and Giulio; Danika and Sergio, Kathia and Erik; Kendra and Kelly, Conner, Jacob, and Makena; Val and John, Zack and Ethan . . . you have all voiced your pride and listened to my whining. And, of course, Ken, who never ceases to amaze me in his unbridled sharing of my dreams and his willingness to help me reach them (and for reminiscing about the old Elitch Gardens and starting it all). I am blessed.

AUTHOR'S NOTE

Researching turn-of-the-century Elitch's Gardens, amusement parks, and Denver was amazing. There was such a volume of information that it was difficult to hold back from adding too much texture to this story. In the end, I did, however, manipulate some factual information to fit it into my fiction—namely combining events of 1904 and 1905 at Elitch's.

Elitch's Gardens was created by John and Mary Elitch in 1890. I have tried to represent it as true to life as possible although I did take license with the layout of the grounds and with the bear pit and feeding procedures. The gardens, the animals, the theatre, the orchestra, and the rides all existed as I have portrayed them. I regret I was unable to provide more details of their colorful history and any alterations or errors are mine.

The ostrich cart was real (though Fred's name is fictitious) as was Sam the bear (I created Gertrude as his mate). Mary's animal stock was, at one time, so unique that other zoos purchased from her. Most of the animals were later donated to the Denver Zoo. The theatre was nationally renowned for years and Broadway's Tony Award was named for actress Tony Perry, who got her start at the park.

Early rides at Elitch's included the miniature train (1895) and the Toboggan Figure Eight roller coaster (1904). Ivy Baldwin and his balloon spent several summers at the park. The carousel was actually purchased for the 1905 season, rather than 1906 as I portrayed. I chose to combine events of 1905 and 1906 in order to include Baldwin's balloon, early autos, Tony Perry, and the plausibility that Adolph Zang would have been planning White City at that time.

Changes were made to the design of the bear pit and Ivy Baldwin's balloon in order to craft fictional action around them. The real bear pit had a raised platform in the middle but it was supported by a tree trunk, which the bears climbed. Feedings were done over the side of the pit. Ivy's balloon would have been anchored by the four tether ropes and the steel cable at all times—to my knowledge, there was no winch pin.

Though I created the personalities of the real-life people in my story, I tried to remain true to what I was able to uncover in research. I so hope I was true to Mary Elitch Long—she was, from all accounts, a woman who loved children and all the aspects she included in her park. She was also straightforward and an acute businesswoman. I imagined personalities for Tom Long, Ivy Baldwin, Gustav Weiss, Charles Leopold, and Adolph Zang. There is absolutely no truth to any hint of any effort to run Elitch's Gardens out of business and no indication that competition among Denver amusement parks was ever anything except professional.

Lottie, Caleb, Elsa, Rupert, Edward, and minor characters are entirely fictional. I hope they appear real. I tried to make their inner stories as true to life as possible.

In the years after this story, Elitch's Gardens became known simply as Elitch Gardens. Tom and Mary sold the park to John Mulvihill in 1916 and Tom Long died in an automobile accident in 1920. By this time, expanded floral gardens and greenhouses had replaced the zoo enclosures. Elitch Gardens had become known for its work on hybrid roses and colored carnations and operated its own floral company for a number of years. The focus of the park shifted to amusement rides and entertainment. The famous Trocadero Ballroom was a highlight from 1917 to 1975.

Carousel Number Six was replaced in 1928. It is now known as the Kit Carson County Carousel and located in Burlington, Colorado, where it has been completely restored and is open to the public. More details on the carousel can be found at www .kitcarsoncountycarousel.com.

Mary, known for years as the "Lady of the Gardens," died in 1936. Her death left a large void at the Gardens and within the Denver community at large.

The world-famous theatre operated until 1991 and the building still stands today. It was listed on the National Register of Historic Places in 1978 and named a Denver landmark in 1995. The Historic Elitch Gardens Theatre Foundation is currently renovating the building. The foundation also maintains the 1925 Carousel Pavilion and Theatre Plaza. See the foundation website at www.historicelitchtheatre.org/about-the-theatre for more details.

The last season for Elitch Gardens at its original location was 1994. In 1995, the new Elitch Gardens opened near downtown Denver. Today's Elitch Gardens has expanded to include a water park in addition to the amusement park, theatre and music performances, and beautiful flower gardens. Further information about the park can be found at www.elitchgardens.com.

PROLOGUE

New York City, 1905

Lottie Chase slipped into the house, the moonlight barely bright enough to illuminate her path. Holding her breath, she stepped around the squeaky spot on the floorboard and eased the door closed behind her.

"Did you think I wouldn't notice?"

Lottie jumped at the bitterness in Aunt Aggie's voice. Criminy. She should have expected the old biddy to be sitting guard. She swallowed, then turned.

Aggie sat at the kitchen table, her index fingers steepled upward. "Are you letting every Tom, Dick, and Harry dip his wick or are you bedding one in particular?"

Hot stinging tears pooled at the corners of Lottie's eyes, but she'd be damned before she'd let Aggie see how much power her words had. "I wasn't—"

"Don't you dare bring any more shame on this household. If you bring another bastard into this house, I'll throw you out, like I should have years ago. After all we did for you, taking you in when your ma died, you turned on us, catting around with lord knows who."

"Hush up both of you before you wake the whole neighborhood." Uncle Edward shuffled into the room, favoring his bad leg. He set his candle stub in a wall sconce and leaned against the counter. His summer drawers rode up his tall frame, revealing he'd gained more girth over the winter. "Leave her alone,

13

Aggie. You ended up with a baby of your own to raise—like you wanted—and no one was the wiser. It isn't Lottie's fault you didn't enjoy motherhood." He drew closer, his gaze lingering on Lottie. "She was a kid . . . didn't know what a seductress she was."

His words were soft, caring, but Lottie shivered anyway. He'd said the same thing each time he'd had his way with her. Until she carried Elsa inside her and grew from adolescent to woman. Then, he'd wanted nothing more to do with her.

Wanting to flee, Lottie rooted her feet, shoved the pain away, and drew on her hatred, building a wall. Edward's sweaty white body and his groping hands, Aggie's false accusations that she'd been out whoring, the acrid taste in her mouth every time Elsa called Aggie "mother."

"Girl?" Aggie probed.

"What?" Lottie jerked her head up.

"You shoulda been home hours ago. You let some man grope you?"

"No, Aunt Aggie. I went to coffee with an old friend after we got off work." In fact, Rupert was leaving to seek his fortune. He had been trying to talk her into joining him, had offered her a partnership. She'd turned him down, unwilling to leave Elsa.

Aggie crossed her arms across her chest and faced her husband. "She ends up pregnant again and I'll turn her out. No matter what you promised her."

"You will do as I say," Edward said. "Lottie kept her mouth shut when you claimed Elsa as your own. She has a home here as long as Elsa is in this house."

Aggie muttered under her breath.

"What's all the noise about? It ain't even light yet."

Lottie turned toward Elsa's sleepy voice.

The ten-year-old padded into the room, her thin white nightgown backlit by the wall candle. Elsa's gaze sought Lottie.

The edges of her lips lifted the tiniest bit as their gazes met and she winked, the brief movement quick enough to escape Aggie's notice.

Warmth flooded Lottie and she basked in the bond she shared with her daughter, one Aggie had never been able to sever. Lottie tugged at her earlobe, her special signal that she loved Elsa back.

Elsa yawned, stretching her arms wide enough to pull the gown tight. The first hint of budding breasts drew Lottie's attention and Lottie's heart skittered. When had that happened?

"Here comes my special little girl." A broad smile crossed Edward's face. Fire lit his eyes. "Aren't you something?"

Cold hard dread cramped Lottie's gut. She'd heard those words before, too.

CHAPTER ONE

Denver, 1905

A fierce wave of protectiveness swept Lottie Chase as she watched her daughter traipse toward the ornate sandstone train depot. Once again, Lottie had done what she had to do. She glanced at Rupert Gennick, her one-time close friend, and wondered what had caused him to change so much since they'd been trusted pals. She prayed he'd wait until Elsa was out of earshot before he launched into his tirade. He'd been steaming all morning, ever since they'd missed the San Francisco–bound train and had to wait three hours at Denver's Union Station.

As soon as Elsa slipped inside the building, Rupert glared at Lottie. "I tell ya, baby doll, the kid is slowing us down. I don't see why you're so set against sending her home." He jammed his hands into his pockets.

Lottie glanced up from her bench and reined in the urge to rise and shake him. She knew that look. She'd seen it often enough on the trip. "I've already told you. Elsa is not going back to New York. Not now, not ever." Rupert's invitation to join his trip had offered her an unforeseen chance to save Elsa. Now that Elsa had grown old enough to catch Uncle Edward's eye, Lottie wasn't about to stay there and watch the old lecher prey on Elsa as he'd preyed on her. She peered at Rupert from the corner of her eye, resigned to humoring him until he calmed down. "It wasn't Elsa's fault we were late, you know."

"So you say." He kicked at a stone and watched it roll toward

17

the big iron "Welcome" arch. "You wanted the kid to see the country. She's seen it. It's time to send her home. I didn't sign on to babysit your cousin for the rest of my life. She's in the way. B'sides, you don't send her home soon, her ma's gonna have our skins."

"Nobody's going to have our skins," Lottie said with a certainty she didn't feel. She had no doubt Aunt Aggie was glad to see them gone but she imagined Uncle Edward was livid that she'd disappeared with Elsa. He'd threatened before to pursue her if she ever took the girl away.

Lottie stilled her pounding heart. They hadn't wanted her when they'd taken her in all those years ago. Aunt Aggie had claimed Elsa as her own, intrigued by having a baby to raise, until she'd discovered she wasn't maternal after all. Uncle Edward had been indifferent at first but had grown more and more possessive of Elsa in recent years. A tiny finger of apprehension snaked its way up Lottie's spine. Uncle Edward wouldn't have searched beyond New York for Elsa, would he? Lottie looked toward the depot, wishing now she had followed Elsa to the restroom.

"How're we gonna break into the big leagues with a brat in tow?" Rupert said. "I got things to do, Lottie. Soon as we get to San Francisco, I got people to see, rides to sell. I'm gonna make it big and I don't want the kid slowing things down. I have too much staked on this."

Lottie sighed, tired of this new trait of Rupert's—his constant predictions of his future success. Despite being the son of a renowned amusement ride manufacturer, he'd failed to break into the business thus far. He had big ideas but a serious lack of follow-through. She doubted a change of locale would make any difference.

She glanced at Rupert and pasted a smile onto her face. "Having a ten-year-old isn't going to affect whether or not you

make sales."

Rupert plopped onto the bench and stretched his arms along its wooden back. A slow mountain breeze drifted through the morning air, lifting his blond hair. "I don't see you paying for her tickets or her room and board," he said.

Lottie stared at him. It was the first time he'd complained about the added expense, and guilt stabbed at her. Once she realized the danger Elsa was in, Lottie had seized the chance. Granted, she'd misled Rupert about her own intentions and conned him into bringing Elsa along, but she hadn't had any other choice. Still, he'd put out his own money in good faith, and it wasn't right. "I'll get a job," she offered, "repay you for our tickets."

"We're a pair, Lottie. A team." He rubbed her shoulder with his hand and offered a lazy smile, the same one that had first drawn her to him back when they worked together at Coney Island. His voice was a mellow drawl—the bewitching tool of a master salesman. "That's how it was supposed to be when we planned this. You and me, together, schmoozing the park owners. A doll like you in on the deals and I can't go wrong."

If it were any other situation, Lottie knew she'd be tempted to be his partner, maybe even his girl. When he wanted to, Rupert could charm his way through a person's resistance faster than anything. But she had Elsa to think of. She had to keep her daughter safe, no matter what. "Elsa stays," she said. Her gaze again shifted to the depot.

Rupert's fingers drifted to her neck, the massage now a caress. "And night after night, you share her room instead of mine."

Lottie started, goose bumps rising on her skin. She'd been afraid it would come to this. She'd flirted with him a little, let him kiss her a couple times and allowed him to believe they might become more than friends, but it had been an act. However promiscuous Aunt Aggie accused her of being, she'd never been with anyone . . . except Edward. She shied away, turning her body to the side. "Is that what this is all about? You think that it's only Elsa keeping me out of your bed?"

"You're the one who agreed to board the train without a chaperone and come West with me." His teeth flashed, brilliant in the June sun, and an all-too-familiar glint sparkled in his malachite eyes. "Add in the kisses and the message was pretty clear."

Damn those ill-conceived kisses. They had convinced Rupert to bring Elsa but she'd never offered intimacy and she didn't plan to. The goose bumps turned into a cold, clammy sweat. Uncle Edward used to look at her the same way. Panic rushed through her. Not again. Not ever. She lurched to her feet and glared at him. "Yeah, well, it worked, didn't it?" she blurted.

"Worked?"

She shrugged her shoulders, only now digesting the implications of her hasty words. She affected nonchalance as her mind scrambled to put together some sort of plan. "You brought us along."

"You suckered me?" Still sitting, Rupert leaned forward and shook his head.

Elsa emerged from the far door of the depot, and Lottie let out the breath she hadn't realized she'd been holding. "I had no choice," she said, her gaze on Elsa.

"Well, I do," Rupert said, rising. He spun Lottie around until she faced him. Fear sliced through her at the angry set of his mouth. "I got several choices. Being suckered isn't one of them. It's time we got on with what you've been promising, Lottie, whether you meant it when we left New York or not." His grip softened, but the glint in his eyes remained. "I'm crazy about you. But I'm tired of your games and the stories you can't keep straight. No more babysitting your cousin. Send her home and let's quit pussyfooting around."

Lottie drew a breath and met Rupert's stare. "She's my daughter, damn it, and I'm not sending her anywhere."

Shock replaced the lust in his eyes and his hand dropped away. "Fine, baby doll. Have it your way. From here on out, you're on your own."

Lottie stared at the purse she'd removed from her trunk and swallowed the bitter taste in her mouth, hiding her rising panic from Elsa. The purse was empty. After Rupert had Lottie's trunk pulled from the baggage room, he'd left her and Elsa to fend for themselves. She'd expected nothing less. What she hadn't expected was to discover the rat had broken into the trunk and filched her stash of money.

"Lottie?" Elsa asked from her seat on the bench. "What are we gonna do now?" Her azure eyes, so like Lottie's own, flickered, bright with threatening tears.

Her stomach rock hard, Lottie closed the trunk and plunked down next to Elsa, responsibility weighing heavy on her. "We're going to find a job."

"In Denver?"

"Yes, pet." Lottie ignored the doubt in Elsa's voice and drew her close. She knew little about the city, other than it was home to Elitch's Gardens. The owner, Mary Elitch Long, had visited Coney Island several times. Her zoological park and botanic garden was one of the country's newest amusement parks. It was testament to Rupert's cockiness that he'd centered his attention on San Francisco, overlooking Elitch's growing reputation and considering Denver's amusement parks too small to be bothered with. A good salesman should always know his marks.

There was another park in Denver, Manhattan Beach, but Lottie guessed Elitch's Gardens would be her best prospect. She'd stand a better chance of being hired by a female owner and it was an environment she knew well. And, if Uncle Edward did pursue her, he wasn't likely to know about the small park.

Releasing Elsa from the hug, she stood and looked toward the street. "Let's be on our way," she told her. Spying a porter, she waved him over and inquired about the park's location.

"Northwest of town, ma'am, out in the Highlands area." He glanced at the trunk. "I could hire you a coach, if you want. Otherwise, you can catch the Denver Tramway." He pointed to Sixteenth Street. "That route takes you over the Platte River where you'll connect to the Berkeley-Elitch's loop. It'll take you right to the gate at Thirty-eighth and Tennyson."

Lottie thanked him and dug through her pocket. Pulling out her few remaining coins, she counted them and sighed. "Looks like it's the tramway for us." She nodded to Elsa. "Are you ready?"

Elsa stared at the trunk and swung her feet back and forth under the bench. "We're taking that on a tram?"

Lottie held back a sigh. Elsa had never known her as anything but an older cousin and her attitude was less than respectful on occasion. At some point, she'd need to tell her the truth. But for now, there were enough changes in her young life.

"I don't have enough money for a coach, pet," she said, keeping her voice light. "All we need to do is drag it to the corner over there."

Elsa rolled her eyes and stood. "If you say so."

Lottie gripped the leather handle of the steamer trunk, tilted the monstrosity on its edge, and tugged. The metal edging grated against the stony ground and Lottie winced. The heavy trunk stalled, and she pulled harder.

"I don't think you're going to get very far," Elsa noted.

"Maybe we'd get farther if we were both pulling."

Elsa scrunched her face in dissatisfaction, then grasped the handle and tugged. "Ouch."

"Could we try pulling at the same time?" Lottie said in tired frustration.

Elsa dropped the handle. "I don't want to. It's heavy. This trip isn't fun anymore. Let's just get back on the train and go home."

Lottie set the trunk back on its end. "Elsa, pet, I'm sorry. I didn't mean to be grouchy." She crouched in front of her usually cooperative daughter and caught her gaze. "The truth is we have no choice. Rupert stole my money. We can't afford tickets home, not until I earn more." A stab of guilt poked at her for lying, but this wasn't the time or the place to reveal the truth. She'd get a job first, then tell Elsa they were never going back. "If I'm going to find a job, we have to get on that tramway."

"Can't we leave the trunk and send someone back for it later?"

"I don't have enough money to put it in storage, and we can't just leave it on the street. We don't have a choice, Elsa, and I need your help."

Elsa bit her lip, then nodded.

They grasped the handle, tipped the trunk, and pulled. They crunched across the gravel toward the far corner of the block, inching their way through the downtown crowd, pedestrians parting for them as if they were trained elephants. The only offers of assistance were shouted by drivers of horse-drawn cabs intent on overcharging them.

By the time they reached the corner, Lottie could feel the sweat dripping from her brow. Beside her, Elsa wore a sullen expression.

The rail lines ran through the center of the dirt street. Between the iron tracks lay a third rail, which carried the tramway's electric current. Lottie watched the wooden car approach. The paint on the lower half of the car had faded but the wood above it had been polished, as had the plow-like metal apparatus attached to its front. The car slowed as they tugged the trunk into the street. The driver stared at them from the center window.

He loaded the trunk amid much grumbling as Elsa stomped aboard and plunked onto a wooden bench. She slouched, arms akimbo. Lottie paid the fare and settled next to Elsa. The inside of the car was hot and airless, despite the lowered windows, and she could hear the muttered frustrations of other passengers as they commented on the delay caused by the trunk.

The situation repeated at the transfer point, but the ride quieted as they traveled northwest. Passengers disembarked along the way. As the tram neared the park, they were the only ones remaining. Lottie dabbed at the sweat on her brow, ruing the loss of the breeze that had cooled them in front of the station.

"I'm tired," Elsa said, her feet kicking against the wooden side of the rail car with each swing of her legs.

"We both are." Lottie heard the frustration in her own voice and wished she could bite it back. She reached for Elsa and squeezed her shoulder. They were nearing the end of the line. "We're almost there," she said.

"Elitch's," the driver announced as the vehicle slowed to a stop. He grabbed the trunk and tugged it toward the steps, then moved around it and hoisted it off the car. It landed with a thud in a cloud of dirt. "Good thing it wasn't crowded, miss. Don't bet on me being able to lug that thing back downtown. Once the gardens close, I'll be too full."

Lottie pulled out two of her last precious coins and tipped the man, then watched him pull away. She and Elsa stood at the empty side of the road as Lottie told herself not to worry. If she projected an air of confidence, she could convince whatever employees she encountered that she had an appointment with Mrs. Long. Then, she'd persuade Mary Long to hire her. It was all a matter of how she presented herself.

Elsa blew a sigh and turned to Lottie, her arms crossed again. "Now what?" she asked.

"Now, I find myself a job." Lottie gazed at Elsa and smiled, as if doing so would make it happen.

"Who the heck is that?" Old Man Farnum asked Caleb as he pointed toward the front gate.

Caleb Hudson glanced up to find the most vibrant woman he'd ever seen, dust and all, a rose amid wilted foliage, her confident stance projecting life and energy despite her bedraggled trappings. His chest tightened. Like a misplaced cutting, she stood across from the park entrance with a battered steamer trunk and a ragtag kid who looked none too happy to be there.

"I'll check," Caleb said but, as usual, the inept old animal tender was already shuffling away, his attention elsewhere. Caleb's curiosity was piqued. Women who looked like that didn't just crop up like weeds. She had to be lost, all the way out here in the sticks with a trunk. He grinned and strode through the arch of the wooden building that served as the gate to Elitch's Gardens, then crossed the road until a couple feet away from the pair.

"We came for the job." The kid made the announcement, then waited, as if he was supposed to know how to respond to it.

"What job?" he finally asked. Though the park hired summer help—local youth—to run the ticket counter and the rides, all the positions were filled.

The kid looked at him like it was obvious, stubbornness written all over her face. She exhaled and blew her bangs upward. A handful, no doubt about it.

Caleb shifted and glanced at the tawny-haired woman,

25

wondering if she would take the child to task.

Her limp hair hung like corn silk, strands escaping from what once might have been a stylish Gibson Girl hairdo. Her sweat-stained travel suit hugged a trim figure—one that raised Caleb's pulse despite the soiled clothing. She waved a worn hat in a fruitless attempt to create a breeze. "The job Mary Long promised me," she said.

"Here?" Caleb stared at her. The woman had to be confused. Elitch's was an amusement park, not a secretarial pool or downtown shop.

"Yes, here." Exasperation filled her voice, giving it an edge of disdain.

His shock settled, and he digested her words, doubt creeping up his spine. He'd filled the role of unofficial foreman for years and was always informed of any changes. Elitch's had a full staff, and Mary hadn't said a word about adding anyone. "Ma'am?"

The woman stared at him with morning glory eyes, wide and round and startling. Eyelashes wispy as fountain grass swept down, then back up. She drew a breath. "You do work here?"

"Yeah." Caleb drew his own breath and eyed the kid. She looked about ten or so, a younger version of the woman, and appeared tired as all get-out. Tired and hot and not at all happy. A kid in need of attention. Mary would be fussing over her in no time.

The woman tugged on his sleeve. "Well. Then. Perhaps you could direct me to Mrs. Long, Mr. . . . ?"

"Hudson. Caleb Hudson. The gardener." He left it at that.

"Ah, the gardener." She reacted as he expected, placing him in a subordinate role. He didn't bother to correct her. Few folks knew Mary Long had mothered him for more years than his own had or that he'd been her right-hand man from the time John Elitch had died and left her alone with the fledgling park.

26

He'd play along, see what the woman was up to.

The kid slid to the ground, her back against the trunk, and sighed.

Caleb glanced at the woman, wondering what was filling her head to drag a kid and a trunk all the way out on the tramway line. Then again, if she intended to scam Mary in some way, she might have brought the kid along on purpose. It was no secret that Mary loved children. He eyed the woman again.

"Season's well under way, Miss. All the jobs are filled. There's nothing here for you and your . . . sister?"

"I'm Charlotte Chase. Lottie." She extended a long slim hand. "And this is Elsa, my . . . cousin."

The slight pause made him even more nervous. Something wasn't right and even though Mary was astute, kids were her weakness. She'd taken him in, after all. He needed to divert this Lottie Chase before she wiggled her way into the park.

"There'll be another tram along in about an hour. You can catch a ride back to town, then." He paused and nodded toward Elsa. "I could maybe fetch you some lemonade, while you wait."

Lottie's lustrous eyes widened and she laughed, a light airy sound, and Caleb's skin tingled. "Oh, but we're not waiting," she said. "If you could take us to see Mary Long, I'm sure everything will be squared away. Elsa, stand up now, so the man can bring the trunk."

"You want me to haul that trunk in?" He stared at the two-by-four-foot behemoth as Elsa rose. "Best if you wait here. We're just going to have to haul it right back out."

"Oh, but we won't." She gave him a wide smile. "We're not leaving." Then she turned and marched across the road, the youngster following.

Caleb jogged a few steps after them, remembered the trunk, and uttered a silent curse as he returned to it. He ought to just leave the thing where it was, but it wouldn't be responsible.

Besides, Mary would have his head if he did.

What kind of woman showed up at an amusement park with a kid and a trunk, trying to bluff her way into a job? He shook his head. She strode toward the park entrance, the purpose in her step adding just enough sway to catch his attention. Damn, she was a looker. But quick. Already, she was under the wooden gate, charming her way straight past the teenage gateman. Caleb's gut told him she was smarter than she appeared. She'd bear watching, that one.

He grabbed the trunk handle and dragged the blasted thing across the road and through the gate, dropping it behind the gateman's counter. The woman and the girl were well into the park.

Lottie stood with Elsa, her face animated as she pointed out the attractions announced on the signage. Elsa's moodiness dissolved, and her eyes grew round as she noted the bear pit and the lions, and the miniature train.

"And there's a roller coaster," Lottie's own eyes were full of excitement.

"Oh, Lottie! Look!" Elsa turned in the direction of the arrow pointed toward an octagonal brown and white building. "They have a theatre."

Caleb approached, shaking his head. Their fascination seemed genuine enough. Maybe his suspicions weren't so well grounded after all. If they had ulterior motives, why would they be so entranced by the park?

"You know," he said to Elsa, "Frederick Perry and his daughter, Antoinette, are appearing this summer. She's eleven."

"Truly?" Elsa said. "I'm ten."

"I thought you were about that age. Maybe you'll have time to look inside later and meet Tony, after the matinee."

It was funny, how much alike folks were. The little ones flocked to the miniature train. The teens eyed the roller coaster.

Adults, and some of the kids Elsa's age, raved about the theatre. Old folks headed for the trees and the picnic grounds and everyone liked the zoo animals.

Few mentioned the gardens anymore. When John and Mary Elitch bought the sixteen-acre farm back in 1888, it was the apple and cherry orchards that had drawn the couple. Two years later, they'd added flower gardens, pathways, and a few animals, deciding to open the gardens to the public.

Caleb glanced at the wide tree-lined paths and envisioned more sculpted flower beds on either side. Mary had grown the park, adding a world-class theatre and a few rides. They'd taken Caleb in, and he had tended John's gardens, even after John died and Mary had remarried, but there was potential for so much more. Caleb had found peace here. There weren't many quiet refuges left in the growing city, and other folks needed them as much as he did, whether they knew it or not.

Once he followed through with his plans, folks would appreciate the flowers and the quiet gardens as much as the other attractions. Their reverent whispers about the floral sanctuary would echo as loudly as the laughter, applause, and wild shrieks.

"Excuse me?" Lottie was saying next to him.

He jerked his attention back to the woman, disappointed that he'd allowed his mind to wander.

"I said, where would I find Mary Long?"

Caleb tilted his head. He reckoned Mary'd be feeding the bears right about now. He debated taking Lottie to Mary's husband, Tom Long, instead, but Tom was apt to be in the back of the theatre, catching the end of the matinee. He didn't know which leading actress was on stage this afternoon but, either way, Tom was certain to be sitting in. He'd take her to Mary, but if she so much as tried anything funny, he'd escort her out of the park himself.

"Mary's most likely in the zoo area." He strode in the direction of the animals, leaving the Chase girls to follow him this time.

He took them past the miniature train and the turnoff for the roller coaster, penned lions and monkeys, noisy seals, a lazy elephant, and a round pit with two black bears. The discordant smells of wild animals lingered in the air, scents mingling as they passed from one enclosure to the next. Ahead of them, a group had gathered. Children's laughter rang out, drifting in the thin mountain air.

"Looks like we missed the feeding but Mary's up ahead, with the ostrich. She'll take a little spin, then you can meet with her." Caleb led them through the crowd and stopped in front of a light four-wheeled carriage. Mary Elitch Long sat solo in the small seat, holding reins that were attached to a harnessed ostrich. She tapped one of them and the animal trotted down the gravel path.

Elsa's mouth dropped open, and she glanced at her cousin.

Lottie smiled, her eyes dancing. "Thank you," she mouthed to Caleb and warm satisfaction crept through him.

His gaze drifted to her lips. They were fuller than he'd anticipated, lush as cultivated roses. His body tightened, and he shifted.

Elsa watched the ostrich cart with avid fascination, enchanted. Caleb shook his head. It was too bad her cousin would have to haul her all the way back downtown in less than an hour. It wouldn't take long for Mary to call her bluff and send them on their way.

"Mr. Hudson? What kind of job do you think Mrs. Long will have for me?" For the first time, doubt shadowed Lottie's eyes.

Caleb smiled at her and decided to play along. "I don't know. Season's more than half over, Miss Chase, and Mary's already hired on everyone she needs. What are your skills?"

She batted her grassy-lashed eyes, and the doubt seemed to

melt away. "I can swindle boys trying to knock over pins with a baseball out of two-bits at a time, and I can hawk sideshow attractions. I can sell spun sugar to kids who swear they can't eat another bite and entice them to spend their last pennies trying to toss rings around bottles." Seduction filled her voice, and Caleb swallowed, hard. "I can talk grown men into making fools of themselves to win a prize and impress me. I can pump up a crowd and talk them into one more ride, even if they're dead tired." She paused. "And I can scream louder than anyone else on a roller coaster."

Caleb stared at her, his opinion of her plummeting despite his rising pulse rate. A screaming, sugarcoated huckster! She was just what he'd suspected and he'd been right to distrust her.

CHAPTER TWO

Lottie's face grew hot. How stupid she'd sounded! Skills, indeed. Caleb Hudson must think her half-insane and a tart to boot. Men as attractive and assured as he were not easily fooled. She flashed him a self-confident smile that belied her churning stomach. Her flushed cheeks would be seen as flirtatious rather than embarrassed but it was too late. Whatever she said at this point would come across as manipulative. She could see the judgment in his etched face.

Elsa pulled at her sleeve, her keen eyes filled with awe. "Can you believe it, Lottie? An ostrich pulling a cart?"

Lottie squeezed her small shoulder, thankful Elsa hadn't heard her blunder. "It's something, huh?" She glanced across the oval pathway as Mary Long slowed the gangling bird to a halt. She'd have to watch herself, now that she had Elsa depending on her. For too many years, she'd relied on acting a flirt in order to earn her way. All she'd had to do was find the easy marks and pour on the charm. She cringed as she realized she pretty much was a tart. Or at least she had been. Now that Elsa was with her, she'd need to reform and be responsible.

The problem was flirting and manipulation were her only skills.

She watched Mary Long unhitch the ostrich from the light harness that encased its body. The small crowd drifted away toward other attractions until only a few curious onlookers remained. Elitch's was small, nothing like Coney Island's multiple parks, where Lottie had spent most of her time over the past ten years. The place was quieter, less rough-and-tumble than Coney Island. A quick survey revealed few of the carnival games she'd helped run and no sideshows to lure people into.

Darn, she wished she'd been observant enough to have noticed this before reciting her swaggering list of skills. She wouldn't make her way as a huckster here; that was for sure. But the park had potential. She had seen it in the eyes of the children as they rode the miniature train and in the eager expressions on teenagers' faces as they rushed toward the roller coaster.

What was it Rupert had said? With the break they could get from his father, selling several of the new amusement rides could earn them enough commission to live for a year. Maybe it was just as well he'd gone on without her. She could sell a ride with the same ease as he could, couldn't she? Once she secured a job, she'd talk to the owners about their future intentions. If she could broker a sale, she and Elsa could survive a few months without worries. But first, she needed to convince Mary Long to hire her.

Elsa tugged on her arm. "Can I go see the ostrich? Up close?"

Lottie smiled at her daughter, her chest tightening. She'd shared so little with Elsa. Aunt Aggie had fulfilled her duty, taking eight-year-old Lottie in when her mother died but had never mothered her, especially after Uncle Edward had begun paying attention to her. The couple had claimed Elsa as their own, commanding Lottie to earn her keep. It was the only way Aunt Aggie would allow trash like her to live in the house. It hadn't mattered that she wasn't what Aggie said—Aggie believed what she wanted, and no one had cared much how she earned the money—only that she contributed and kept out of the way, that she stayed away from Elsa.

She shook off the memories, hating how worthless she'd felt

all these years, and turned her attention to Mary Long. Caleb and Elsa had already made their way over to the middle-aged woman, and Elsa was petting the exotic bird under Mary's tutelage. The bird's tufted head rested on Mary's shoulder, its fine feathers standing up like freshly toweled baby hair. As Lottie approached, Mary said something to the bird and it lowered its head to Elsa's level. Elsa giggled and ran her hand over its downy head while the animal emitted a low satisfied moan that sounded almost like a cow mooing.

"Mrs. Long?" Lottie said, ignoring Caleb.

He stood beside Mary, his critical eyes assessing her. She ignored him, no matter how easy on the eyes the man was, and concentrated on landing a job.

"Yes." The woman hung the harness on a hook inside a small shed, then extended her hand. "I'm Mary Elitch Long."

"Charlotte Chase . . . Lottie. And this is my cousin, Elsa." Elsa nodded and continued to pet the bird. Lottie shook Mary's hand, noting its strength, and projected as much self-confidence as she could muster. "We've just arrived in Denver, and I'm looking for a job."

"So Caleb tells me." Mary turned to the gardener, firm determination gracing her features. "I'll handle this, Caleb. Tell Farnum to finish the feedings."

Caleb glanced at Lottie, his lips pursed together.

A chill went up Lottie's spine.

"If you don't mind, Mary, I'll stay here for a while," he said, his boldness surprising Lottie.

Mary considered Caleb, then tipped her head. "I do mind. We'll discuss it later."

Caleb flashed Lottie a wary look before striding away from them.

Mary, on the other hand, eyed Lottie with frank appraisal. "You'll forgive my surprise," she said. "Elitch's attracts very few job seekers. We are a bit out of the way."

Lottie nodded, recalling the five-mile trip from downtown, and straightened her posture. "Yes, you are. But, you're also very well known."

Mary positioned the cart behind the shed, talking as she worked. "So you were aware of the business before you made your way here? What draws two young ladies to a zoological garden and amusement park?"

"Previous experience. I worked at Coney Island."

"In New York?" Mary stopped and eyed Lottie again, this time with a little more interest.

Lottie's mouth stretched into a confident smile. She'd caught Mary's attention, at least. "Yes, ma'am. At several of the parks, over the past ten years."

Mary placed a wooden block behind the rear wheel of the cart before closing the door to the shed. "And you decided to come west?" She turned to Lottie and raised her eyebrows. "To Elitch's Gardens?"

Lottie debated her answer, knowing some explanation was needed. She didn't know the woman, and she couldn't tell her the whole truth with Elsa standing just a few feet away. "We were in a bad spot," she said, pride spurring her to continue. "I had an opportunity to get us out. It didn't work as planned, and we're stranded in Denver." She brushed her lavender travel suit and stood tall, formulating her sales pitch without a second thought. "Elitch's has a reputation, Mrs. Long. I have experience. Once here, it didn't take much deduction to know this was the best option for us."

Mary crossed her arms and assessed Lottie. "What kind of experience?" She glanced at Elsa and the ostrich. "Have you worked with animals before?"

Lottie drew a breath. She'd already noted the lack of carnival games and sideshows. Telling Mary she was a good huckster wasn't going to get her anywhere and Caleb had told her all the jobs were full. If there was an opening, she couldn't afford to lose the chance at it. She had helped feed the elephants a time or two, when the trainer's scantily clad assistant had been ill. It was mostly showmanship rather than animal care but it wouldn't be an out and out lie.

"Yes," she said, reasoning she'd learn if Mary gave her a job.

Mary smiled. "Well, you've caught my attention. Let's get Fred settled and we'll talk about it further." Mary turned and started down a dirt path. "Bring him along," she said over her shoulder. "Let's see how you do with him."

Lottie glanced at the big bird and wondered how in the world she was going to coax him to follow Mary. He stood next to Elsa, nuzzling her neck as the girl beamed. Lottie tilted her head toward Mary and said, "Come on, Fred."

Fred refused to move and made another mooing sound.

Lottie stared at him and pushed away the bothersome little voice that told her she wasn't good enough to do even a simple task like getting an ostrich to move. "Come on, boy. Let's go with Mary."

He lifted his head and stared at her with woeful eyes. Elsa grinned.

"He might need some herding," Mary called from twenty feet away, her brows lifted in playful challenge. Then, her eyes lit on Elsa, and her mouth lifted into a smile. "Come along, Elsa. You can walk with me and tell me all about your trip. Let's leave your cousin and Fred to follow."

Lottie squashed back a groan as Elsa scampered over to Mary. She had no idea what Elsa would reveal to Mary, but she couldn't run after them, not when Mary had tasked her to herd Fred. Herding? How the dickens did one herd an ostrich?

Goodness, she told herself, she'd dealt with manipulating men every day for years. It couldn't be that hard to make an ostrich do what she wanted. The elephant trainer at Coney Island had simply patted the animals on the rump. It shouldn't be that much different.

Lottie shrugged and swatted the bird's feathery body.

Fred made a startled "woo" sound as his coffee-brown eyes widened. He trotted forward, his head shifting from side to side with a jerk. Then, like a giant chicken, he was off, bobbing his way forward before suddenly lifting his wings and swerving to the side in aimless reaction to whatever seemed to catch his attention. He strutted down a sculpted garden path that bordered the picnic grounds. Lottie shook her head and started after him.

With each long step, Fred's legs pumped harder, his two-toed feet pointing forward. His brown and white tail feathers lifted upward with each movement, teasing Lottie. Every few steps, his throat vibrated with a deep, bass three-syllable wooing sound. Along the path, strolling picnickers gasped as they scrambled to get out of his way—their jerking responses serving only to frighten Fred further. Children stared, then doubled over with laughter.

Lottie, losing ground behind the ungainly ostrich, was not amused. Sweat ran down her face. Breathless, she gritted her teeth, hiked her skirts, and trailed after the spindle-legged bird. A group of boys linked arms in front of Fred, chaining across the path and slowing him. Lottie neared and dove for the ostrich just as Fred screeched and swerved, his large feet tearing through sculpted flower beds. Petunia petals flew upward, filling the air with pink confetti. Alyssum buds scattered like snowflakes as Fred zigzagged onward, dirt flying behind him, and Lottie landed face down in a bed of bright blue lobelia.

She rose onto her knees, sputtering. Her chest heaved and sweat dripped off her chin. Laughter rose behind her, and she had no doubt the picnickers were having quite the time. Oh, Lord, she hoped Mary Long couldn't see her. She spit out a small green leaf, and pushed herself back until she was kneeling. Where was the damn bird?

She glanced around and spied him. He was stilled at the far edge of the picnic grounds, between rows of empty wooden tables, nibbling up scraps from the ground as he stared at her from the corners of his eyes.

"It's about time you stopped, you overgrown turkey." She stood and smoothed her skirts, then stalked forward.

Fred continued to eye her and uttered another set of resonating woo sounds.

Panting, she strode toward him. She wasn't sure if birds could read expressions or not but if they could, Fred would have no problem understanding she was not happy. In fact, she was downright incensed. "You no good buzzard," she muttered under her breath. "By the time I get ahold of you, you're gonna wish—"

Fred's spindly leg flew out, grazing Lottie's hip. The force knocked her to the ground. She landed on her rear, pain coursing through her, a long gash ruining her once-smart traveling suit. Stunned, she stared at the tear, then at Fred, still picking away at the ground.

"Are you all right? Are you hurt?" Caleb Hudson jogged toward her from behind a nearby shed.

She shook her head, still dazed. She doubted she was about to get a job as an ostrich herder. Her eyes stung with embarrassment.

Caleb hunkered down in front of her. "Miss Chase?"

"I'm all right," she mumbled, staring at Fred as her animosity churned. She bit it back and tried to make her tone light. She didn't want or need his pity. "My dress will never be the same, though, thanks to that monster."

"You're lucky he didn't kick you straight on. You could have been seriously hurt." Caleb helped her to her feet, his initial concern shifting until he was staring at her as if she was insane. "What were you doing?"

What the heck did he think she was doing? "Herding him for Mrs. Long," she said with an over-bright tone, batting her eyelashes for good measure.

Caleb's jaw dropped. "Herding him?"

"She said to bring him along. I just gave him a little pat on the rump and he took off."

"And you chased him?" Caleb shook his head and stalked over to the shed. Moments later, he returned with a rope in hand and approached Fred, murmuring as he extended his other hand. Fred lifted his head, sniffed, and trotted forward to investigate what Caleb offered him. Caleb eased a loose rope around Fred's neck and led him back to Lottie. "You don't chase ostriches. You put grain in your hand and lure them."

"You do?"

"Yes, you do. Use a rope if they get balky. And if they start booming instead of lowing, you leave them alone."

"Booming? Lowing?"

"Lowing—the cow sound—is what they do when they're content. Booming—the woo, woo, wooooooo—is a warning. You're not telling me you didn't notice the difference?"

"I noticed. I just don't speak ostrich."

Caleb shook his head as he opened his hand and let Fred take another nibble, then turned and began walking down the now deserted path. "That's all it takes, then put the rope on and lead him—" He stopped and glanced back at the damage Lottie and the ostrich had carved. "Hell! You ran that bird through my gardens."

"I didn't run that bird anywhere, Mr. Hudson," she said as she caught up to him. "He ran of his own accord, thank you very much. I merely ran after him."

"You destroyed them. Three flower beds!"

Lottie followed his gaze. The sculpted beds were a mess, endless bare patches where plants had been uprooted and scattered like snowflakes. The bitter taste of incompetence rose in her throat. "They're just flowers," she ventured, determined to counter the self-recrimination before it took hold. "They'll grow back."

"They're ruined." Caleb stalked to the edge of the bedding area. "For the rest of the season. It looks like a herd of sheep wound its way through there. It's a park, Miss Chase. It's supposed to be peaceful and well-ordered. What were you thinking?"

"I wasn't. I was rounding up an ostrich." Leave it to a gardener to fuss over a few flowers. Still, the sculptured gardens did make the grounds more inviting. It would take a lot of work to replace them. Guilt tightened her chest. She stood behind him, again unsure. "I'm sorry."

He shrugged but didn't turn around.

"I could help you plant more," she offered.

"Don't bother. I'll do it myself." Silence stretched, then he turned back toward her. "It was an accident." He didn't sound convinced, but Lottie guessed it was as close as he'd get to accepting her apology.

She offered a wavering smile. "All right, then. I guess I should find Elsa and talk to Mary about that job she promised me."

Caleb stared at her, his eyes narrowing. "You can't possibly be serious," he said. "You expect Mary to give you a job after you've managed to scare Fred to death, ruin a whole section of public gardens, and almost get yourself killed?"

A sudden flash of Mary and Caleb in deep conversation, about her, filled Lottie's mind. She turned toward the path. She had to speak to Mary first.

"Oh, no, you don't," Caleb said, as if reading her mind. He grabbed her hand and led her to the nearest bench, towing Fred along with them. "I don't trust you." He pulled his hand downward until she sat. "I'm taking Fred to his pen. Then, we'll go see Mary. Together."

He glared at her. "You just sit right here and wait for me."

Lottie waited until Caleb and Fred were out of sight, then stood and hurried down the path. If that infuriating man thought for one minute that she was about to sit there and wait, he had another think coming. The way he'd glowered at her, she wouldn't put it past him to hightail it straight to Mary and tattle. If she and Elsa were to survive, Lottie needed to find Mary and offer her own version of events before Caleb did more damage than she could undo.

Her best option was to head back the way she'd come. Someone along the way would know how to find Mrs. Long.

As she marched along the worn route, she took note of the flower beds. Caleb had been right—they were devastated. Winding trails disrupted his meticulous patterns. A second wave of guilt rose, along with memories of Aunt Aggie's constant complaints of Lottie's worthlessness.

Then thoughts of Uncle Edward exploded in her head, nauseating her. A cold sweat crawled across her skin and the urge to flee threatened to consume her. The roller coaster beckoned. In minutes, she could be whipping around turns and sailing over rises, screaming as if nothing mattered but the moment and its exhilarating freedom. Coasters had been her escape ever since he'd begun to prey on her. And after, as she'd fled the pain of losing Elsa to Aggie.

For ten years, Lottie had battled guilt and loss. When it hurt too much to bear, she had spent more time at Coney Island, riding one thrill ride after another, working there so she wouldn't have to bear the pain of being shut out of her daughter's life. But now wasn't the time for escape. This time, she had a chance to save Elsa and be her mother. She wasn't about to relinquish the opportunity.

Lottie swallowed and gathered her bearings. She'd passed the picnic grounds, now all but deserted despite the lingering scents of fried chicken and apple pie that made her stomach growl. Ahead, people were grouping together, moving toward the exit. It was closing time. If she didn't convince Mary to hire her soon, she and Elsa would be out the gate, too, and she couldn't let that happen.

Hustling forward, she spied an older man picking up trash and asked where to find Mary Long. He directed her down another path, to a small gray bungalow. She approached, assumed a self-confident air, and knocked on the door.

Mary answered, a wide smile on her face. Behind her, in the parlor, Elsa sat on the floor. Kittens crawled over her lap.

"You've found us," Mary said, holding open the screen door. "Come on in. Elsa and I have been having such fun while we waited for you."

Lottie entered, strategizing. There was no way to avoid a discussion of her failure to "herd" Fred and the ruined flower beds. She'd need to confess that, straightaway, before Caleb arrived. Lottie took a seat in a pretty pink floral wing chair and waited, unsure of how to start.

Mary sat in the opposite chair, behind Elsa, whispering something in Elsa's ear as she did so.

Elsa beamed, then rose and walked toward the open kitchen doorway, kittens trailing after her.

Mary gazed after Elsa with tenderness, then looked at Lottie, clasping her hands on her lap. "So, tell me about Fred. How did you do?"

Lottie's smile wavered. "Not as well as I'd hoped," she said. "Ostriches behave a bit differently than elephants."

Mary laughed. "I suspect they do."

"I made an assumption, Mrs. Long, and it didn't pan out. Fred didn't respond as expected when I patted him on the rump."

"Oh, no! You didn't?" Mary interrupted. She leaned forward, her eyes twinkling. "He took off, didn't he?"

Lottie plunged ahead. "I made the mistake of chasing him. By the time he slowed, we were at the back of the park. We . . . uh . . . we also ruined three flower beds."

Mary sobered. "Fred's all right?"

Lottie nodded. "He's calm and locked in his pen, thanks to Caleb." Her thoughts flashed to the gardener with his whiskey-colored eyes and his strongman chest, and his anger. "I'll help him repair the damage."

"We'll see. Caleb's a solitary soul." Mary sat back in her chair and assessed Lottie. Her perusal took in Lottie's rumpled dress and ruined hat while Lottie fought the urge to defend herself. After a moment, her eyes stilled, locking gazes with Lottie.

"Ma'am?" Lottie offered.

"You don't have quite the experience you indicated, do you?" Mary asked, her voice quiet despite the stern set of her mouth.

Lottie drew a breath, knowing the jig was up. Mary Long was not an easy mark. "I've worked with elephants, never with ostriches." That much was the truth.

"And other animals?" Mary pressed.

"No," she admitted. "But I am a quick study. I've worked at Coney Island for ten years, mostly with sideshows and games. I work hard and I'll give you my best effort. But I will require some instruction."

Mary nodded. "I suspected as much when I asked you to bring Fred back by yourself. Thank you for being frank."

Lottie's stomach knotted. She'd been honest but she'd also just told Mary she had none of the skills needed here. She doubted the woman would take a chance on her when a local farmhand would handle animals with more ease.

Silence stretched as Elsa came back into the room, a plate of cookies in hand. She set them on the table, then turned to Mary. Mary smiled and nodded at Elsa. Only then did Elsa take a cookie herself, biting into it as she curled up at Mary's feet, leaning against the woman's legs as if she belonged there while the kittens mewed for her attention.

Lottie's eyes widened at the implication. Fear crept up her spine. Elsa and Mary had become very good friends in a very short time. What if Elsa had told her that Lottie had taken Elsa away without so much as a word to Aggie and Edward? "Mrs. Long?"

"Yes, dear?"

"Has Elsa told you anything about us?"

Mary sighed, and her mouth thinned. "Enough for me to know you need help." She paused. "Children don't belong on the street, Lottie. I'll offer you a place to stay and find a job for you. Farnum's slowing down—you can be his assistant."

Her steady gaze bore into Lottie. "But make no mistake, young lady. There will be no more chasing ostriches. If you endanger my animals again, I'll send you on your way."

Caleb neared the empty bench. Sure enough, Lottie was no longer there. He hadn't expected she'd stay put but he wasn't sure where she'd gone.

He turned and glanced back down the empty path. The place was almost deserted. Even lazy Old Man Farnum had been headed for the exit, muttering under his breath. It was too much to hope Lottie had simply walked out the gate at closing time.

He'd wager she'd gone to find Mary.

He strode toward the cottage, intent on putting a stop to whatever it was Lottie Chase was set on accomplishing. A woman like that had no business in a place like Elitch's. Dressed in impractical lavender chiffon—chiffon that clung to her curves and made her look soft and touchable despite how travel worn it had become—chasing an ostrich as if she wanted his feathers for her hat. He reined in a smile at the image of how she'd looked with those corn-silk tendrils of hair peeking out from under that hat. Tussled, he guessed you'd call it—like she'd just been well and thoroughly kissed.

Cursing, he reminded himself she was nothing but a delicate lilac left out in the wind too long, pretty and sweet-smelling but dropping blossoms all over the place. She didn't have an ounce of experience in animal tending. That much was obvious. His mind seized on her self-proclaimed skills—scam and manipulation. Damn! He should never have let her get near Mary.

For years, ever since John and Mary Elitch had taken him in as a boy and given him his first job, he'd done what he could to pay back their generosity. After John died, he'd protected Mary, turning away those who wanted to take advantage. There'd been more than a few unscrupulous men those first few years, but he'd always been there. Even Tom Long had been scrutinized for months after he'd arrived to manage the theatre.

Something told Caleb, deep in his gut, that Lottie Chase was dangerous. He increased his pace and tallied what he knew. Flaxen hair, wide eyes, wispy eyelashes, a body that would tempt a priest, and a sultry voice that knew exactly how to play a man. She was used to getting what she wanted. Add her innocent act and the kid, and she had the goods to take over like hollyhocks in a flower bed. Damned if he could work out what Lottie's game was, though.

Whatever she had in mind, he wasn't about to be taken in by any of it. She hadn't shown up here out of chance. She'd targeted Elitch's and brought along the charms needed to tempt both Mary and Tom.

And him, too, if he was truthful. He should have rousted Tom out of the matinee and let him deal with her. By now, she'd have Mary so convinced she was helpless that Mary would refuse to listen to what he or Tom said.

Lottie'd done more than a fair share of collateral damage already. The flower beds were a loss. It wouldn't have been so bad, had she run Fred straight through. Instead, they'd zigzagged all over the place. He could fill in the damaged areas with transplants if there weren't so many of them, but he didn't have enough greenhouse stock this late in the season. The best he'd be able to do would be to try and create some symmetry, tear out plants in some areas and use them for fill elsewhere, maybe create a small winding pathway of painted gravel. It wouldn't be neat but he might be able to maintain the illusion of peace.

He neared the tidy bungalow that served as the Longs' summer home. Known by all as "the cottage," it lent a hint of hominess to the park with its white picket fence and curlicue trim. It was just one more way Mary Long had made the Gardens uniquely peaceful.

Tinkling laughter greeted him as he entered the small garden within the picket fence. He could see Mary through the open window, chatting with Lottie in the parlor. Unease poked at him and he rapped on the door.

Inside, Mary raised her head and spotted him through the screen. "Door's open, Caleb."

Stepping in, he closed the door behind him, then entered the parlor. The younger girl was nowhere to be seen while Lottie sat in one of Mary's wing chairs, a glass of lemonade in her hand. Her tattered hat lay on the floor, just below her shapely crossed ankles, delicately tucked to one side. His pulse quickened, and he raised his gaze only to encounter blond tendrils framing laughing eyes. Drawing a breath, he cursed himself for his susceptibility to her charms.

"You're still here," he said to her.

"But of course. Mary and I needed to work out my employment details. Leaving before I did so wouldn't be very productive."

She'd grown sassy, now that she'd worked her way in, and he didn't like it. It was obvious that she'd charmed Mary, and that it was past time for a few revelations.

"You don't actually plan to hire her, do you?" he asked.

"Oh, but I do," Mary said. "Lottie'll do fine."

"Doing what?"

"I'm to be an animal keeper," Lottie said.

He narrowed his eyes at her. "With all your vast experience?"

"I'll have you know I'm a very quick study, Mr. Hudson. I love animals. I'm willing to work hard." She paused and stared at him. "I need this job."

Caleb looked from Lottie's morning glory eyes to the determined set of Mary's jaw and knew he was in trouble. Maybe if he spoke to Mary alone, he could convince her to see reason. "Can I speak to you in the kitchen, Mary?" he asked.

Offering Lottie an apologetic glance, Mary rose and led the way from the room.

Caleb followed. Once inside the kitchen, he closed the door and paced the room. "She chased Fred through the park for heaven's sake. She knows nothing, nothing, about animals. And she ripped those gardens up without so much as a second thought to what she was doing. That's carelessness. Is that what you want in an employee?"

"Fred did what I expected he might do. He suffered no harm and no doubt got some needed exercise. The flower beds will recover. Once you set your skills to them, I suspect you'll enjoy crafting the changes. And, I'll wager, tongues will wag in town and we'll have record crowds for the next week."

He stared at Mary, unable to believe what he was hearing. Lottie Chase had worked her charms all right and worked them well. He'd never seen Mary so blithe.

"She has no skills and less common sense than Fred."

Mary waited, letting him pace out his frustration.

He slowed and leaned against the counter. "Mary?"

"When John and I took you on, you'd never seen a bear, and you didn't know the difference between a weed and a flower. You needed our help and we gave it to you."

Caleb sucked in a breath. He'd been a child, not some itinerant confidence man. He glanced away, seeing Elsa in the yard beyond, and his heart sank.

"It's the kid, isn't it?" he said.

"Elsa, it seems, has an interest in theatre. I thought she could spend time at the playhouse. She's about the same age as Tony Perry. She also seems to like flowers. It wouldn't take much to set her to weeding the gardens."

"Lottie's a huckster. I don't know what her game is yet but I'm pretty sure she's using Elsa to con you."

"Caleb Hudson, that's enough. While Lottie was chasing Fred through the park, Elsa and I had a talk. There's more to this situation than you realize and I'm not about to turn those two out on the street. I've hired Lottie and that's that."

Caleb's certainty faltered and, for a moment, he wondered if he might be wrong about Lottie's intentions. But what if he wasn't? "Mary—"

"That's that, Caleb. Now let's call Elsa in and we'll all have some lemonade."

Caleb swallowed and shook his head. He'd never talk Mary out of her decision, not with Elsa involved. He'd bide his time, learn what he could about Lottie, and enlist Tom to help. "If it's all the same to you, ma'am, I'd just as soon not. I'm not too happy with that woman right now and the less I have to do with

Lottie Chase, the better for all of us."

"Oh, dear," Mary said.

Alarms sounded in Caleb's head. "Mary? What else did you do?"

"Do? Why, nothing." She sighed. "Except Farnum stopped by a few minutes before you came. He quit when I told him I had hired a woman assistant for him. I need you to train Lottie."

CHAPTER THREE

Two long days later, Lottie swiped her forearm across her brow and wondered what the devil had possessed her to think she wanted this job. She'd just finished mucking the lion pens. Never in a hundred years would she have believed two small lion cubs could produce so much odor-laden waste. She pinched her nose and reached for the fetid pail, then trudged toward the far end of the Gardens to dump it.

She winced as the weight of the wire handle cut into the blisters that the heavy buckets had worn on her hands. Gads, she wished she hadn't lost her gloves. Keeping animals was more work than she'd imagined, but she was determined to prove she could do the job. Elsa's future was at stake.

It was her first solo day and she was exhausted. But the last pen was clean, fresh straw lining the floor. She'd piled the soiled straw into a large wheelbarrow that Caleb would later move to the garbage area.

Cleaning the cages was heavy, rote work. Early in the day, before the Gardens opened, she shut the animals inside their cages and mucked the outdoor areas of their pens. Then, once the animals were shooed outside, she closed the gate and cleaned inside before opening the gate again. She had little to keep her mind occupied except her own thoughts, and she missed the constant customer interaction that had been part of her job at Coney Island. She hadn't even had time to form friendships with the part-time employees. Too much time alone

50

meant a resurgence of memories she didn't want to dwell on. She'd be glad when Caleb started training her for the other duties of her position.

She and Elsa had settled into a spare room in Mary's cottage. Mary doted on the girl, as she did on Tony Perry, the young actress who lived nearby with her parents. Tony and Elsa had become fast friends and spent hours at the theatre together. The rest of the time, she helped Lottie feed the animals or was with Mary. Warmth flooded Lottie. For the first time ever, she and Elsa had a real chance at forging a relationship. Already, they'd grown closer; Lottie was glad they'd settled here.

Elitch's was a wonderful place for the youngster. Her sullenness was fading, but Lottie knew they would have to talk about the future. She'd need to tell Elsa she wouldn't be returning to New York at the end of the summer, as expected. But first, Lottie knew she must prove herself worthy enough for Mary to keep her on during the off-season. Only then would she have the confidence to ask about long-term employment.

Dumping the waste into a compost bin, Lottie wiped her dirty hands on the work smock covering her wrinkled pastel yellow dress and turned back toward the animal enclosures where she was to meet Caleb. Today, he planned to teach her about the public feedings. She'd heard that audiences gathered at the pens to watch baby lions drink from bottles and grown bears dance for their dinners. Folks said the bears were so tame they followed Mary around like dogs.

Lottie wasn't sure she wanted bears following her around the park, but she looked forward to working the crowds during feeding time. Nothing took a person away from feeling blue like a good crowd. Except, of course, an exciting ride. She neared the animal pens just as fevered screams rose from the amusement area. Oh, how she craved a good ride on a roller coaster. Goose bumps tickled her skin as she anticipated finishing today's tasks in time to catch the final run of the day.

"Where have you been?" Caleb sat on the ground behind the lion pen, away from public view, a thin horticulture volume in his hand.

Lottie lifted the pail and flashed him a smile. "Dumping waste. Why?"

"I've been here for almost twenty minutes. I've got more important things to do than wait around while you have your head in the clouds." He frowned as he stood, tucking the book into his back pocket. "You might fool Mary but you and I both know you're a charlatan." He spared a quick frown at her dirty smock, then strode down the path. "Besides, I have my own work to do."

Lottie fought the urge to brush off her apron and throw the bucket at his head, hating it that she looked like a farmer. Caleb Hudson might like flowers, but he was no sissy. With every movement, muscles rippled under his tight work shirt. She damned her racing pulse. No matter how many times she regretted telling him she was a huckster, the damage had been done. She wished he hadn't taken her so seriously, but it didn't matter. He was determined to think the worst and was giving no quarter.

"Yes, I know," she muttered. "You've been very good about reminding me." He never wasted an opportunity to let her know how much he resented having to teach her the ropes. She set the pail behind the pen and followed, matching her pace to his, glaring at his chiseled body and ignoring his opinions. She dredged up some enthusiasm. The happier she appeared, the more he glowered. It was a small victory but all she had.

"Where's the kid?" he asked.

"With Mary." Lottie felt her spirits lift. "She's become her right arm."

"And Mary's glued to her just as fast. Am I right?"

"You are. But I sometimes think I should have Elsa with me."

"Don't." His voice softened, devoid of the judgment Lottie expected. "Mary loves kids. Shame she never had any of her own." He stopped at one of the small sheds and pulled out two pails. A fishy odor wafted through the air until he contained it with a hinged lid. "You ready?"

Lottie swallowed. "As I'll ever be."

They neared the bear pit. A crowd of people stood in a circle three and four deep, their hands on the metal railing of the enclosure, eager gazes on the black bears below. Here and there, children had clambered onto the railing and sat, legs swinging, as protective mothers clutched them around their waists. Others perched more precariously. Excited chatter filled the air, along with the sharp musk of bear.

Shuffling their way through people, they neared the wrought iron gate at the top of the stairway. Caleb nodded and handed Lottie a key to the padlock. Below, one of the bears stopped its pacing and stared upward. Lottie's heart pattered as she realized the stairway in front of them led straight into the pit. The stone stairs clung to the side of the round enclosure, winding down to the bottom, iron bars on their exposed side.

Lottie stopped. "He knows we're coming," she said. Criminy, her hands were sweating! Though not as large as grizzlies, the two black bears were not to be toyed with.

"Of course he does—he can smell the food, even with the lid on. Besides, he knows what time it is. Always, always, feed the animals on time. Bears in particular. They'll be halfway up the stairs to meet you if you're not."

Lottie turned, unable to stop herself from gawking. "Halfway up the stairs?"

He nodded, dead serious. "Bears are smart. We haven't found a latch yet that they can't work open. They get hungry, they search for food. We're twenty minutes late and they're getting impatient. Be. On. Time."

"They get out?" She heard the panic in her voice and locked her knees together. It wouldn't look good if she ran screaming from the pen. She needed this job too much to let fear get in the way. If she left, Caleb would waste no time telling Mary she was inept. She glanced at the crowd, letting their expectancy buoy her confidence. "Isn't that dangerous?"

"It could be," he said, moving past her. "Mary hand-raised almost all of the animals from birth. We've never had a problem and most of them appear lovable as lap dogs. She waltzes with the bears, if you can believe it. But they're wild animals. Don't ever mistake them for pets, no matter what Mary says."

"They can just open the gate and come out?"

"They can. Do they? Not anymore. Some of the visitors got frightened. That's why we use padlocks now. But they could still get riled up if you're too late. Feed them on time and there's no risk of a problem." He entered the gate and started down the steps. "Are you coming or not?"

She drew a breath, pasted on a smile, and followed him down the narrow stairway. The larger bear still paced the pen, lumbering back and forth with great waddling steps. Seeing them on the stairs, the bear raised his head, then stood on his back legs.

Lottie's heart pounded but the crowd oohed and aahed. She took another step down.

At the bottom of the stairs, Caleb paused and handed her the pails before unlocking the padlock on the bottom gate. Lottie pressed against the wall and kept her eyes on the bear as it raised a foreleg high into the air. A wave? A swipe? Lottie wasn't sure but its grayish claws seemed to slice the air. A shiver ran up her spine and her feet felt like they were stuck in quicksand.

"Lottie? Let's go. I don't have all day here."

She stared at the bears.

"Lottie. Sam and Gertrude are waiting. And the crowd's getting anxious."

The crowd. Crowds she could handle. She glanced upward and pushed away her fear. Folks leaned over the railing, curious about the delay. She could make out the muttered grumbles of the kids. She drew in a breath and nodded to Caleb. "Let's go, then."

They slipped through the gate and into the open pit, moving with caution toward an elevated platform at its center. The second bear peered at them through dark eyes, then stretched into a standing position and waddled toward them.

"Toss berries over to the far side of the pen," Caleb advised in a serious tone and took the pail of fish from her. "They'll go after the food. Keep them interested over there until I get on the platform and open the fish pail. They're trained to wait for the release of the scent. If they come back in this direction, throw more berries to distract them."

She glanced at the bears. *Be rational.* If she stood here quaking, the bears would know it and the crowd would, too. Show. No. Fear. The crowd wanted a show, after all. The animal keepers at Coney Island parks didn't cower in the corner. She drew a breath, lifted her head, and waved at the crowd.

As the bears drew closer, she reached into the pail and scattered berries across the pit, aiming for the far wall. Once the bears lumbered away, Caleb moved toward the twenty-foot-high platform, his steps smooth and unafraid. Each time the bears turned in his direction, Lottie made another theatrical toss.

Caleb climbed up the secured ladder to the platform and opened the lidded pail. Below him, the bears caught the escaping scent of the fish—their cue that the feeding was about to start—and moved toward the ladder, no longer interested in the berries. Lottie stood against the wall, ready to bolt for the gate, holding her breath as the larger bear neared the ladder and reached out. The crowd oohed again.

"Easy, boy." Caleb stepped off the ladder and stood on the small platform. Below him, the large bear circled, his appetite now whetted. The female, Gertrude, sat on her haunches. Caleb reached into the pail and pulled out a small fish. Both bears raised their heads, nostrils quivering.

"Let's dance," Caleb said loudly.

The larger bear, Sam, bared its teeth and roared. Caleb ignored it as Lottie shrank against the wall next to the gate. A scant twenty feet away, Gertrude stood and turned in a circle. "Good girl," Caleb praised in a soft tone and dropped the fish into her mouth. She swallowed, nodding as she did so, then returned her gaze to Caleb. He repeated the command and she performed a second time.

The crowd applauded, sounds of satisfaction rising as they smiled at the performance. Lottie's pulse quieted. If she could make it across the pit and up the ladder, she'd have no problems. If the crowd wanted dancing bears, she'd have them doing the polka. Or at least a slow waltz. Maybe she'd let a few crowd members toss in a fish or two. Heck, maybe she'd get the kids to throw the berries while she crossed the pen. Back at Coney Island, someone would be selling berries just for that purpose.

In the center of the pit, the other bear approached the platform, now ready to perform for his dinner. Caleb pulled another fish from the pail and held it above Sam's head. The animal rose and pawed the air. Caleb raised the fish again. "Dance," he said.

Sam stared at him in a short battle of wills, then swiped his paw at the ladder. The crowd gasped. After a tense moment, Sam dropped to the ground and circled before sitting and extending his forelegs. Caleb dropped the fish into Sam's waiting paws as the crowd applauded.

Lottie laughed. Sam was stubborn, it seemed. She'd have to

determine a strategy for how to best use that. Caleb didn't say much up there but she might get some good laughs if she invented a few one-liners for use in such situations. This needed to be a show, not just a feeding.

With both bears now responding well, Caleb finished the feeding and descended the ladder. At the bottom of the ladder, he waited for the bears to approach in one last search for food. Sam stood, lumbering in place as he stared at Caleb. Lottie's skin prickled as Caleb waited out the animal's scrutiny. She slid the gate open and slipped into the stairway.

Caleb kept his pace slow, allowing Gertrude to sniff the empty pail while he avoided eye contact with Sam. Once Gertrude was satisfied there was no more, she turned away. Sam grunted, flashed a final intense gaze toward Caleb, and followed his mate. Caleb released a breath and glanced toward Lottie as the crowd applauded him.

Lottie waited just outside the gate, her knuckles grasping at the iron rails.

Caleb approached and closed the gate behind him, his shoulders rising and falling. "You all right? Your face is pasty as a whitewashed wall." He fastened the padlock, then nodded for her to precede him up the stairs.

"How did you know they wouldn't attack?" she asked.

"I didn't. But Gertrude is almost always docile, and I saw nothing to indicate she'd act otherwise." Caleb reached around Lottie and opened the gate at the top and waited for her to exit, then secured the lock. "Sam was more obstinate than he should be, though." He shrugged. "Funny Old Man Farnum didn't mention it. Mary might need to work with Sam a little."

"But what if he'd attacked?"

Caleb stopped and turned to her. "I'd pray you had the sense to throw out a few more berries." He paused, staring at her.

"Don't look so worried. He'd already eaten. He couldn't care less about more food."

"And if he decides he doesn't want to play games for his food or doesn't like it that the pail is empty? What then?"

"Then you drop to the ground and play dead." He moved toward the shed.

"You what?" She'd never heard of such a thing.

"Never look him in the eye. Never run. Just let him think he's the boss, and he'll leave you alone. If he's eaten, you're not food. Let him think he's in control and he won't bother with you. In the end, he'll follow Gertrude away. She's the real boss."

Caleb took the berry pail from her hands and set it inside the shed with his own, then turned back to Lottie. "If you can ride those damn roller coasters, going lord knows how fast while the wooden trestle shakes, and the wheels threaten to leave the track, you can do this. The bears are a whole lot more predictable, if you ask me."

"I'm not asking you." Lottie felt her face redden at the implication that she was too afraid to do the job she'd been hired for.

"Look, you told Mary you wanted the job. Either you'll do it, or you'll be on your way. It's not like there are other openings, and I can't be here every day."

His hot arrogance was gone but his distrust was still apparent, even in his quiet reassurance. And she liked it less with every passing moment.

"You were scared, too. I saw it," she ventured.

His expression softened. "I had a couple moments," he admitted. "That wasn't Sam's usual behavior. Next time, we take whips in with us, just in case. Tomorrow, you go up the ladder. You'll learn the job, and you'll learn to do it without visible fear." He sobered further. "They can smell the fear."

"I'll be ready," she told him. She swallowed. She could do this. And she'd be damned if she would let Caleb smell her fear, either.

Lottie peered across the breakfast table, watching Elsa stuff Mary's fresh pancakes into her mouth, and her heart swelled. Elsa was carefree and happy, adjusting well to life at the amusement park. They both were, really. They'd been in Denver just two short weeks but already Lottie felt as if they belonged.

"Did Miss Mary tell you?" Elsa asked, a drip of syrup running down her chin.

Lottie pointed to her own face, reminding Elsa to use her napkin. "Tell me what?"

"I get to help Tony say her lines."

"Run lines, dear," Mary corrected from the kitchen where she was pouring coffee.

"Run lines," Elsa mimicked, beaming with the news.

"Really?" Lottie asked, in mock surprise. Mary had consulted her yesterday with the idea, seeking Lottie's approval before she vouchsafed the idea to Elsa. Elsa had taken to the theatre like a natural and Mary thought she might take on the role of understudy. But first, the director wanted to observe her stage presence. Running lines with Tony would be the first step toward taking the stage. "And here I thought I would take you with me to feed the animals today," Lottie teased.

Elsa swallowed, clearly disappointed. She'd helped Lottie once before and hadn't been pleased at Lottie's insistence that she remain safely outside the pen and tote pails. "Yes, ma'am," she said, as Mary approached the table.

Guilt surged in Lottie's throat, and she patted Elsa's hand. "No, pet, you go to the theatre. I was teasing."

Elsa beamed, finished her last slice of bacon, and wiped her hands. Glancing first to Lottie, then to Mary, she asked, "May I be excused?"

Mary nodded once, her gaze on Lottie.

"Go ahead. But you're to mind Tony's parents and the director. I'll check on you when I've finished the morning feedings."

" 'Kay." Elsa rose from the table, rousing a dozing kitten from her lap, and deposited it in Lottie's hands before the feline knew what was happening. "Take care of Boots for me." She kissed Lottie on the cheek, hugged Mary, and was out the door in seconds.

"Well," Mary said, "she's a bit of a whirlwind today."

"She's excited. I can't believe how well she's adjusted."

"And you? Caleb said you're almost ready to feed the bears solo?"

Lottie set the mewing kitten onto the floor. "I think so. I've worked them for close to a fortnight and he said I'd feed them alone tomorrow while he watches from the stairs."

Her pulse quickened at the mention of Caleb. He infuriated her most of the time, but his strong presence also drew her in . . . she sighed.

The man didn't trust her. He'd made that more than clear. And who could blame him, after she'd made a fool out of herself. She'd all but thrown it in his face that scamming was her only skill.

"Lottie?" Mary's voice jerked her back to the present.

"I'm sorry . . . my mind was wandering."

"Caleb says the bears have adjusted to you and the change in their routine, that they're responding well. Do *you* feel ready? Having Caleb tell me you've learned the tasks is quite different from hearing you say you're comfortable."

"I'm not scared to death anymore, if that's what you mean. I don't know that I'll ever be as trusting of them as you are, but I know the procedures, I've learned their personalities, and I'm alert. And, I know how to put on a show." Her thoughts jumped to the ideas she'd generated. She had big plans for the bear feeding—plans that would impress both Mary and Caleb with her showmanship and prove her worth to the park. "I think you'll be pleased with some of the—"

"Mrs. Long? You in there?" Ivy Baldwin, the mustached balloonist who ran the sixty-five-foot-diameter attraction, stood outside the screen door. "I've got a problem with one of the guests. I got her back on the ground but she's still feeling a little green. I thought you'd want to know."

"I'll be right there, Ivy. Let me get the smelling salts."

"How can I help?" Lottie asked.

"Pull a pillow out of the linen cabinet and ready the sofa, just in case. I suspect she'll be fine after some water and a few minutes back on the ground, but we'll bring her here to rest if she needs."

"Anything else?"

"No, dear. You have animals to tend. A few folks get dizzy every summer. They simply need a little extra attention." Mary disappeared into the kitchen, then returned with a small vial. "We'll talk later," she said as she slipped out the door.

Lottie readied the sofa, then gathered the dirty dishes and took them to the kitchen, quickly rinsing them before leaving for the animal pens. Throughout her day, she thought often of her plans. She suspected Caleb might be less than thrilled with the changes she envisioned for the feeding. He didn't seem to take change too well, whatever it was. But she knew salesmanship and how to play a crowd. If there was one thing she'd learned at Coney Island, it was the better the show, the bigger the crowd. She suspected she could double the crowd for Mary Long. And once she did, Mary would be sure to keep her through the winter and forward into future seasons. By then, she also hoped to sell Mary several rides.

Lottie hummed as she returned from the garbage area with

her empty pails. Crowds loved to be involved and she could see no reason why the show couldn't expand to include some of the spectators. They'd remain safe at the top of the pit but, at the same time, they would have a role in the show. A bit of theatrics would also draw a larger audience. Showgirls in skimpy costumes had always been a part of the Coney Island elephant shows. Both magic shows and circus tents employed female assistants who did little beyond flirting with males in the crowds. All drew in more people. There was no reason Elitch's should not be doing so.

Lottie had intended to broach her ideas to Mary—this morning would have been the ideal opportunity. She would make a point of discussing them this evening, before her solo debut tomorrow. They would need to have a costume made, of course, but Lottie did have an idea for the interim.

She set the pails in the shed, grinning at the clothing she'd already chosen and placed there, sure Mary would appreciate her creativity. Then she pulled out her dainty locket watch to check the time.

Goodness, she'd dawdled away the afternoon with her plans. It was well past time to start the feedings. She set the empty waste pails in the shed, wondering what was keeping Caleb. As a rule, he was here, leaning his firm body against the shed while he waited for her return, his brown eyes watching her.

She shivered and shut out the distracting thoughts.

Filling both the berry pail and the fish pail, she anticipated the feeding. Gertrude was as docile as she'd been the first day, and Sam seemed to be adjusting to her presence. As long as his timetable wasn't too disrupted, the male bear behaved well.

Lottie pulled out her watch and checked the time again. Apprehension poked at her. Where was Caleb? If they waited much longer, Sam would not be on his best behavior. She glanced down the path, debating, as her worry increased.

If Caleb didn't show up soon, she'd have no choice but to start the feeding on her own.

Caleb tossed his tools in the shed and jogged toward the bear pit. He knew he was late and concern crawled over him like a persistent itch. Sometime in the past few hours, his pocket watch had fallen into the flower beds and, with the skies overcast, he'd lost track of time.

He could hear the excited murmur of the crowd and hoped the bears weren't becoming impatient. The finger of worry scratched harder. Lottie should be waiting for him but he knew, in the pit of his stomach, that she'd gone ahead without him.

He'd told her never to be late and he knew she was sharp enough to take that advice to heart.

At first, she'd struck him as having no sense whatsoever. But that wide-eyed innocence was misleading—even if it did make his pulse race. Over the past week, he'd seen more than the kissable mouth and swaying hips that had first caught his attention.

To give her credit, the sharp smell of animal dung that used to hover over the pens had lessened since she took over Farnum's duties. She worked hard and kept the cages clean. He knew she didn't like the work, but she kept at it anyway. And, in the bear pit, she'd caught on at once. She had spunk, despite having first appeared scatterbrained.

Rounding the monkey cage, he spotted the throng clustered around the bear pit. An expectant quiet filled the air, and Caleb's gut clenched. She hadn't waited. She was in that pit all alone, without him there to step in if there were problems.

He sprinted to the pen and wormed his way through the knot of people. Their attention was riveted on the action below and he prayed Lottie remembered everything he'd told her. Panting, he reached the top gate and fumbled with the latch. He peered downward and gulped.

Lottie stood at the bottom of the ladder, a whip in one hand and a bucket of fish in the other. She wore blue slippers on her squarely planted feet, her slim legs revealed under what looked like a blue wool bathing costume. Good lord! His pulse raced at the sight of her bare calves peeking out beneath the red piping at the bottom of the pants. The suit hugged her curves and he could imagine how it would cling to her if wet.

Sam and Gertrude circled. Lottie cracked the whip, fully in control. She waited while the bears stepped back, then switched it to her other hand and mounted the ladder. There wasn't an ounce of fear evident. For a moment, she leaned away from the ladder, one well-shaped leg extended, one arm outstretched with the pail of fish and the whip. The crowd roared in appreciation.

Caleb swallowed.

She climbed the ladder as handfuls of berries rained into the pit from above, distracting the bears.

Frozen in place, Caleb held his breath, concern over the changes in procedure drawing his eyes to the bears. Both Sam and Gertrude were chasing berries. Caleb shifted his gaze back to Lottie.

The top of the bathing suit hung past her hips, barring him from a coveted glimpse of her bottom. Every few steps, she struck a suggestive pose, her rear thrust to one side. The crowd applauded with catcalls and whistles. Caleb's groin tightened.

Lottie reached the platform and maneuvered onto it, opening the pail and leaving it and the whip at her feet, then looked down at the bears. As if she'd just discovered their presence, she framed her mouth with her hands and formed it into an "oh." The audience cheered in response.

She was the epitome of a damsel in distress, playing the crowd. Her eyes grew round as she peered at Gertrude and

Sam. She sashayed, provocative as a lily luring bees on the small square that was her stage.

Caleb glanced at the bears and realized they were not as entertained as the audience. Below Lottie, Sam and Gertrude had scented the fish. They began to circle and Sam emitted low growls while Lottie stood there with no clue that the bear thought he was being teased. Caleb catapulted down the stairs.

When Sam stood and roared, Lottie jumped. Like a melodrama ingénue, she batted her eyes and appealed to the crowd for help. Sam roared again, and the audience went wild.

Finally, she turned to the pail of fish, pretending to notice it for the first time as the crowd cheered her on. She lifted a fish, made a show of not liking its smell, and waved it over the edge of the platform.

Caleb paused at the bottom gate, unsure how the bears would respond to yet another change in their meal routine. Lottie was too busy being the center of attention to realize she was teasing them by waving the fish. Sam and Gertrude had been trained to expect their feeder to hold the fish steady.

Caleb reined in his fear. Lottie seemed unaware of his presence. If he yelled, he might surprise her and cause her to stumble. He waited for her to drop the fish, hoping the meal would appease the animals.

"Dance," Lottie called.

Below, Gertrude stood and shuffled as she'd been trained. Caleb released his breath.

Lottie dropped the fish into the bear's waiting mouth. The crowd applauded. Lottie fed Gertrude several more times before the female bear lumbered away, content, and slumped down near the outer wall of the pit. Lottie reached for another fish and waved it over Sam's head, unwittingly baiting him more. "Dance," she repeated.

Sam roared a third time and swiped one powerful foreleg at

the ladder. It shook, and Lottie's expression faltered for a moment before she recovered. Still, fear filled her eyes and Caleb's gut clenched.

Lottie continued to wave the fish, her confidence melting. "Dance," she said.

Sam batted the ladder again, more angry with each passing moment. Lottie's chin wobbled and her smile shook.

She tossed the rest of the fish into the pen but Sam's fury had overridden his hunger.

Caleb opened the bottom gate, knowing he needed to distract the bear. If Sam became irate enough, he would swipe at the ladder until it was shredded. If Lottie was on the ladder when he did so, she'd tumble to the ground like a rag doll. He glanced at her, a silent plea for her to stay put when he yelled.

Then, from the platform, Lottie spied him. She drew a shaky breath and reached for the whip, throwing it in his direction. She tipped the fish bucket over, revealing it was empty. It was all up to him.

He nodded at her, relieved she'd had the sense to toss the whip. He stepped into the pit as Lottie climbed onto the ladder, clutching it with both hands.

She stared at Caleb, and he wondered if her heart was pounding as hard as his. Sam swiped at the ladder again, and Lottie tightened her body against it, gasping.

Caleb grabbed the whip and cracked it. A hush settled over the crowd as Sam turned from the ladder. Caleb strode forward, his eyes on both bears. Gertrude still lay at the edge of the pen but Sam paced, his dark eyes flashing. Caleb hoped like hell Lottie didn't freeze on the ladder because he couldn't spare her any attention. He cracked the whip again, forcing Sam to back away from the center of the ring.

Without warning, a slew of berries poured into the pen from above, and Sam jerked around, his eyes dark and fierce. Caleb saw Lottie from the corner of his eye. She scrambled off the ladder just as Sam spotted her. The bear lunged forward at a full run. She stared at him, then at the gate.

"Drop." Caleb yelled and raced forward, whip extended.

Lottie's mouth opened in shock, but she fell to the floor of the pit and curled into a ball.

Sam stopped, confused. Caleb cracked the whip. "Yee-aah."

The bear took a step backward.

Caleb strode forward, cracking the whip again. Without looking at Lottie, he ordered, "Go."

She rose with care and ran for the gate.

Caleb moved away from Sam, steadily backing toward the gate as he swung the whip. He moved through it, shoved the latch into place, snapped the padlock, and ran up the stairs.

Below him, Sam roared and raced for the gate.

CHAPTER FOUR

Lottie was too stunned to resist as Caleb pulled her up the stairs and out the top gate of the bear pit. Her legs moved, adrenalin driving them. Her breath came in spurts.

Holy criminy.

Caleb swung the gate shut and jammed the padlock together. Taking her hand again, he led her through the buzzing crowd. At the nearest shed, he opened the door and pulled her into the private quiet of the semidarkness.

The damp closeness inside the building held a lingering scent of bear musk. It clawed at Lottie and she panted, gulping for air. Her legs shook.

"Lottie?"

She tried to concentrate on Caleb's voice but her eyes refused to cooperate. She looked around, her mind blank except for the residual fear.

"Deep breaths, Lottie. Everything's okay. Calm down." Caleb steadied her. His warm hands rubbed the goose bumps on her bare arms. "Shhhh."

She shivered, her mind only then grasping that the bears were no longer a threat. She clung to him. His strong chest lay beneath her, cradling her head as she concentrated on the beat of his heart. She could have died in that pit. She pressed closer and a soft whimper escaped her lips.

"My God, Lottie," Caleb murmured. "I could shake you until your teeth rattle."

"H . . . hold me. Just hold me."

His arms tightened around her and he stroked her hair. Lottie melted into him, savoring the security.

"Are you all right?"

She nodded. Sheltered within his arms, her response caught in her throat. Warmth spread through her, his solace satisfying something deep within her. She touched his cheek. A hint of afternoon stubble scratched her palm. Craving for his unexpected tenderness flooded her. Rising onto her toes she kissed him.

His lips met hers, tentative and uncertain until he retreated. Then he trailed light kisses up her cheeks and across her eyelids, his lips warm and soothing against her eyes. "Shhh," he whispered, as his mouth returned to hers.

She pressed into his kiss. Wanting this inexplicable closeness. Needing to affirm this new sensation.

He pulled his mouth away. "My God," he choked out.

"I was so scared," she whispered.

"I know. Me, too. But you did good. You kept your head." Stepping back, Caleb drew a breath, then exhaled. "Lottie, Sam thought you were teasing him. You changed the routine. He was hungry, and you just kept waving that fish at him."

She gulped. She hadn't even considered the bears would respond to something that minute. "I didn't know."

"They're creatures of habit. You can't spring changes on them. Mary and I would have told you that, if you'd mentioned what you were planning to do."

"I started to talk to Mary about it. But she got called away. I planned to explain after dinner. I thought I had until tomorrow." Even as she said the words, Lottie knew she wouldn't have thought to mention such a small detail as waving a fish. Aunt Aggie had been right—she was worthless. "You didn't come. I wanted the show to impress people, and now Mary'll fire me."

"Mary's not going to fire you."

"She's not?" Lottie shifted, searching Caleb's eyes.

He was serious. "But you are going to get a good set-down. Lottie, what you did was not only careless, it was dangerous. You could have been hurt bad, or killed."

"But it was a good show," she said, her enthusiasm weak.

"It was a hell of a show." He paused, his face alight with appreciation before something akin to distrust flickered in his eyes.

His expression shifted, taking on a hard edge as the words lingered between them. His hands dropped away from her, and he stepped back. "Elitch's is a family park. Scantily clad women twitching their butts on a platform isn't what we do here." His voice hardened. "This isn't burlesque, Lottie. You might have gotten away with using your body to charm men in New York but you can't do it here. I'm on to you. I may not know what your goal is, but I recognize a game when I see it."

Confused at the abrupt change in his reaction, Lottie drew back. Her gut tightened at the rejection and she stared at him.

He stared straight back. "You'd best put your clothes back on, girl, because you've reached a dead-end on this route."

Caleb stalked out of the shed, leaving Lottie dazed. She sank onto a folded tarpaulin and swiped at the annoying wetness in the corner of her eyes.

She swallowed, her emotions a mixed-up jumble of resentment, humiliation, and disappointment that she didn't want to deal with. She hated how these feelings raged inside her, clamoring for attention.

She drew her legs onto the tarp, hugging her knees as she dropped her head onto them. For a few moments, she'd felt

70

treasured. Caleb's tenderness had wrapped around her, soothing her, tempting her to let down her guard for the first time in
ten years and open herself up to him. Then she'd ruined it. She
ran her hands down her bare calves and told herself it didn't
matter.

Her reaction to Caleb's comfort had been wrong. Her greedy
response—that kiss—revealed her for what Edward had always
said she was. She'd tempted Caleb, just as she had her uncle.
No wonder Caleb had stalked away from her. She led men on.
Uncle Edward had twisted her into a cheap doxy.

Memories crept around the edges of her mind until Lottie
rebelled. Damn it! She wouldn't be this way had not Edward
exposed her wanton nature. She should be angry instead of
ashamed. Anger she could deal with. She could direct it at a
target and spit it out of her system.

She stood and picked up the empty tin pails, shoving them
onto the shelf. They clanged together, punctuating her indignation.

Who did Caleb think he was anyway? How dare he think he
could kiss her, touch her? Just because he'd been tempted didn't
mean he had the right to give in to it or be angry with her over
it. She ought to have punched him.

Indignation driving her, she strode out of the shed, slammed
the door shut, and stormed toward the roller coaster.

An hour later, Caleb shoved his trowel into the moist black dirt
of the greenhouse bedding table and hacked at the dandelion
that had somehow grown up among the new petunias.

Damn Lottie Chase.

How in heaven's name had he let down his guard enough to
take her in his arms? How had he let himself respond to her kiss
that way? The root snapped off, free to sprout back. Caleb
jammed the trowel into the dirt, swatted at a fly, and leaned
back against the next table.

He exhaled.

After he'd pulled Lottie out of the bear pit, his intense relief that she hadn't been harmed had overwhelmed him. He didn't even like the woman but he'd felt the need to cherish her like a tender rose, one whose scent was so intoxicating that he couldn't resist breathing her in.

He couldn't afford to fall under whatever spell she was weaving. Mary depended on him. If he slipped, let Lottie under his skin, and something happened to Mary, he'd never forgive himself. He'd faltered in Cuba, failing the men who had depended on him. He wouldn't survive if it happened again.

Familiar, heavy guilt pooled around his heart. His chest tightened and he gulped for air, fighting for sanity. He struggled to keep the memories at bay, to maintain his precarious hold on today.

Then he heard the scream.

It waded through the distance. His mind registered it as someone on the roller coaster but it filled Caleb's senses anyway, surrounded him, multiplying.

He clutched his head, willing it not to explode as the screaming echoed. The air grew damp, sticky, and sweat dripped from his skin. The jungle surrounded him, its chaos cloying. Mosquitos buzzed, diving at his face. Gunshots, over and over and over. And the endless screaming. The soldiers lay on the hill above him, their agonizing cries stretching time into eternity. He clawed at the ground, trying to move through the overgrown thickness of the native groundcover to save the men he'd sent to their deaths, his painful limbs refusing to move. The scent of blood, the smell of death filling his senses as he struggled to stay conscious.

Caleb stood, panting, until the memory faded, and only guilt and the buzzing fly remained.

His fault. His.

★ ★ ★ ★ ★

Evening seemed to stretch forever. Lottie plopped into a wicker chair amid the flowers of Mary's back garden and sighed. It had been a long day. Phantom shivers of fear still pulsed down her back. She dreaded having to discuss the incident with Mary. Her emotions still battled over the scene with Caleb. And, she was tired, more so after holding her temper in check during Elsa's bedtime protests.

The back door of Mary's cottage swung open and footsteps crunched on the gravel pathway. Lottie looked up to Mary's worried countenance.

Tom Long stood next to her, a lantern in one hand and concern on his face. His typically sparkling eyes were dark under his graying temples, and his strong jaw twitched.

Lottie's stomach knotted.

"Are you ready to talk about what happened?" Mary asked in a no-nonsense tone and Lottie shivered all over again. She settled into the chair opposite Lottie. Tom placed the lantern on the picnic table, adjusted its wick, and sat on the bench. As if one, he and Mary both turned to Lottie, waiting.

Lottie wiped her hands on her lap, concentrating on Mary. "I had some ideas for the bear feeding, changes I intended to discuss with you this evening. When Caleb was late, I knew I needed to feed them and felt confident I was ready. I decided to make the changes without talking to you. Things went wrong."

Mary nodded, her mouth drawn into a thin line. Though her hands were folded on her lap, her thumbs circled one another.

Lottie swallowed.

"We're told Sam was quite upset?" Mary said.

"I made a mistake," Lottie admitted. There was no point in denying what was obvious. "He thought I was teasing him."

Mary arched one eyebrow. "And were you?"

Heat crept over Lottie's face. "I didn't intend to but, yes."

"Were the bears in danger?" asked Tom. His voice, though not stern, was firm enough to give Lottie pause. He was asking about far more than whether or not the bears had been injured.

Lottie considered her answer before speaking. "No, sir, I don't believe so."

"And the crowd?" he asked.

"No." Lottie shook her head.

"But you were," Mary said.

"Yes, ma'am."

Silence stretched around them, disturbed only by cricket chirps and the scent of roses in the cooling evening air.

At length, Tom leaned forward, hands on his thighs. "Lottie, we need to know. Is Sam violent?"

Again, Lottie weighed her response. "I don't think so. No." She glanced at Mary. "Caleb said last week that Sam's training had slipped, but Caleb worked with him and he was better."

"So you don't believe Sam's become unpredictable? Beyond control?"

Lottie looked back at Tom, realizing he wanted confirmation that she had truly understood his question. "He was only responding to what I did, I think. I was scared to death but he was fine until I was unpredictable."

Tom sighed and leaned back. "That's good to hear. I would hate to have to put him down."

"Put him down?" Lottie stared first at Tom, then Mary.

"If he's become violent, we would have to, dear," Mary said.

Lottie shivered. She hadn't given a thought to the more far-reaching consequences of her actions. "It was my fault. Not his."

"Nonetheless," Tom said, "we'll stop his strolls for a while, to be on the safe side." He spoke of their long-standing habit of allowing the bears out of the pit for chaperoned exercise in the park each evening. "And you need to tell us immediately if he

74

shows any hostility during feedings. Any."

"Yes, Mr. Long."

Tom stood. "I'm headed to Caleb's cabin. For safety's sake, we'll check on Sam together, make sure he's calmed down." He caught Mary's gaze. "I'll leave you ladies to discuss the rest of our concerns."

They waited as Tom made his exit, Lottie's thoughts tumbling to Caleb. She blushed again before squashing her feelings, then turned to Mary. "Do you want me to pack our things?" she asked, fighting to keep her voice steady.

"No, Lottie. Everyone makes mistakes." She reached out and patted Lottie's knee. "It's just that this one could have gotten you killed."

"I know."

Mary stood and offered Lottie a brief hug. "Let's go in and have a cup of tea."

Lottie followed her into the house and gathered cups as Mary filled the tea kettle and set it on the stove. They busied themselves preparing the hot brew, then settled at the kitchen table, steam rising from their cups as the aroma of strong black tea swirled around them.

"I think we need to discuss the show itself," Mary said, her tone both frank and curious. "What were you trying to do out there?"

"I thought, if it were a show and not just a feeding, the crowd would be more entertained." Lottie offered a half smile, her enthusiasm for the plan dampened considerably.

"Well, I suspect they were entertained far beyond their expectations today."

Lottie grinned, remembering the response. "They loved it."

Mary chuckled. "The men, in particular, from what I heard."

"And the kids," Lottie added, fighting a blush. "The kids loved it. They were part of it."

Mary raised her brows in question. "Part of it?"

"I let them toss the berries."

"Ah, yes." Mary sobered and took a sip of tea. "These would be the berries that ended up scattered all over the pit rather than thrown in a direction that would lead Sam and Gertrude away from you? The berries that later rained down in a torrent and angered Sam further?"

The air went out of Lottie's boasting. She hadn't thought. "I suppose so."

Mary rubbed Lottie's hand. "You see, my dear, when you give up control without strict instructions, people respond in a haphazard manner. Those children had no idea they were supposed to distract the bears, did they? They didn't know dumping the berries on top of Sam was a mistake."

Lottie shook her head and stirred at her tea, the silver spoon clinking against the white china cup.

"And you. Caleb said he explained about waving the fish."

"Yes, ma'am." She looked Mary in the eye. "I didn't intend to tease. I thought it would be more dramatic than simply holding the fish out and dropping it."

Mary nodded. "And the flirting with the crowd? The costume?"

"All the acts at Coney Island—"

"This isn't Coney Island, Lottie. Our park is for families. I'm not a prude, dear, but Elitch's has a wholesome reputation. Bare legs and suggestive movements are not part of what we are known for. While I have no doubt that the men loved your show, it was not appropriate."

Though Mary hadn't been preachy, her words were firm and Lottie accepted them at face value. Wanton behavior had no place here. Caleb's abrupt withdrawal had implied much the same thing. Lottie's gaze dropped. "Yes, ma'am."

"I think there were a few parts of your act that could enhance the show. But they will require Sam and Gertrude be trained first, so they aren't threatened by your movements." Mary stood, crossed to the stove, then refilled their tea cups. "I'll work with you for a few weeks, to help retrain them. Black bears aren't known to be volatile but Sam hates sudden changes in his routine. Perhaps we could add a small pail of berries up top for the kids. And one for you in case you need them."

"Yes, ma'am."

"You put the cart before the horse, that's all." Mary returned to her chair and smiled at Lottie. "Your ideas are sound, except for the blatant promiscuity. And even that would be acceptable, were we a different sort of park. Perhaps we can compromise here. I don't want you to feel your instincts are wrong. Just use your head."

"I will."

"Make sure you do. If you had been injured or, worse yet, killed, what would happen to Elsa?"

A shiver ran up Lottie's back. This, too, she hadn't thought about.

"You know I would have to send her back to New York." Mary's words were cautious. "Elsa told me your family life is not good, that she's afraid of her father."

Lottie swallowed. She hadn't realized Elsa had already begun to fear Uncle Edward, already understood there was something amiss with his attentions. Thank goodness she hadn't waited any longer.

Lifting her gaze, Lottie looked at Mary, knowing deep in her gut that this was a friend such as she'd never had—a friend who cared about her. "They're not our real parents. Mama died," she said, holding back the full story, then added, "Elsa doesn't know."

"They're . . . ?"

"Aunt Aggie and Uncle Edward."

Mary nodded. "And Elsa's fears?"

"She's right to be afraid." Lottie clutched the tea cup, letting its warmth seep into her hands, unsure how much more she should reveal. "Uncle Edward . . . Uncle Edward likes girls that age. We couldn't stay there any longer."

"I see. Then you should not be taking unnecessary risks, should you?" Mary let the subject drop, busying herself with adding sugar to her tea. "You spent quite a bit of time at Coney Island?"

"I spent a lot of time there. At first, I just wanted to be out of the house, away from Uncle Edward." Neither of them needed to hear the words she left unspoken. "Later, Aunt Aggie demanded I earn my keep, and I got a job there."

"At one of the parks?"

"Not at first," Lottie said. "I started hanging out in front of the gyp joints when I was still a kid, luring in customers for them."

Mary frowned at the reference to the gambling halls, all known for their trick devices and rigged games. "Not a good place for a child."

"It was better than home. When I grew older, though, I realized the men who came there had other expectations. I got a job as a barker at Streets of Cairo when I was fourteen. When Luna Park opened, I hired on there."

"Luna Park—my, how Fred Thompson turned Coney Island on its head when he opened that place. Tom and I visit the Coney Island parks every year, after our season closes," Mary said, her eyes sparkling. "Luna Park is now our favorite. There are so many new things to see. The lights, the imaginary cities, the circus acts. And the rides! Oh, how I love the rides."

"Me, too! For a few minutes, nothing else matters."

"For me, it's the thrill of taking a risk." Mary set down her spoon. "But Tom's more cautious. It took me a full year to convince him we should purchase a roller coaster. He needed to make sure it would be safe." She chuckled.

Lottie peered at her new friend, her imagination filling with ideas once again. "Have you ever thought about adding more rides?"

Mary smiled, a fellow conspirator. "We've ordered a carousel!"

"Oh, Mary." Lottie's enthusiasm bubbled. "The kids will flock here when it arrives. Just think of it."

"You're a kindred soul, Lottie, dear." Mary drained the last of her tea.

"Can you imagine if you added even more?" Lottie ventured, unable to stop the visions in her mind. "This place could be the Coney Island of the West."

"Oh, I can imagine," Mary said. "I'm just not sure how we'd do it."

Lottie grinned. "I am, Mary, I am. Put another kettle on to boil and I'll tell you all about it."

CHAPTER FIVE

The next morning, Lottie hummed her way through her morning chores, basking in the summer sun as it warmed her skin and not once minding the stench of the soiled hay she raked from the elephant pen. She couldn't believe how enthusiastic Mary had been at her suggestions.

As she pumped water into the hand-washing basin behind the shed, Lottie's head buzzed with the ideas she had for making Elitch's bigger and better. All while she secured a future for Elsa. Now, she needed to reason out how to convince Gennick Amusements to give her the commission on any rides the Longs purchased.

Last night, she and Mary had exchanged observations about the merits of one amusement ride after another and compared the various parks on Coney Island. The earliest rides had been simple toboggans like the famous Shoot the Chutes water slide at Sea Lion Park and Steeplechase's Ferris Wheel. Each additional ride stretched the imagination further and brought new thrills.

Lottie and Mary had rated each as a potential addition to Elitch's collection. They'd laughed as they shared reminiscences about their experiences at Coney Island and giggled at one another's anecdotes. By the time Tom returned and pointed out the late hour, they had cemented their friendship far beyond Lottie's wildest expectations.

Still, Lottie couldn't help feeling that Tom and Mary would

continue their cautious one-ride-at-a-time approach to expanding the park beyond its current status. Tom's concerns about safety and expense were valid, as was Mary's insistence that all attractions be family-oriented. Together, they were excellent business managers, strong in areas where Lottie realized she had no sense whatsoever.

Her role would be bringing them fresh ideas, from the viewpoint of someone who had observed public reactions firsthand.

Lottie dried her hands, then put her supplies in the nearest shed and closed the door. Pulling a hankie from her pocket, she wiped beads of sweat from her forehead, located her lunch pail, and strolled to the picnic grounds.

She navigated through the shady tree-lined paths of the park. Mary would never create make-believe streets with camel rides and belly dancers. Still, there were rides Mary should consider—rides full of excitement and imaginary worlds.

Lottie found a quiet spot under one of the fruit trees and pulled out her sandwich and jar of sweet tea. Across the way, families munched on picnic lunches. The scent of egg salad filled the air. Children squirmed on the benches and licked their fingers, anxious to get back to the attractions. Here and there, groups of young people clustered, laughing as they consumed their meals, but most of the crowd was comprised of families.

Smiling, Lottie recalled the overwhelming numbers of young people at the Coney Island parks. They flocked to the Old Mill, a simple water ride that drifted through a darkened tunnel, known as the "tunnel of love." Together with the Flying Swings and the Tilt-a-Whirl, it garnered repeat visits from teens and adults alike.

These were the types of rides Elitch's Gardens needed. Oh, Lottie knew the miniature train attracted the children but the profit lay with older riders, those who had money of their own. If there were enough rides to keep them thrilled all day, food stalls could be opened and games established. And, by lighting the rides after dark, people would spend even more money.

She wondered what Caleb would think of the Old Mill, a shiver tickling her. She imagined the two of them, drifting through the cool evening twilight into the darkness of that long tunnel. Would he take her in his arms and kiss her senseless? Gads, if she'd only kept her mouth shut, maybe he'd hold her until she melted away. Just because he cared. Or would he still see her for what she'd become and turn away in disgust?

She pushed the thoughts away, gathered up her lunch items, and walked toward the monkey cage. She bit her lip, puzzling on how to convince the Longs to invest in the rides she envisioned. To her way of thinking, expanding Elitch's wouldn't be as difficult as Tom and Mary feared. The key lay in how good a deal she could broker with Rupert's father.

The only problem, as she saw it, was how to best contact the company. She didn't know squat about how to purchase rides— Rupert had told her he had that side of their partnership taken care of. He'd said they'd make the most money dealing with his father's firm. But now, without Rupert, she'd need to convince his father she was knowledgeable enough to negotiate a sale. Rupert had made it clear his father was a closed-minded recluse who relied on a small clique of trusted salesmen. His father might accept her as Rupert's partner, but he would never consider doing business with a stranger. Without Rupert's association, could she convince his father to do business with her? Besides, Rupert had been so secretive about the man that she didn't even know how to contact him.

What she needed was a letter of introduction. And it had to be from a member of Gennick's inner circle.

Her stomach knotted. Like it or not, what she needed was Rupert.

She doubted she could trust Rupert, not after seeing the lecherous look in his eyes. But, if she didn't have to see him . . . Granted, he was angry about the way she'd used him. But she knew him well enough to realize how well groveling worked to soothe his vanity. If she begged his forgiveness and promised to pay him back, she might be able to convince him to send her what she needed.

She'd simply swallow her own pride, forget he'd stolen her last dime, and write to him in care of the hotel in San Francisco. She was accustomed to doing what had to be done. It was just a letter, after all.

Caleb glanced across the flower bed to where Elsa knelt, plucking weeds. The early evening air had cooled, and he delighted in the silence of the empty park. He loved the quiet hours after the crowds were gone, and the screams no longer threatened.

Before the Longs had purchased the first amusement ride three years ago, the park had been more peaceful. But the miniature train hadn't disturbed him. Children's laughter hadn't affected him like the screaming roller coaster riders. Caleb exhaled and set down his trowel.

"You done?" Elsa asked, grinning at him. The smile lit her face. She'd helped him every night for almost a week, and she was a far different child than the sullen little girl who had arrived at the park with Lottie.

Caleb smiled back and felt his heart tug. She and Lottie were about as opposite as two cousins could be. He was taken with Elsa. She had an ingenuous nature that was hard to resist. But, he'd need to make sure his soft spot for Elsa didn't let him cave in to Lottie's manipulations.

"Guess so," he said. "My weeds are all gone."

"You didn't have as many," she quipped. She sat back on her heels and studied the flower bed. Located immediately inside the front gate, it was weeded with frequency. This evening, there had been few weeds when they started, and Elsa had done a fair job of catching those under her assignment. She picked out the remaining stragglers and brushed her palms together.

"How come we gotta get 'em all?" she asked.

"The way I see it, folks have all sorts of busy thoughts in their heads, things they have to worry about, and things that make them angry and sad and confused. When they see pretty flowers and smell their quiet scents, without weeds to mess them up, they remember how good life can be. They can forget about their cares for a little while. Flowers are simple things but they can bring a lot of peace."

"And weeds are clutter? Like all those thoughts?"

"Yep." A slow warmth pooled around his heart at the ease with which Elsa had grasped the concept. It was one of the many things he liked about the kid. "Gather up what you pulled and put it in there." Caleb nodded to a wooden bushel basket, then stood and scratched at the stains on his denim waist overalls. Giving up, he dumped his own pile of weeds into the basket and offered Elsa a hand.

She clasped it and stood. "Need help?" she asked.

"I can get it. You can go on up to the cottage."

"I don't mind, really. Lottie'll just tell me it's bedtime, anyway." She rolled her eyes. "I'd rather stay and help."

Caleb hoisted the basket, understanding her reluctance to surrender on such a balmy summer evening. "Grab up the trowels, then, and we'll drop them off in the shed." He waited while Elsa did so, then ambled down the path. A cicada sounded in the distance. Otherwise, the only noise was the crunching of their feet on the gravel.

They walked in companionable silence, stopping to drop off

the trowels and lock the shed. Then, they continued on to the trash area.

"So, you're liking it here?" Caleb asked her, though he already knew the answer.

"Oh, bunches," Elsa said. "We were gonna go to San Francisco but Rupert and Lottie had a fight, and we ended up all alone. By the time we got all the way out here, all I wanted to do was go home. But then we met Mary, and everything turned out perfect."

He wasn't surprised they'd been traveling with a man. It fit the picture Lottie had created of herself. Or at least the one he'd painted of her. An inkling of doubt poked at him. He'd believed she'd targeted Elitch's on purpose. Elsa's information didn't mesh well with that assumption.

He recalled his heady reaction to holding her in the shed and the disturbing stab of distrust that accompanied it. Could it be possible she *had* been seeking comfort instead of scheming to soften him up?

Uncomfortable, he concentrated on Elsa's words instead. "Perfect?" he prompted.

"Holy cats, what isn't great about living in an amusement park?" Her cheeks grew pink as she waited for him to react to the slang expression. When he didn't, she continued. "Mary said I can ride the train any time I want, and I can go with Lottie when she rides the coaster. There are animals to look at, a jar of homemade cookies in Mary's kitchen, and I have a best friend." She paused. "I never had a best friend before. And I absolutely adore the theatre. I'm gonna be an actress, just like Tony is. Lottie and Mary said I could."

Caleb chuckled at her enthusiasm, then sobered. "Don't you miss your folks?"

Elsa's smile dampened, and she shrugged. "I guess."

Her response caught him off-guard. "You guess?"

She didn't answer right away, kicking instead at a wad of paper that someone had neglected to pick up from the walkway. "They're not my folks, you know."

Caleb stopped and squatted down, setting the basket on the ground as he reached for the paper. "What?"

Elsa shrugged again. "Everybody thinks I don't know but I do. I heard Lottie tell Mary they're really our aunt and uncle. I think maybe I'm Lottie's sister." She caught Caleb's gaze, staring hard. Her voice was tremulous. "But I don't think anybody else is supposed to know."

His heart lurched for the poor kid. How the hell was a person supposed to respond to news like that? People didn't confide in him. Not anymore. He swallowed. "But you're telling me?"

"Why wouldn't I? You listen instead of pooh-poohing me like I'm a little kid who doesn't know anything." She'd recovered her composure, a matter-of-fact tone replacing her earlier anxiety. "Grown-ups talk about important stuff like that. Besides, we're friends and friends trust each other."

Caleb sucked in a breath. If Elsa knew better, she wouldn't. He didn't have much of a track record with trust. But she'd picked him, and he guessed he'd best steer her to the person she should be talking to about this.

"That's a pretty big piece of news to overhear," he said. Unsure where to put his hands, he leaned on the basket. "Did you talk to Lottie about it?"

Elsa shook her head. "Not yet."

"Don't you think you should?"

"I reckon Lottie'll talk to me when it's time." Elsa smiled at him, then inclined her head. "Let's go."

Caleb straightened. Out of his element, he thought it best to follow her lead. "You don't seem too shook up about it," he noted as they continued down the path.

"That's 'cause I'm calmed."

"Calmed?" It was a strange expression, though it sounded oddly in character for her.

"I heard Tony's dad say it in the play and I like the word. It's how I feel, too."

Caleb tried to wrap his thoughts around the concept, unable to quite grasp it. "I wouldn't guess there are too many girls who would be calmed to learn her folks aren't really her folks."

"Maybe not." She skipped ahead, then stopped and turned around. "But I was lots more bothered when I had a mother who never hugged me and a papa who looked at me funny. Now, I feel better 'cause they're not my folks after all."

Caleb stopped, too, as possible scenarios filtered through his brain. The words were heavy in what had been left unsaid, and he wasn't sure if he'd understood. Or if Elsa understood it herself.

Clearly, the couple hadn't loved her the way a kid deserved to be loved. It could be as simple as that . . . but there was something in Elsa's eyes.

"Lots of folks don't hug much," he offered.

"She didn't hug me. He did."

Caleb's stomach knotted at the venom in her voice. Good-night! If Elsa was saying what he thought she was saying, there was a whole lot more to Lottie Chase than he'd credited. Had Lottie known? Was protecting her sister the real reason she'd traveled here?

He stepped forward, knowing he was an interloper, that this was a family matter. Stopping as he reached Elsa, he squatted in front of her. "That's a pretty big thing," he said, looking her in the eye. "The kind of thing sisters might want to talk about together. I'd guess Lottie would want to know how you feel."

"Do you really think so?"

He nodded. "I know so." He offered Elsa a reassuring smile, his thoughts drifting to Lottie and everything he'd just learned.

It looked more and more possible he'd been wrong about her.

Lottie pushed an empty wheelbarrow toward the large storage barn at the back of the amusement park, sweat dripping from her brow. The heat was stifling today. Not for the first time, she wished Elitch's had a refreshing water ride.

There was a patch of land along the picnic area that would be exceptional. She'd noticed it after she'd started her duties, trekking toward the animal pens with her loads of grain. There was ample room for a straight coaster at one end and a pond at the other. All the Longs would have to do is remove a few trees. Later, she'd talk to Mary about the idea.

But first, she needed to settle things with Caleb. It was time to make peace, more so now that Elsa seemed so taken with Caleb. Last night, in the wake of Elsa's praises of the gardener, Lottie had realized she was being petty. She needed to give him the benefit of the doubt.

Leaving the wheelbarrow next to the barn, she walked back toward the cottage. With closing time near, the picnic grounds were quiet, and she expected he'd be starting on his evening maintenance. Sure enough, at the end closest to the main hub of the park, Caleb stood, pruning a row of shrubs.

His muscular arms were bare where the sleeves of his cotton work shirt had been torn away, and his tanned skin grew tight over his biceps as he squeezed the large sheers. Powerful as a trapeze artist without the extra brawn that spoke of too much body-building. The sheen of perspiration on his skin glistened just enough to capture Lottie's attention.

Her breath quickened in appreciation.

She approached, memories heating her cheeks despite her intention to put them behind her. She readied herself for the censure in his whiskey eyes.

Caleb lowered his sheers and turned to glance at her. "How'd your day go?" he asked, his voice holding no trace of the anticipated disapproval.

Lottie blinked, her defensiveness melting. "Fine," she said, unsure of what else to say. "The bears are adjusting to the new routine."

"I thought they would."

"So, you're trimming bushes." The idiocy of the statement shouted at her, and she shifted in front of him. She hadn't expected polite conversation any more than she would have expected him to take her in his arms.

"Part of my job." He offered a disarming smile.

"You don't get tired of it?"

"The routine is peaceful. I get to stand in the shade, shape growing things, muse on life. Most times, I wait 'til the area's quiet. It soothes me."

Muse on life? Lottie wasn't sure how quieting she'd find such activities. It seemed that thinking on life did nothing but roil her up and make her want to run. "I'd rather live life."

"Live life?"

"Experience things. Do something exciting. Have some fun."

"Ah," he said, raising his eyebrows. "Run helter-skelter as fast as you can?"

"How else do you get to feel the wind in your face?"

"Yeah, but don't you miss out on how warm and peaceful it is when you stand still and feel the sun or smell the roses?"

Lottie frowned, pondering his words. She was surprised at how much sense they made, phrased that way. Still, she couldn't imagine life void of the excitement that had buoyed her so generously. "You have no sense of adventure, do you?"

"I've had my fair share of adventures." His jaw tightened.

"And you didn't find them exciting?"

"Excitement isn't all it's cracked up to be." He snipped at a

89

few more branches, then closed the catch on the sheers. "Walk you up to the cottage?"

"Sure. If you don't think it will be too much excitement for you."

He offered a fleeting smile. "Touché."

They walked toward Mary's house, Caleb preoccupied with his own thoughts. Lottie felt his withdrawal and glanced at him. His face had clouded.

"Elsa says you're growing special roses in the greenhouse," Lottie prompted, reluctant to surrender their brief, companionable give and take.

Caleb nodded, his expression again softening. "I'm working on a new variety, for the rose garden."

"Why not use ordinary roses?"

"These will be better, fuller, more color, more scent."

Lottie noted the pride that filled his voice and warmth filled her. She liked this side of Caleb, liked his acceptance of her, his willingness to share.

"So, making these new roses, that's excitement for you?"

"I guess it is." He smiled, this time a wide, full expression that filled his whiskey brown eyes, too. "Not much in the way of adventure, the way you like, but crafting something new brings a lot of satisfaction."

They crunched down the gravel path, the noise of the crowds stronger as they neared the main area of the park. The miniature train's horn sounded as it thrummed along the track, children's voices raised in laughter echoing after it. Just shy of the roller coaster, the clickety-clack of wheels filled the air as the string of cars inched up the incline of the wooden hill.

Lottie's anticipation built as she watched the cars climb. A few minutes and they'd crest. Pent-up energy would explode as the riders began their fall. She held her breath, waiting for the release that always surged through her when it happened—even if she was only watching from the ground.

"Elsa said the two of you have had your share of adventure this summer," Caleb said, interrupting her musing.

"In what way?" she evaded.

"Traveling all the way from New York City, getting stranded in a strange place, taking a job in an amusement park."

"Oh, well, yes. I guess we have." She skirted around the question in his words, nervous about his motives, worry over Elsa gnawing at her.

"That fellow that left you here? What's he to you?"

Lottie's breath caught as she recognized interest in his tone. Caleb wasn't probing about Elsa—he was interested in her. Her mind scrambled for an answer that would let Caleb know Rupert had meant nothing. "Just an easy mark. Someone to get us from there to here." Her face burned as she realized what she'd said and how he might interpret it.

Screams pierced the air, and Lottie's heart jumped.

Beside her, Caleb stopped, staring. His face paled as his chest rose and fell in a rapid staccato. Sweat beaded on his forehead.

"Caleb?" His eyes remained blank, reminding her of Uncle Edward when he grew angry at her. "Caleb?"

As if pulled from a dream, his gaze settled on her, hostile and accusing.

"What's wrong?" She knew she sounded weak, and she hated it.

"Go away." He ground out the words.

She raised her head and met his eyes, unflinching.

"Go. Leave me alone. I don't want you here."

She gasped, then turned and strode away before he could hurt her again.

CHAPTER SIX

Caleb slowed his breathing as Lottie disappeared down the path.

It's just a roller coaster. Just a roller coaster.

His mind chanted the refrain until the steaming jungle no longer surrounded him, his men no longer cried out for help and the smell of blood dissipated. He wiped the icy sweat from his brow with a trembling hand and continued across the park, detouring away from the crowds, relieved that he hadn't collapsed in front of Lottie.

Most days, the screaming was a bother. He hated it, but if he remained diligent, he could squelch his response. It was when he was caught unprepared—when the screams surprised him—that he relived his actions on that god-forsaken Cuban hill.

Damn. Damn. Damn.

He shouldn't have to live his life in a constant state of heightened awareness. In fear that someone would see his weakness, realize he'd given that irresponsible order, then failed to protect those under his charge. Soldier's heart, the doctors called it, that sudden reliving of his worst memories. And it would never go away.

He detested having to be vigilant all the time, hated that damn ride and what the screams did to him. And he hated it that Lottie had been there to see his weakness.

He wasn't sure why it mattered what she thought. He wasn't even sure he liked her, at least not until today. He was drawn to her, more than he wanted to be. Her spunk was unquestionable, and there was no denying that she hid some interesting curves under that shapeless work apron she wore. And a manipulative spirit, he reminded himself.

Yet, today, when she'd intimated that she'd only used that fellow she was traveling with to get away from New York, he saw something more in her expression, heard what she hadn't said. He no longer believed she was as shallow as she implied with her frivolous quips.

It irritated him that he'd been short with her, that he'd demanded she leave, yelled at her. He knew she didn't understand. She'd believe he thought the worst of her again. His heart heavy, he kicked at a stone.

His only other choice would have been to let her see his loss of control, his failure, his guilt.

He wasn't ready to let anyone get that close.

For three days, Lottie did her best to avoid Caleb Hudson. She altered her route whenever there was a chance she'd encounter him. She reversed direction, made excuses, and changed her plans so often that it was almost laughable.

Except she wasn't laughing.

She'd never allowed any man to exercise that much influence over her behavior. Not since Uncle Edward. Yes, she'd stuck her foot in her mouth. But she'd done that before and she was apt to do it again. It had never seemed important.

But the look in Caleb's eyes when he turned her away had stung. Beyond being attracted to him, it mattered to her what he felt, that he thought badly of her. The man compelled her to examine herself in ways she'd never before allowed.

Warmth crept through her body, quickening her breath. The way those whiskey eyes scrutinized her awakened moist tingles in the small of her back. Even now, thinking about it, she felt the spark stir, as it always seemed to just before he grew judgmental.

She shrugged off the tender twinge in her heart and circled past the center of the park. As she strode toward the cottage, she turned her thoughts to Elsa. She'd finished her tasks early, in time to round her daughter up and bake cookies. Never mind that she made lousy cookies. It was the fun that mattered, anyway.

As she neared the front porch, she heard voices inside.

Dear heaven, don't let it be Caleb. The thought jumped at her like a jack-in-the-box clown, and she paused to even out her breathing.

At the creak of the door, Mary called out. "Lottie? Is that you?"

"It is," Lottie answered, forcing more cheer than she felt into her voice.

"You have a guest, dear."

A guest? Lottie glanced down at her soiled apron. She looked a wreck and must smell even worse. But, aside from Caleb, there was no one that would be visiting her and she wasn't about to tidy up for him. Not after the sting he'd left her with.

"Lottie? Come in and say hello."

Lottie's heart skittered at the sound of the familiar voice. "Rupert?" She stalled.

"Hello, doll," he said, rising to his feet. His honeyed drawl coated her uneasiness, diverting her like a familiar addiction.

She swallowed and stepped further into the parlor, reminding herself he couldn't be trusted, despite that candied tone. He'd made demands, stolen her savings, then abandoned them. She scrutinized his expression, trying to make sense of why he was here. "You are the last person I expected to see."

Rupert's gaze raked across her, and he lifted his eyebrows in a silent question.

Lottie stared back, chills creeping up her spine.

"Mr. Gennick has been telling me about his trip to San Francisco," Mary said, filling the void of silence.

Rupert smiled, his eyes heavy with emotion. "I told Mrs. Long how surprised I was when you refused to get on the train with me. I shoulda never have left you here, no matter how big the misunderstanding. I was just so worried about being late and losing out on the sale." He paused. "And I guess I was hurt. Gads, I've missed you. And the kid."

He was smooth, she had to give him that. If she didn't know better, Lottie would have wondered if that had been all there was to it—a simple misinterpretation. But she did know. She'd grown up watching him persuade people to believe him. He'd worked for a few years in other areas but, if anything, his skills of persuasion had only improved over time. The silky smoothness was nothing but a sticky-sweet coating hiding the fact that he was a huckster, like her.

She straightened her spine and drew a breath. "What are you doing here?"

"Looking for you." He grinned. As usual, his voice was full of charm and his eyes alight with a sincerity few ever questioned. "I want to make things right."

"Make things right? You left us."

Mary stood in one fluid movement. "Why don't I leave you two alone? I haven't seen to Fred yet today." She brushed past Lottie, patting her arm as she scooted around her. "I'll stop by the theatre, find Elsa, and we'll visit the old bird for a while."

Lottie turned, anxious to avoid being alone with Rupert. "Mary . . . you don't have to—"

"Thank you so much, Mrs. Long," Rupert interrupted. "It looks like Lottie and I have a lot to talk about. I think I made a bigger mess of things than I guessed."

"You think?" Lottie sputtered as Mary slipped out the front

door. Her mind scrambled past possible motives for his arrival here and seized on the only one that made sense. He'd come to steal the sales commission away from her.

And if she wasn't careful how she played it, he'd do exactly that. She couldn't let him know how close she was to making a sale. She had to divert him. She pulled her mouth into a pout and willed tears to form in the corners of her eyes.

Rupert's mouth tipped into a persuasive smile. "Come on, doll. You're not gonna hold a grudge, are you?"

"You left us," Lottie said, punctuating her words with a finger to his chest. "You dumped my trunk and left it. After you stole my money out of it."

Rupert stepped back and cocked his head to one side. "You owed me for two tickets."

"You left me with nothing."

"And you misled me. Suckered me." His deceptive eyes filled with conflict. "Used me and left me hurt and angry."

The truth in his words stung. Lottie had used him, and she couldn't deny it. It had been the only way to get Elsa away from Uncle Edward, and Lottie knew she'd do the same thing again. Of course, Rupert had been angry. But hurt? Lottie sighed and abandoned the pointless argument. They'd been, were, two peas in a pod. She'd do better to concentrate on the present and how to outmaneuver him. "Yet, now you're back."

"Aw, can't a fellow change his mind? You have no idea how worried I've been about you, doll. Thinking about you and the kid all alone. I'd have been back for you in a heartbeat if my heart hadn't been so broken."

She held back a snort. "I don't know that you even have a heart."

"I've been pining away, figuring you wired your uncle for a ticket home. Thought I'd lost you forever."

"Lost me? I was never yours to lose."

"Don't be angry, doll. I didn't know what I had 'til you left me. Then you sent that letter, like a beacon to guide me back to you."

"Give it up, Rupert," she said, opting for the direct approach. "We both know better. All I wanted was a letter of introduction."

"And all I want is another chance." He paused and ran his hands through his hair, then expelled a heavy breath. "All the crap aside, doll, I was glad to get the letter." He met her gaze and shrugged. "I was wrong. I pushed for too much, too fast. Maybe I can get to know the kid more. We can take things slow—see what develops."

Lottie shook her head. "I'm not looking for a boyfriend."

He sighed and shoved his hands into his trouser pockets as he turned away. He paced the room as the silence stretched. When he turned back, his expression was void of all his usual maneuvering. "How about a friend? One who's sorry."

"All I need is the letter." She batted her eyelashes, hoping it would convince him she was as scatterbrained as he so often thought. "I want to ask him about working for his company, maybe as a secretary or something."

He stepped back to her. "Secretary? Nope. You want to make a sale, doll. Pop doesn't cater much to independent women, or to people he doesn't know. I told you that. If you contact him yourself, he'll throw away your letter—even if I provide an introduction. The least I can do is set things up for you, play the middleman with Pop. Maybe make a few suggestions here and there on which equipment model to order."

Indecision washed over her. He knew her too well. There was no way she was going to convince him she didn't have a sale in the bag at Elitch's. She'd have to make sure he never found out the true extent of her plans. She raised her gaze and met his. "And what do you want in return?"

He opened his palms. "Nothing, doll. You've made it clear you don't want me. We'll just make the sale, and I'll be on my way. No strings attached."

"None?" Hah.

"None. Maybe I could sign on here, maintenance or something for a few weeks. I'm good at that, you know. I could get a feel for how things are run, help you make a selection from the catalog."

Disgust settled firmly in the pit of her stomach. She'd play his game, but only because he had her over a barrel. She didn't have enough money saved to run. "We make the sale, then you leave, no strings attached."

Assurance lit Rupert's face. "I promise, doll. I promise." He extended his hand.

Lottie shook it knowing that Rupert Gennick had never kept a promise in his life.

Two hours later, Caleb circled around the outdoor pavilion as the last notes of the afternoon orchestra concert wound down. The melody stuck with him, humming through his mind, as the musicians stowed their instruments. He waited for the crowd to disperse so he could check the flower boxes lining the walkway.

From the corner of his eye, he spied an unfamiliar figure hunched over the track of the miniature train; the kid who ran the ride was nowhere in sight. A finger of worry scratched at him, and he picked his way through the throng of people.

"Is there a problem?" he asked.

The man pivoted and shoved a shock of blond hair from his eyes. "Nope. Everything's under control."

The unease deepened. "According to . . . ?"

"The name's Gennick." The man straightened and offered his hand. "Ride maintenance and repair."

Caleb shook the hand, his memory trying to place the name.

Neither Tom nor Mary had said a thing about planning to hire anyone but the name seemed familiar. "Since when?"

"Hired on earlier this afternoon." Gennick wiped his brow with a worn handkerchief. "Sorry, I didn't catch your name."

"Caleb Hudson. Gardener."

"Glad to know ya, Hudson. This is some place they got here, huh?" He shoved the handkerchief into a rear pocket and shifted his weight as the small talk lingered between them.

Caleb eyed the man. Gennick's clothes were worn but not shabby. Caleb ruled out his being a bum. On closer look, though, the clothes were a bit too clean for a man who handled maintenance work. There wasn't a single oil stain on them. Caleb's unease began to form its way into a knot. "Tom hire you?"

"Mary."

The knot tightened. Who was this guy? "She say why?"

"Nope." He crossed his arms and threw a glance at the miniature train. "But I reckon it might have something to do with the fact that there hasn't been a lick of maintenance on these rides in weeks. She said the old guy up and quit."

Caleb bristled. Since Old Man Farnum had walked off, he'd done his best to ensure the rides were safe. Granted, maintenance wasn't his trade, but he did all right. "They get checked over every night," he said with an edge, crossing his own arms.

"Not by anybody who knows what they're doing."

"Not that complicated." Caleb stretched his fingers out of the fist they'd formed. He drew a breath, knowing anger wouldn't gain anything. Not if he wanted to determine the man's game. "You talk Mary into thinking she needs a specialist?" he said instead.

"I know rides, saw a few things right off. You don't want to fool around when safety's involved. I'll turn things around, teach someone else to take over when I leave." Gennick turned back to the miniature train, abandoning all traces of posturing.

"You leaving soon?"

"I reckon I'll stay the rest of the season, maybe winterize the rides for the Longs."

"But you aren't planning to stay?"

"I'm a rolling stone, Hudson. Got things to do, places to go. I'll be around, then I'll be gone. I need to earn some money, I've got a skill to ply." He glanced back. "You got a problem with that?"

Caleb pondered. The man had been casual, then defensive when questioned. Both normal reactions. He wasn't slick with any of his answers. Still, the situation didn't set right. It was almost as if he was guarding secrets. "I have a problem with strange men who just show up and wrangle themselves a job—especially one working with the equipment."

Gennick nodded. "I'm treading on your territory, huh?" He picked up a handful of tools and stuck them in his pocket, then offered Caleb a slow glance. "Look, sorry if you were insulted when I said I saw things weren't up to snuff. Not your fault." He turned back toward the equipment. "Wouldn't expect a gardener to know about all the little details, after all."

The last words were soft enough that Caleb might have missed them had he not been on his toes.

"What's your game, Gennick?"

"No game," he said, his attention still on the train. "Itinerant ride mechanic. That's all. Soon as I fix things up and put a couple dollars in my pocket, I'll be on my way. No need to get riled up about it."

"Not riled up. Just careful."

"Then we're of a like mind."

Caleb stared at the man, unable to shake the gut feeling that there was more to him than he let on.

★ ★ ★ ★ ★

Rupert watched Caleb turn and leave, feigning disinterest in the gardener. Any man who dug in the dirt for a living had to have a few screws loose but he sure as heck didn't want to discount the yokel as stupid. Rupert had seen his kind before, and they always caused trouble. He had enough worry as is.

Lottie was creating a mess, and he couldn't afford to let it get any worse. Hell, when he'd spotted her at Coney Island at the launch of the summer, he'd been pleased. It had been a few years since he'd last seen her, and she'd turned into a real doll—one with the skills he needed.

Way back when they were young, she'd shown up on the Coney Island boardwalks looking like a lost waif, and he'd taken her under his wing, taught her how to con. She'd taken to it like a fat lady to a sideshow. And she was gutsy—there wasn't a ride on earth she feared. She'd been his sidekick, and they'd had some great times together until he moved on to work as a mechanic.

He'd forgotten about her as he honed his skills and worked his way up the ladder. One day, he'd open his own park. Maybe then he'd catch his old man's attention. Maybe then, the smug son of a bitch would quit denying his own damn son, and Rupert would be more than a long-ago-forgotten bastard of a showgirl.

Rupert spat at the ground and gathered his tools, fighting to keep from throwing them into the toolbox. He glanced back at the miniature train and the huge hot air balloon that dominated the park and snorted. Trains, balloons, animals, and flowers. The Longs didn't have a clue what it took to build a true amusement park. His park would put them to shame.

For now, he needed to gain their trust. Once they saw how loyal and productive he was, he'd point out how easily the old-style amusements malfunctioned. No one would be the wiser and he'd have the Longs clambering to purchase new rides. From him. He'd milk them for a profit and move on—one step closer to his dream. But if he wasn't careful, Lottie Chase and her newfound independence would ruin everything.

She was supposed to be his ticket to the top. When she was a kid, she was a good con but now, with that body, she was unbelievable. She could talk a man into things he hadn't planned, and Rupert had no doubt she could persuade park owners into buying more rides than necessary. And she was just needy enough that she trusted everything he said. Or at least she had.

Hoisting his toolbox in one hand and the oil can in another, Rupert stowed them in the small shack, his thoughts still on Lottie. He'd had no trouble talking her into going on the road with him. She'd signed right on to his plan to travel the country, hitting the big parks to sell rides for a couple years until he built up the cash and connections he'd need to open his own park. By then, he'd have found the prime location for it, too.

Hell, Lottie wanted his attention so much that she'd never questioned his explanation for working menial labor at Coney Island. He'd told her how important it was for a successful businessman's son to learn all sides of the business, and she'd nodded at his wisdom. She'd swallowed that bit about the big discount they'd get from his old man and the huge profit they'd make. She'd never asked about other manufacturers and hadn't a clue who Rupert really intended to purchase from. He doubted his old man would give him any kind of discount at all but Lottie didn't need to know that. Let her go on accepting every bit of crap he told her—including how much her share would be.

Then, she'd brought that damn kid with her and everything started to go to hell.

His great plans to bed her and keep her dependent on him

while he used her wiles to con park owners had failed. She'd brought the kid along, then goaded him into a temper tantrum. He'd reacted without thought, dumping her, only to regret it. In a childish snit, he'd spent his time in San Francisco wasting money instead of earning it. Though he'd made a few contacts that might prove valuable, he'd failed to sell any rides and had been down to his last dime.

Then, she'd written him for a letter of introduction, of all things, and opened the door for him to reel her back in and put his plans back on track. He'd asked around, once he knew she'd remained in Denver, and learned Elitch's might be worth his time and effort after all. The park was ripe for expansion. He'd make a little money here, then move on, with Lottie in tow. She was his good-luck charm, after all. Together, they'd con a few more park owners into buying more rides than they needed at inflated prices. In no time, he'd have the money back in his pocket.

This time, he'd play the game a little smarter. When Lottie had let slip the kid was hers, he'd filled in the blanks. Her protective fussiness, her refusal to send word back to New York, her hatred of her uncle all these years—it hadn't taken a genius to figure out what had happened. When he left Denver, he hadn't given a thought about it.

Now, it would be his ace in the hole—one he planned to use.

Just as soon as he convinced the Longs the rides they had were unsafe and needed to be replaced.

Caleb stored his spade in the toolshed and glanced at his new pocket watch. Almost four hours since Ivy Baldwin's balloon had last risen above the park. He shook out his shoulders and double-checked the time. Something wasn't right.

Ivy was meticulous at keeping the lifts on schedule. Short delays occurred from time to time but four hours? Caleb closed the shed door and strode toward the center of the park. Even from a distance, he could see that the balloon sat there, empty, Ivy Baldwin absent. With a run, Caleb turned toward the cottage. Nearing, he heard Tom's concerned voice, then the overtly smooth cadence of the new maintenance man, Gennick. Caleb's muscles tensed.

Crap.

He slipped through the side gate and into the yard.

Tom and Gennick sat at the picnic table.

Tom was slumped, his hands clasped in front of him. "I don't see much choice. How long?"

"A day at least. Maybe two, if I can't find the parts." Gennick shrugged, as if whatever he referred to was out of his control.

"What's going on?" Caleb asked.

"Rupert found a damaged winch."

Caleb shook his head. "Not on Ivy's machinery. Not a chance."

Tom stared at Caleb, then Rupert. "It's a risk we can't take. Keep it closed. Remove the step stool and rope it off. Rupert, go to town and get what you need—we have an account at Allis-Chalmers on Tremont. I'll telephone and authorize you to get what you need. The sooner we get the part, the sooner we can reopen it." Tom stood, shaking his head. "I'd have thought Ivy would have caught this."

Caleb eyed Rupert. Ivy *would* have caught it. Rupert shrugged again, the action too casual, too offhand. Caleb's skin prickled. "Where is Ivy?"

Tom sighed. "Family emergency. He left for Colorado Springs at noon. Rupert here stepped in." He stood and crossed the yard. "I need to get back to the theatre. You go ahead into town and get what we need."

Caleb waited until the gate banged shut, then turned his gaze back to Rupert Gennick. "What's your game, slick?"

"No game, flower boy." A slight smirk crossed his face. "Just doing my job."

"Ivy's crew checks that balloon every night."

Rupert rose and swaggered toward Caleb. "Then his crew needs replacing."

"Like hell."

"Curse all you want, gardener." He stepped closer. "It don't change anything."

Caleb moved to the side. "What were you doing with the balloon anyway?"

"Just checking on it. The old man got the call, sent his crew home, and took off. I stopped to see that everything was battened down, saw there was a problem." Gennick rocked on his heels, checking his fingernails.

Heat flashed through Caleb's veins. "I don't believe you."

"Protest or no, the balloon isn't safe." Gennick thrust out his chest and a slippery smile graced his lips. "Like I told Tom, that's the problem with old-fashioned attractions like these. Things go wrong. Lucky I caught it. 'Course the ride could be down for a couple days. The winch is old, hard to find parts for. You don't have that problem with modern rides. Things rarely go awry and the parts are plentiful."

Suspicion morphed into irritation. How could Tom fail to see through the greasy con Gennick was feeding him? "Ivy would have made repairs at the first sign of trouble."

"Well, he didn't. And now the Longs have a problem."

Caleb moved forward, fists balling. "You're the problem."

"Stick to your flower beds, chump," Gennick said, raising his hand in an overt gesture of polite refusal of physical involvement. "Leave the complicated maintenance to someone who knows what he's doing. This park's been in an amateur's hands too long already."

The insult burned but Caleb tamped down the sting and

wondered at Gennick's motives. "Whatever it is you're trying to pull, the jig is up."

"No jig, Hudson. Just a maintenance expert pointing out what happens with old rides and untrained help." Gennick stepped back, not bothering to hide the sneer on his face.

His heartbeat stampeding, Caleb followed. "You conniving son of a—"

Gennick threw up his hands, refusing the bait. "Save it, Hudson. I need to catch a trolley, make it into town before the store closes. Unless you want me to pin an extra day's delay on you."

Caleb bit his tongue and watched the smug interloper saunter away. He didn't believe Rupert's story. Hell, he doubted the mechanic had even looked at the winch, let alone that there was a problem with it. Ivy was too meticulous to let something like that go. He'd check the balloon for himself, just as soon as he located Ivy's maintenance log and proved the slippery maintenance man was a liar.

Lottie shrugged her aching shoulders in an attempt to rid herself of the knot that had formed at the back of her neck. It had been a long day. She could swear the animals had gotten together and planned to soil their pens more than usual, all on the same day. She craved a bath.

Rupert had kept at her, too, piling on his own version of refuse. Bringing her ice cream and lemonade. Toting buckets and pushing wheelbarrows. He was so solicitous, it made her downright nervous. He'd turned on the charm with Elsa, too, until Elsa had quit scowling at him and offered a smile.

Lottie knew from experience that when Rupert Gennick ingratiated himself, nothing bode well.

The man was hard to resist. Rupert had a knack for sliding right under her skin and diverting her from her cares. He was fun to be around. He'd been a pal since they were kids and had taken her mind off her troubles those difficult months after Elsa had been born and Aunt Aggie had made it so uncomfortable to stay around home. But this summer, he'd changed, he'd pushed for more than Lottie was willing to give. She would need to stay alert and ahead of his game.

She sighed and trod toward the cottage, for once thankful for the peaceful tranquility of the closed park. To the left, Ivy Baldwin's hydrogen balloon sat a couple feet above its pad, a huge rope net around the silk air-bag. Four sturdy tether cables were attached to the head-rail to anchor it to the ground. Ivy and his crew were nowhere to be seen, probably already in their nearby rooming house, settled in for the evening.

She neared the sixty-five-foot balloon, watching it sway in the evening breeze, and caught sight of a beaded reticule perched on the dark railing of the eighteen-passenger willow gondola.

Someone might be at home, fretting about her lost purse. Lottie would take it to Mary, see if they could find out to whom it belonged and contact the woman. If the lady had a telephone, they could ease her worry this evening.

Lottie veered off the path, toward the balloon. She stepped close, stumbled over a loose rope, and steadied herself on the edge of the gondola siding. The reticule toppled into the basket. Cursing her clumsiness, Lottie peered over the side of the basket and spied the purse. It lay on the gondola floor amid the dirt and clutter Ivy had left to be swept out first thing in the morning.

Lottie frowned at the handbag and debated with herself. Ivy never allowed other park employees in the basket unless he was present. Still, she hated to leave a valuable item lying there. She climbed up the step stool beside the balloon, frowning at its height. Didn't Ivy normally tie it off closer to the ground? She sighed, grabbed hold of one of the ropes attached to the basket ring above her, and hoisted herself up until she could sit on the side of the gondola. Then she swung her legs over the side.

The basket rocked and she reached for one of the tether cables. Too late, Lottie recognized there was no tension. She tumbled forward, swinging on the cable. The gondola lurched.

Her heart stuttered at the unexpected pitching, and she dropped into the basket, her hands burning from their slide on the rope. She reached for another cable, finding it slack. With stark clarity, she realized the cables weren't anchored and the balloon was rising. *Oh, lord.* "Help! Anyone? Help."

"Lottie?" Caleb's voice sounded from under the basket. "Be still, I'll find the winch pin."

The precarious basket jerked, then tipped as the balloon sprung further upward. Sweat broke out on Lottie's skin.

Jump.

She ducked the loose cables, hurried to the lower edge of the swinging basket, and peered over the side. A pile of sandbags lay atop a single anchor cable, causing it to lurch to the side. Bit by bit, the rope was sliding loose, the balloon tipping further aside as it rose higher. Caleb scrambled from under the basket, rose to his feet, and ran for one of the opposite ropes.

Shaking, Lottie yanked on the nearest cable and pulled, her feet scrambling to climb out of the gondola.

The basket lurched again.

"Stay put," Caleb yelled. "She's going to jerk loose any second."

His voice sounded distant, nearly drowned out by Lottie's heartbeat thrashing in her ears. She gasped for air, throwing one leg over the railing.

The gondola jolted upright and Lottie tumbled to the floor. She stared upward, dizzy, as the balloon began to ascend with speed. Her chest burned, tremors shuddering through her as her mind began to clear.

She fought to control her breathing.

An arm wrapped around the top of the gondola. Grunting, Caleb hoisted himself over the side and dropped into the basket.

Lottie struggled to her knees as Caleb managed the ropes above them. Standing, she edged toward the side of the basket.

"Stay put, I said." Caleb warned, "Let me get control of this thing."

"But—"

"No buts, Lottie." He reached for her, pulled her close, his hard muscles enfolding her until her heart raced again. "I need you to listen to me. Do you understand?"

She nodded, her tense body calming as she leaned against him.

He released her, working the ropes as the last of the pitching settled, and the balloon rested on the sway of the light summer breezes. Then he faced her.

"There's a reason Ivy doesn't let anybody in when he's not here, you know."

"Yep. I figured that out."

"Yet here you are."

"I guess a person assumes four tether ropes would hold one woman," she mumbled.

"They would," he said, "if they were hooked to their anchor rings." His brow knit for a brief moment. "I unhooked them so I could run the winch, try to see what was wrong with it. You didn't notice they weren't attached?"

"I didn't check. You didn't notice someone was in the balloon?"

"By the time I figured out it wasn't the wind and that someone was stupid enough to get in an untethered balloon, it was too late to crawl my way out in time." He adjusted the ropes again.

Lottie watched his strong arms as he worked to control their ascent, breathing easier as their lift slowed. He seemed to know what he was doing. Her shoulders relaxed, and she offered him a wavering smile.

"I was tempted to just let you go," he said.

Her eyes widened. "Let me go? Are you crazy?" She stared at him while gentle buoyancy lifted them.

"You do have a tendency to get yourself in some strange predicaments." He shook his head. "There's a steel cable hooked onto the bottom of the gondola. It's attached to a winch so the balloon can be reeled back in. But I had the pin pulled out and couldn't find it among the grass clippings before the ropes pulled loose. Criminy, Lottie, I didn't even know you were there. What were you doing?"

"Retrieving that." She pointed to the purse, lying on the floor. "I thought someone would be missing it."

Caleb shook his head, a slight smile stretching his lips. "I put it on the gondola rail. I was going to take it to Mary later."

"Why did you have the cables loose?"

"Gennick said the winch was faulty. The only way to check it was to release the balloon."

"So what happens now?"

"The cable will hold us from rising too far up. But we'll climb 'til it plays out." He glanced at her. "I could have let you go up alone."

She stiffened.

"It would have been a good lesson on rules." He sobered. "But you were panicked. I didn't want to risk you jumping before I could find the pin and pull you down."

She shuddered, recalling her frantic attempt to escape the balloon. "Thank you."

"If we're lucky, someone on the ground will spot us, find the pin, turn on the winch's engine, and reel us in. If not, we take it down ourselves. I assume you don't know much about bringing a balloon down on your own?"

"That's a fair assumption."

"Ivy taught a few of us. Never thought any of us would need to put his lessons to the test, though."

She watched him lean back against the side of the basket, unsure just what to make of him. He was an enigma—closed and judgmental at times, responsive and open at others. This was not the same man who had grown cold and turned her away a few days ago. Catching his gaze, she shivered.

Unable to look away, her mouth parted. The air grew heavy around her. She swallowed, then moved to the opposite railing, determined not to make a fool of herself again.

"I didn't mean to be so abrupt the other day," he said.

She bristled. "Yet you were."

"I'm sorry, Lottie. I . . . I don't do well with screaming roller coaster riders." He turned away, shoulders stiff.

Roller coaster riders? Lottie stared at him. "I thought it was me," she blurted, her face heating.

Caleb turned back. "You?"

"What was I supposed to think? I made that wisecrack and you told me to go away."

"Hell, Lottie, I don't even know what you said. Those screams filled the air and I wasn't prepared." Pain crossed his face and her heart caught.

"Prepared for what?"

Caleb swallowed. "The screams took me by surprise. Set off bad memories. For a minute, I was somewhere else." He paused. "I'm sorry I snapped at you. You had nothing to do with it."

Lottie offered a wavering smile, wishing he'd say more. Knowing he wouldn't. "I wish I'd known," she said.

He smiled back, his eyes warm. "Me, too." She stepped to the opposite railing, her arms braced behind her as she leaned back, watching the center ropes sway in the breeze.

The stillness of the evening surrounded them, bringing a calm peacefulness. They drew slow breaths, comfortable in the coolness of the evening air.

Caleb shifted. "You intrigue me, Lottie." His voice was deep against the silence.

Goose bumps dampened the small of her back. Goose bumps! She started.

He smiled.

Lottie closed her eyes, her chest pounding. She wanted to run but there was nowhere to go. When she opened them again, he was staring at her.

"Caleb?"

"Yep?"

Her mouth refused to work, words stuck in her throat along with her breath. Heat inundated her, desire clambering for recognition. She swallowed.

"Gads!" she blurted.

Caleb's rich laughter filled the air, surrounding her until she joined in. Then, the humor drifted away and they stood, across the gondola from one another, speechless and panting. Then the intensity overwhelmed her and Lottie turned away, her gaze shifting to the vista beyond the basket.

"Oh, my!" She stared downward. "Would you look at that! How high do you suppose we are?"

"A thousand feet, maybe more. The cable's fifteen hundred feet long so we can climb higher before I take us down."

"Let's let it play out." Her nerve endings jumped in excitement, and she couldn't keep it from her face.

Caleb chuckled. "You're not afraid of heights, then?"

"Oh, no. Not as long as I know we have a way down. This is exhilarating. You can see all of Denver from up here." She turned to the west. The evening sun shimmered through the peach and lavender clouds, dropping beams of light on the snow-tipped peaks. "And just look at the mountains."

Caleb nodded. "Elitch's Gardens looks a lot smaller from up here, huh?"

She bent her head and looked around. The basket had drifted and the grounds were no longer under them. "Goodness. Just look how far they seem from the city."

"Five miles, from downtown. A few farms around."

Lottie peered downward. "Jeepers, would you look at all that land!"

"Yep." He straightened and reached to sort through the various ropes hanging above them. "Guess I'd better open up the vent, take us back down. Doesn't look like anyone's noticed we're up here. Least not anyone at Elitch's."

Lottie laughed, thinking about how many Denver children were pointing at the balloon. She watched Caleb for a moment and allowed the serenity of the moment to stretch on. Then she glanced over the side again, drawn to the open patches around the Gardens, her thoughts jumping.

"If Tom and Mary would buy up that land, there'd be all kinds of room to expand the park. That land beyond the orchard, they could put a larger coaster in there and still have room for a couple other rides. And it's empty to the south, too." She stood and turned to Caleb, her mind racing with ideas. "How many acres do you suppose that is? I can imagine it built up. We could add five, maybe ten attractions. Big ones."

Caleb's mouth drew into a thin line. "The Longs aren't adding any more rides. Only the carousel they ordered. That's it. Mary wants to build up the theatre."

Lottie considered his words only briefly. After all, hadn't Mary been as enthused as she was about adding rides? "I can almost hear the crowds. Kids laughing and screaming, can't you?"

Caleb shook his head. She couldn't leave well enough alone,

could she? The ride, and their conversation, had been peaceful, sociable. She'd been a picture, her initial fear of her own desire, then her unfolding joy in the moment was so genuine that his heart had constricted, watching her. Now, here she was, going on about the park yet again.

"Can you imagine it?" she repeated.

"No. I can't." Caleb knew his voice had become brittle but he didn't care. How could she think of taking a beautiful sanctuary and surrounding it with acres of cheap thrill rides? Diminishing the culture Mary so loved by transforming the area into a common playground instead of a family garden? And how could he be so damned attracted to her?

He located the vent line and pulled the rope to release hydrogen from the vent at the top of the balloon, frowning. Nothing had been wrong with the winch. Rupert was either inept or playing games, both troubling scenarios. Then, Caleb himself had been irresponsible, failing to take precautions when he checked the winch. Ivy wasn't going to be happy. Not about the carelessness or about the expense of having to refill the balloon. It took some twenty tons of scrap iron and the same amount of sulfuric acid to make enough hydrogen to charge the bag, the damn thing was so huge.

Lottie was chattering about expanding the park and how well she could envision it from up here. No matter how desirable the woman was, her ideas troubled him. Expanding the park went against everything he and the Longs had discussed. He'd already seen the sway she had with Mary. She may not have sabotaged the balloon, but now that she'd been up in it, he doubted she'd let her ideas die away. If he wasn't careful, she'd soon have Tom and Mary sold on her ideas.

It was time to get off his duff and tell them about his vision for the park.

CHAPTER SEVEN

"Caleb?" Tom's voice echoed as he stepped through the greenhouse door the following morning.

Across the muggy, sunlit room, Caleb tossed a final shovelful of worms onto the compost heap and turned to his friend and employer. "Thanks for coming over," he said. "I thought we should talk, and I didn't want to worry Mary." He strode down the aisle, wiping his hands on the wet rag he'd slung over his shoulder earlier.

"Shall we sit?" Tom nodded to a pair of wobbly wooden stools and lifted a quart jar. "I brought cold tea."

Settling with care on a stool opposite Tom, Caleb took a swig from the proffered jar and returned it.

"You look at the balloon?" Tom asked as he set the jar on the table.

"Me and Ivy both. There's nothing wrong with it."

"But the runaway?"

"My own carelessness. There was never any threat of a problem with the winch."

Tom's brow knitted. "Then what's going on?"

"There's something about that new mechanic that doesn't sit right with me. He either doesn't know what he's doing or he was trying to mislead you."

"Look, son," Tom's voice was patient, filled with familiar tolerant understanding. "I know it's in your nature to protect Mary." He paused. "Gennick came well-recommended as a

115

mechanic—letters from Fred Thompson himself."

The owner of Luna Park, Coney Island's premier park. He was a man of sterling reputation and a personal friend of Mary and Tom. As Caleb should have realized, Mary was too smart to hire someone without references. Still, his gut told him things weren't all they seemed.

"He's slick, Tom. Too slick."

"Lottie said he used to be a huckster, before he became a mechanic. I suppose one doesn't lose that."

Caleb's gut flinched. A huckster? He should have known. No wonder things were odd. "We need to keep an eye on him. If he's working a confidence game, we need to be one step ahead of him."

"I'll watch him."

"Another thing. Ivy said the maintenance log is missing entries."

"Missing entries?"

"Nothing's entered for the past couple weeks."

Tom eyes widened. "Ivy wouldn't allow such incompetence. Did you talk to the employee who was supposed to be adding entries?"

"He swears everything was done and logged." Caleb reached for the tea, uncomfortable with the implication. Taking a swig, he passed it to Tom. "Ivy wants to believe him but he hadn't checked the book himself. He's never had reason to."

"So you think Rupert removed pages to make us think there was a problem?" He set the jar back on the table.

"No proof . . . Just things that don't make sense and a feeling in my gut." Caleb paused, trying to gauge Tom's thoughts. "Why'd he show up here?"

"Mary said he's a friend of Lottie's. They parted on less-than-good terms. I guess she wrote him, and he took it upon himself to show up and try to win her back."

"So, Mary's matchmaking?" That made more sense. "I wondered why she felt the need for a mechanic."

Tom rolled his eyes. "She was also trying to save you the extra work. Since Old Man Farnum left, you've been picking up the slack. It seemed like an opportunity, having a bona fide mechanic ready things for winter."

"Are you implying I don't know what I'm doing?"

Tom laughed. "I'm saying you're a gardener at heart and that you've had your hands full with maintenance and training Lottie."

"True enough. But I still don't trust Gennick."

Tom stood, smoothing his trousers, and picked up the jar of tea. "I'll talk with Mary, decide what we want to do. In the meantime, let's have Ivy maintain the log himself."

Caleb nodded, recognizing the importance of diligence. He'd do the same, only his eyes would be on Gennick.

Caleb rubbed his eyes and blinked in the gathering darkness of his small cabin. The evening had gotten away from him again. After long days tending the gardens, keeping a sharp eye on Gennick, and performing extra safety checks, he'd spent the past two evenings in the cramped quarters sketching out his garden plans, growing frustrated when the drawings failed to do justice to the intricate visions in his head.

He needed to translate his visions to paper before Lottie had a chance to sway Mary into thinking she needed more amusement rides. For too long, he'd kept his ideas to himself, content to pursue changing one small area at a time. Mary and Tom had no clue how widespread his dreams for his adopted home really were.

And it sure hadn't helped the process with thoughts of Lottie intruding every few minutes. She complicated his life and he wasn't sure how he felt about it.

He exhaled a heavy breath and fingered his lithographic crayon. Determined to avoid her tempting distraction, he concentrated on the drawing in front of him. His ideas included not only expanding the groomed flower beds, but adding quiet grottoes and a modern greenhouse to replace the current small glass-enclosed bedding area.

When he'd returned from Cuba, he'd had little interest in continuing the architectural studies he'd begun before the war. Instead, he'd found solace in creating landscapes, using his training to craft sculptured gardens for Elitch's. He'd poured over botany books, even taken a few classes at Colorado State University. The landscapes in his head found their way into the designs he created. The peace and structure of the place he'd come to regard as his own easing his painful memories of chaos and turmoil.

Still, he envisioned more. The grottoes would be sanctuaries of escape. They'd serve others, just as they would him—secluded glens blocking out the busy upheaval and worries of life. Folks needed a place of peace and calm.

But the new greenhouse would be his special place—a place where he could create life rather than destroying it. For months, he'd wanted to experiment more fully on new varieties of roses, on developing vibrant colors and rich fragrances. And he imagined finding a way to make the small white garden carnation something more than an accent flower in bouquets—fuller, in all the colors of the rainbow, perhaps. Most people had no idea how much joy there was in such simple things.

But to do that, he'd need more than a bedding room. He'd need a full scale conservatory with controlled temperatures and space to experiment.

Caleb tucked the crayon into its box with the rest of the set and glanced down at the drawings on the table. Satisfaction tugged at the corners of his mouth. The plan was balanced. The new grottoes were tucked into already secluded spaces. Intricate flower beds stretched along new pathways, some of them with sculptured clusters of roses, others with a variety of low plants chosen for their colors and ease of care. In a few places, he'd included meandering beds of wildflowers to suggest more natural panoramas. The new greenhouse structure ran the length of the orchard, its panels facing south and west to catch the sun's heat. A public room graced one end, accessible from the park, so that visitors could enjoy rare hothouse treasures, a grotto onto itself.

It was a good plan. Better than good.

And a hell of a lot better than a bunch of loud carnival rides with screaming noise that threatened a man's peace of mind.

The following evening, Lottie paced the cottage kitchen, nervous and wondering where Tom and Mary were. She'd intended to present her plans tonight, and she was unsettled. For days, Caleb had filled her senses, distracting her from her feeble attempts to translate her ideas to paper.

Too much rode on this presentation. She couldn't let desire for Caleb interfere with her presentation. Somehow, she had to convey how the park could be improved by the addition of more rides, how much pleasure people could find in such a setting. After all, amusement parks had saved her once. They could save her again . . . if she was successful with this pitch.

If not, there'd be no commission. At the end of the season, she could be out of a job, and she and Elsa would be living hand to mouth.

Earlier, she'd settled Elsa backstage with Tony Perry for the final theatre performance of the season, promising the fretful youngster she could spend the night with Tony. In just a few days, the acting troupe would be on their way, and both girls were already melancholy. When Tony's father had suggested

119

Elsa might stay over at their nearby rental quarters, Lottie had sought Mary's advice regarding Elsa's safety, then given in to her daughter's soulful pleas and ceded her approval.

She'd thought that having Elsa with the Perrys would provide her uninterrupted time to present her ideas to Tom and Mary. Except the Longs were nowhere to be found. She'd expected them to be settled in the cottage parlor, as was their habit this time of evening, especially after she'd told them she needed a few moments of their time.

She fingered the newsprint she'd spread with such care on the table and frowned at a graphite smudge on the drawing. Her inept illustrations were evidence enough of her amateur status. She didn't need pencil smears to call more attention to it. She pulled a worn eraser from her pocket and bent to rub at the mark.

The rasp of the screen door broke the silence, and Lottie jumped.

"Hello, Lottie," said a familiar male voice. "Where're the Longs?"

Lottie straightened and stared at Caleb, her heart pattering at the sight of him. Since the balloon incident, she'd been so busy with the plan that they'd seen each other only from a distance. He stood with the door still open into the dusk, his whiskey eyes peering into the quiet kitchen.

"They're not here." She flinched at the edginess in her voice. "Sorry," she said, as much in apology as in regret about their absence. She'd missed Caleb these past few days and didn't want to set him off the way she invariably seemed to do. She shivered. Missed him . . . heck, she hadn't been able to get him out of her mind. But right now, she wished he wasn't there. She was nervous enough.

He smiled at her and entered, fully at home, then crossed the lighted kitchen. "They told me to come on over."

Lottie shrugged her shoulders, feigning nonchalance as her nerves jumped again. "I've been waiting for them, too."

He glanced at the table. "What've you got there?"

"Plans," she announced, with a hint of pride.

"Plans?" He moved closer, wariness crossing his features. "For what?"

"Amusement rides."

"You've got to be kidding." His words were slow, drawn out in a way that made it impossible to miss his annoyance.

Frustrated irritation slammed through her. There it was again, that sudden irrational testiness of his. She stared at him, unable to fathom his reaction. "Why would I be kidding? Tom and Mary could turn this place into a first-class amusement park. With all the land around here, they could put in gabs of rides. Elitch's could be the Coney Island of the West." She pointed to the newsprint. "I've drawn it all out."

"No." He shook his head, a curt movement that spoke volumes.

Lottie's hackles rose at the reproof. "What do you mean, no?"

"I mean no. Why on earth would they want to be the Coney Island of the West? That doesn't fit with their vision at all."

"But Mary loves rides. She loves pleasing the kids. Expansion would be a smart move for her."

"You don't know a thing about Mary. She loves the theatre, and the animals, and the orchard. Turning this place into a gaudy circus would be against everything she's strived for."

Disbelief mingled with Lottie's impatience. Caleb Hudson had no idea what he was talking about. "Amusement parks don't have to be garish," she explained. "They can be very tasteful. And there's room for theatre and animals, too."

"Melodrama and slapstick?" he asked with a bitter tone. "Vaudeville and variety shows? Petting zoos and menageries?

Camels parading in an imitation of an Egyptian marketplace?"

"Sophisticated suggestions of faraway places. Entertainment that takes people away from the cares of their everyday lives."

"That isn't what Tom and Mary want."

Lottie gasped at his rude insistence. What was wrong with the man? "Isn't what they want or isn't what you want?"

Caleb's jaw clenched. "I've known Mary since I was a kid, and I know a damn sight more than you about what she wants."

"Then you've spoken with her about this?"

"Well, no, but—"

"Well, I have," Lottie interjected, her voice rising with an unwillingness to take any more of his petty reprimands, "so it seems I know a damn sight more than you about what she wants."

"Good lord. Do you two know folks can hear you halfway across the park?" Tom's voice came from outside the screen door. He pulled it open.

Mary entered, tsking. "I'd wager neither of you knows a damn sight more than the other about what I want," she said as she swept past Tom and into the kitchen. "You're as bad as a couple of scolding monkeys. Hush up and be still, the both of you."

Tom followed, stopping to stare at Caleb and Lottie with his arms crossed. "Couple of fools is more like it."

Lottie's face heated. Across the table, Caleb's chin lowered.

Mary looked from one of them to the other, frank disapproval in her eyes. Her mouth pinched, and she shook her head.

Tom pulled out a chair, waited until his wife was seated, then joined her. His mustache twitched but he didn't say a word. Instead, the silence stretched as Lottie and Caleb stood before them.

Lottie fought the urge to shift her feet like the errant schoolgirl she felt. Caleb shoved his hands into his front pockets, his expression one of strained neutrality.

"We'll hear Caleb first," Mary announced. She glanced at Lottie. "He asked this morning," she explained. "Your request was made this afternoon."

Lottie let out her breath and tried to relax.

Caleb approached the table and unrolled a sheet of butcher paper, laying it over Lottie's washed-out newsprint. Grabbing the salt and pepper shakers from the counter, he set them on opposite corners of the paper, then anchored the remaining corners with the sugar bowl and the empty creamer.

Lottie stared at the well-crafted drawing, her shaken confidence fading further. The park was laid out in meticulous detail, each path and attraction illustrated in tinted crayon. Each scaled flower bed unique enough that she could distinguish the plants in it. New features were sketched in colorful glory. There were no smudges anywhere.

Caleb leaned forward, explaining his ideas for the existing flower beds first. Gathering self-assurance, he went on to describe the new garden areas and the grottoes with their low stone benches. He outlined the improvements he envisioned for the pathways near the theatre and the outdoor orchestra pavilion. His voice filled with enthusiasm, he discussed the long, low building he had drawn next to the orchard—the combination greenhouse and orangery. Passion lit his eyes as he touched on the tropical plants he had in mind and the experiments he would undertake.

Lottie swallowed. Caleb's design was appealing and well-thought-out. She glanced at Tom and Mary. Tom's face was rapt with interest. Mary nodded, digesting Caleb's vision with attentive concentration. Her eyes lit as Caleb emphasized the theatre area. Lottie's stomach knotted. Had she misinterpreted Mary's zeal for amusement rides?

Lottie shifted her feet as Caleb finished his presentation. Silence stretched as all eyes turned to her.

"Lottie?" Mary prompted. "Your turn, my dear."

Caleb lifted his drawing away, revealing Lottie's smeared doodle. She'd put mis-sized squares and rectangles on the paper to represent current buildings and curlicues signified garden areas. Everything was dull gray. A lump lodged in her throat.

She coughed, then drew a breath.

"I . . . uh . . . Mary and I talked a few weeks back about amusement rides. With the fast pace of the world now, more and more people find themselves caught up in making a living. We work longer hours to keep up and often carry worries with us wherever we go. One of the first things I learned when I started working at Coney Island is that people need an escape. Even those with little money will spend some of it to get away."

Lottie glanced at both the Longs, saw their interest, and relaxed a little.

"One of the things Luna Park, on Coney Island, does best is offer that escape. The park is a magical, enchanted area lit by millions of electric lights that attract people. Each segment of the park creates a world apart from the everyday, places the average working man and his family will never actually visit. Then, amusement rides take people further from day to day reality. Riders are thrilled. They enjoy speed and taking chances. They feel the heady thrill of abandon. And they can do it all without taking any real risk. They come back again and again to do so."

"But aren't lights and expanded hours expensive?" Tom asked.

"The additional costs are offset by the increased numbers of people. You continue to charge a reasonable, even cheap, admission fee. That brings more customers in. Then, you apply additional fares for tickets to the larger, most tempting attractions."

Across the table, Tom nodded his understanding.

Lottie chanced a glance at Caleb's crossed arms and closed

expression, then chased his unspoken rebuke from her mind before it dampened her enthusiasm. She turned back to the newsprint and pointed to it.

"My drawing shows the attractions you have now. Here and here are the theatre and pavilion. You keep that portion of the park as a cultural area." She shifted her hand. "But here, where you have underused space, you could add more attractions to complement what you already have. Along the side of the orchard, you could put in a water ride. If you expand to the empty land next to the park, you could add several more coaster rides."

She went on to describe the rides in more detail, ignoring the gray rectangles she'd drawn on the paper and relying instead on Tom and Mary's memories of their annual trips to Coney Island. Their expressions reflected their recollections as Lottie filled in the details on how each ride operated and how the combinations she'd proposed would complement each other.

When she finished, she looked up from the plan and caught their gazes. "Right now is the ideal opportunity to expand," she told them. "The concepts and the rides are still new, and therefore even more exciting."

Mary exhaled a breath. "Expansion takes money, lots of it on the scale you're proposing. Adding rides is a much bigger undertaking than landscaping and a new greenhouse."

"That's true but it takes money to make money. By drawing in more people and adding the extra fees for the bigger rides, you increase your profits. Fred Thompson, the owner of Luna Park, claims he doubled his money back within one season. The secret was in his rapid rate of expansion. By going big, he lured people in, got them hooked, then kept them coming back to see what else he'd added."

"New York has a much bigger population base," Tom reasoned.

"That's true, but I think you'll get a good return, if you select your rides with care." Lottie paused. "That's where I come in. I can not only advise you on which rides to choose and where to put them, I can help you purchase them."

"You what?" Caleb spit out.

Mary quieted him with a look while Tom nodded to Lottie. "Go on."

"I can help you buy those rides," Lottie announced, beaming. "Rupert Gennick's father owns one of the largest amusement ride companies in the country." She paused, ignoring the nagging doubts in her mind. Somehow, she'd find a way around Rupert so she could fulfill the promise. "He's promised Rupert a huge discount. I can negotiate a very, very good deal for you."

She pasted a smile on her face even as Caleb's features hardened, and her heart cramped. She squashed away the pain and told herself it didn't matter.

The following afternoon, Caleb watched Lottie and Rupert Gennick chatting across the open area in front of the pavilion and stabbed at the ground with his spade, nearly severing the delicate primroses he'd cultivated. He scowled at the damage and rocked back on his heels.

He'd known all along that she was a con artist, intent on ingratiating herself with the Longs for her own hidden purposes. Except now, her purposes were no longer hidden. Nor were Rupert's. She and Gennick were in cahoots. She'd revealed her money-hungry intentions, put it out in the open for everyone to see, but no one seemed to notice it but him.

Last night, he'd tried to tell Tom and Mary they were being set up. He'd insisted Lottie and Rupert had invented the abandonment scenario to gain Mary's sympathy. Even the story of Elsa being in danger might be a lie for all they knew. And everything pointed to Rupert staging mechanical problems with

126

the balloon. Without the balloon, people would crave other excitement.

Tom had looked stern and reminded him not to accuse unless he had proof. They'd discussed the issue with Rupert and he'd agreed he might have been overzealous about the winch, citing a belief that it was better to be safe than sorry. Despite Caleb's gut feeling, there was nothing to indicate there was anything more to the incident. Mary had cited Rupert's glowing recommendation and reminded Caleb the man was supposed to be a master ride mechanic. Neither of the Longs seemed willing to acknowledge they might have been deliberately fooled.

Even Caleb had been played, though he hadn't mentioned that to Tom and Mary. His pride stung enough just having to admit he'd been suckered by a pair of innocent eyes and a set of curves. Lottie had wormed her way past his wall of reserve and had dug her talons in so far he'd likely bleed by the time he shook her loose.

Hell, they all would.

Tom and Mary didn't have the money to invest on the scale Lottie had proposed. She'd take all they had while destroying the original vision Mary and the late John Elitch had for their gardens. Before you knew it, riffraff would take over the park, drowning out the culture just as the rides would overrun the peace of the garden areas. It'd be just another amusement park. No longer a sanctuary, no longer a place for families, no longer unique. Hoodlums would abound, and parents would no longer send their kids unescorted for Mary's weekly "children's day."

A sour taste settled in Caleb's mouth. He'd promised John Elitch he would always look out for Mary, and he'd failed.

He stood, his gaze shifting upward.

Lottie stood with Rupert, her hand on his arm, an enticing smile gracing her animated face.

The acrid mix of failure, of being duped, and a foreboding

127

sense of loss bubbled into anger. Caleb shoved the trowel into his back pocket and used his handkerchief to dab at his forehead as he tempered the urge to march over and throttle the both of them.

Being duped he could live with. Wounded pride was a small thing. Loss of the gardens was bigger, but he reckoned he'd live with that, too, if it came down to it, no matter how distasteful he found it. But failing to protect Mary was not an option. And if it took a breakdown of costs, a cutthroat examination of the impact of Lottie's proposed changes, and proof that Rupert Gennick was setting up a con, then he needed to get busy.

CHAPTER EIGHT

Elsa kicked the empty pail. It tipped and rolled with a clatter across the floor of the shed. Lottie jumped.

Glancing at her daughter, Lottie bit her lip and drew a ragged breath. Elsa's continuous sulkiness, now in its third day, was wearing on them all. Ever since the acting troupe had departed, each day grew a little worse. Particularly since Lottie herself was on pins and needles waiting for Tom and Mary to pass judgment on her expansion ideas. Thank heavens she and Elsa were finished feeding the animals, so she could take the youngster home and they could both relax.

She glanced at the overturned pail. "Can you get that?" she asked, forcing calmness into her voice.

Elsa crossed her arms and stuck out her lower lip. "The only time you ever want my help is when there's work to do. I'm tired of cleaning cages and filling buckets. You never let me do any of the fun stuff."

Lottie reined in her anger and reminded herself to act like a parent. "I won't have you doing anything unsafe. Besides, I expect your help when you've created the work."

"You were gonna pick it up yourself a second ago."

Elsa's sassiness grated on Lottie, but she knew she couldn't allow herself to be pulled into a shouting match. She needed to correct Elsa's behavior. That's what Mary would do. "But now I have to walk across the shed to do it. So it seems like you should do so instead."

"It's five whole feet."

Lottie nodded. "Yes, but that's five feet more than it was before you kicked it."

"Feeding the animals isn't my job."

"And picking up after you isn't mine." The words flew out like a slap, harsher than Lottie had wanted. She wasn't at all sure she had the patience for her new role. She'd played such a small part in Elsa's upbringing—Aunt Aggie had made sure of that—and she knew very little about raising a child. She sensed Elsa knew it as well.

The ten-year-old stared at her, her fiery eyes challenging Lottie's precarious authority. "Then send me back to New York," she baited. "Nobody asked you to take me with you when you left."

Lottie exhaled. She'd wondered how long it would take Elsa to circle around to their flight west. "I am not sending you back to New York," she said.

Elsa stamped her foot. "You aren't the boss of me and you can't make me stay here. Not if I don't want to."

"You are not going back."

"You don't have any say-so in it. You don't run my life."

Lottie bit back the retort that was on the tip of her lips. She drew a deep breath and tried to think. While she didn't want Elsa to think it was acceptable to sass, she knew the girl felt alone. Her only friend was gone and the closing of the theatre had robbed her of her favorite activity. Still, Lottie had to squelch any talk of returning to New York.

Meeting Elsa's eyes, she said, "Would you rather have Edward . . . your father . . . running your life?"

Elsa swallowed and shook her head.

"I'm not trying to make your life miserable, sweetheart. I'm trying to protect you."

Tears welled in Elsa's eyes. "I know. I'm just mad 'cause

Tony's gone." Dropping her gaze, she bit her lip. "Edward and Aggie . . . they're not really my parents, are they?"

Lottie drew a breath. "Oh, sweetie." She pulled Elsa close. "How did you know?"

"I heard you tell Mary."

"I'm so sorry, Elsa. I didn't mean for you to find out that way."

"Who am I?"

Unsure Elsa was ready for the whole truth, Lottie scrambled for an explanation. "Mama was Edward's younger sister. She died when I was . . . a long time ago. We never had a father."

"They didn't want us there, did they?" she sniffled.

"I don't think they knew how to be parents. They took us in, raised you as theirs. Aunt Aggie wanted to be a mother. But she never was."

"She never hugged me. Only you did."

"I'm sorry, Elsa. I wanted to make it better for you. I wish I could have been there more."

"I don't really want to go back, you know. I don't like the way . . . Uncle Edward . . . looks at me. It gives me the willies."

Lottie shivered. "I know, Elsa," she said, hugging her tight. "It gave me the willies, too, when he looked at me like that."

They stood, calm settling over them in the silence. Then Elsa pulled back and caught Lottie's gaze. "How come he does that? He didn't used to."

"Edward isn't right." Lottie rubbed Elsa's arm, knowing the answer was inadequate but unsure just how one answered such a question. There was so much that Elsa couldn't begin to understand.

"Then how come Aunt Aggie scolded *me*? She said I was going to turn out loose, like you." Elsa sniffled. "I never did anything and she called me names. The same names she calls you. Ones I'm not supposed to say."

Memories crawled up Lottie's spine like spidery fingers, bringing shame along with the familiar chill. She'd been so humiliated by Edward's leers. Then, his hands had crept over her body, bringing responses she hadn't wanted, responses that had made her feel as dirty as the names Aunt Aggie called her. She'd been mortified when Uncle Edward had explained it was her fault that he'd been so tempted that he'd been unable to stop. The bitter shame of it had haunted her.

But Elsa had nothing to be ashamed of—she hadn't encouraged him the way he'd insisted Lottie had.

Lottie stroked the tears from Elsa's cheeks. Drawing a breath, she offered her a wavering smile. "Aw, Elsa. Neither one of them is right in the head. That's why we had to leave. I would have taken you away a long time ago if I had had a way to get you out of there."

"I'm sorry I sassed you, Lottie."

"I know. It's awful hard not to let things out when you're feeling blue, huh?" Lottie had been cranky herself these past few days, anxious to hear the Longs' decision. The park would close soon, and unless she netted a commission for ride sales, the next few months would be difficult for them both.

She finished stowing her equipment as Elsa retrieved the pail. They exited the shed, and Lottie locked up. They headed down the path, crossing through the near empty picnic area.

"I miss Tony," Elsa blurted.

Lottie squeezed her shoulders. Little girls shouldn't be so lonely, and she guessed it was well past time they remedied that. "I've been thinking . . . Denver seems a pretty nice place."

"Elitch's is a nice place."

"Denver is, too, sweetie. The season only has a week or so left. I need to talk to Mary about keeping me on. If she doesn't, we'll move into town. Either way, we ought to enroll you in school."

Elsa stopped in her tracks. "You mean we'd stay here?"

"I sure don't want to go back to New York," Lottie said.

"Me, neither."

Relieved, Lottie squatted in front of Elsa. "Then, it's a deal. We stay here and you go to school."

"That'd be good." She paused and chewed on her bottom lip. "Lottie?"

"Hmmm?"

"Did Uncle Edward ever do anything funny to you?"

Raw panic churned Lottie's gut. "Funny?" A searing dread filling her, Lottie grasped Elsa's hand and pulled her to a seat at an isolated table. "Sweetie . . . what did he do to you?"

"He told me not to tell," she stalled, her legs swinging under the bench. "He said it was our secret, something special just between us." She looked up. "But I didn't like it. It made me feel creepy."

Cold sweat puckered Lottie's skin. Not Elsa. Dear God, please not Elsa. "Honey, what did he do? Did Edward touch you?"

"Never mind." She poked at the dirt with her toe. "It ain't nothin'."

Lottie stroked her shoulder, willing her to continue. "Please, Elsa, you need to tell me. If it made you feel creepy, then it was something. Did that man put his hands on you?"

"I'm not supposed to talk about it." Elsa hung her head.

The words echoed through Lottie's head. Don't tell anyone. They won't understand our special secret. My God! He'd said the same thing to her, just before . . . if that man had harmed Elsa—

"You need to tell me." She evened her tone, afraid of scaring Elsa further. "Uncle Edward told you not to talk about it because he was doing something wrong, and he didn't want anybody to know." She paused. "He told me the same thing when I was your age."

Elsa looked up, her eyes wide. "He did things to you, too?"

"He did a lot of things to me, sweetie. Things he shouldn't have done." Things she wanted to forget. "Now, tell me what he's done to you, so we can talk about it. I can't help you if I don't know what he did."

Elsa stared at the ground, then drew a ragged breath. "A couple months before we left, he started coming into my room to tuck me in."

Just as it had started for her. "Anything more?"

"He'd kiss me goodnight."

"And?"

"It didn't seem like anything bad." Elsa's words came fast, as if she were trying to convince herself. "You tuck me in and kiss me goodnight."

"But Uncle Edward never did, did he? Not before then?"

Elsa shook her head. "It made me feel funny. And then he came in earlier, when I was putting on my nightgown. And he watched me."

Sour bile rose in Lottie's throat. She'd meant to get Elsa away, before any of this happened. She thought she had. She swallowed. "Did he touch you, Elsa?"

"When he kissed me goodnight, he sort of ran his hand across my shoulder and down my front. Then he started kissing me funny. He said it was our special way of showing we loved each other."

"Did he touch you anywhere else or make you touch him?"

"No." She paused. "Was I bad, Lottie?"

Lottie caught Elsa's face in her hand and caught her gaze. "No, Elsa." She'd been in time. Thank God that monster hadn't gone any further. Still, Elsa showed signs of guilt and confusion . . . the same confusion that had first filled Lottie herself, before Edward had told her again and again that she'd earned her shame by tempting him and Aggie had insisted she was provocative with other men.

Lottie choked back her own humiliation, searching for the right words. Elsa had done nothing to disgrace herself. But, unless someone told her that, Elsa would never realize it.

Drawing both of Elsa's hands into her own, Lottie squeezed them. "I want you to listen to me," she said. "What Uncle Edward did, watching you and touching you and kissing you like that . . . those are special ways to show love. But not for girls your age. Those are things grown-ups do with people they love. Adult men should not do that kind of thing with little girls. Uncle Edward was wrong to do them to you and to ask you to keep it a secret. That's why it made you feel creepy."

Elsa's eyes widened. "I asked Moth . . . Aunt Aggie if it was right for someone to do that to me, and her face got all pinched up. She said it was wicked, and I was going to turn out bad like you."

"No, sweetie." Lottie pushed her emotions back and drew her mouth into an encouraging smile. "You didn't do anything wrong. Uncle Edward did."

"But Aunt Aggie said—"

"Aunt Aggie was wrong."

Elsa digested the words, nodding. She leaned into Lottie's arms and tucked her head against Lottie's heart. Hugging her, Lottie's breath evened as she grasped at the warm peace of the moment.

"Lottie," Elsa murmured, "Aunt Aggie said other things, things about you. That you let men at Coney Island do things to you. But it was Uncle Edward, wasn't it? Uncle Edward did things to *you*, too."

"Yes, sweetie, he did. And it was wrong then, too. That's why I took you away. I'm so sorry I didn't do it sooner."

"Aunt Aggie said I was going to be a slut, just like you were."

"She was wrong." Despite what Lottie knew she had become, Elsa was pure. An aching loss for her own innocence lodged in her heart.

Elsa sat up, her gaze pinning Lottie. "I know what a slut is. Aunt Aggie told me." A tear slid down Elsa's cheek. "Uncle Edward did more things to you, didn't he?"

Lottie's heart skittered, afraid of Elsa knowing. Then she nodded, realizing Elsa knew anyway.

"I think I know what he did," Elsa began in a small voice. "I ain't dumb, even if I don't know exactly how it works. Aunt Aggie said a lot of things to me . . . about you. She said you wanted to do them but I don't believe her. I don't think you did them with the men at Coney Island. I think Uncle Edward made you do them, and he was gonna make me do them, too."

"That's right, pet," Lottie said, desperate to believe Elsa's assertions. All of them.

Elsa's small hand reached toward Lottie, her delicate fingers brushing at the tears on her face. "I think I just figured out something." She drew a breath, then exhaled. "I'm not really your sister, either, am I?"

Lottie's eyes were puffy. It was late, and she was tired. Since settling Elsa in bed, Lottie had been sitting alone in the twilight of the Gardens' picnic area as both memories and sobs racked her body.

She'd spent the remainder of the day with Elsa, tense, answering her questions as well as she could. The tightrope between being honest with her daughter and trying to protect Elsa's innocence was a thin one, and Lottie was exhausted. This had been neither the time nor the way in which she'd anticipated revealing their true relationship. Elsa was young, far too young to grasp all the nuances of what had occurred. But she'd asked, thanks to Aunt Aggie's ranting, and the time for lies was past.

But Lottie hadn't expected the pain that flooded back into her soul along with the truth. For ten years, she'd locked it away, fleeing from it whenever the door cracked open.

Today, throughout Elsa's questions, she'd tried to avoid denouncing intimacy, discussing only the wickedness of an adult man forcing a child into such acts. She knew how important that was. She'd been careful to hold back her own anguished memories and all the filthy guilt she'd carried for so many years. Elsa didn't need to feel that way. No one did.

But they'd welled up, like water behind a dam, until she couldn't hold them at bay any longer. The tears had poured unrestrained once she'd left the cottage.

She hated the tears, hated the horrid images that prompted them. Uncle Edward's groping hands . . . his wet tongue probing into her mouth . . . his smooth, oily words telling her how special she was to him. She'd been silent then, wanting to believe she was special instead of an orphaned niece who was a burden to the family.

If only she hadn't needed to be loved so desperately. That had been her undoing . . . welcoming his first few touches because she hungered for the tenderness that came with them. She'd encouraged him, just like he said. Without knowing it, she'd become a whore, a temptress pulling him back to her again and again.

As Uncle Edward became bolder, that tiny shred of specialness had died away. His increasing demands had made her feel dirty and sordid so that even his loving declarations when he'd finished with her were not enough. He'd taken her virginity just after she turned eleven. The assurances of love had vanished, replaced by the accusations that she'd lured him to it.

And, buried deep below it all was the certainty that she had. She must have.

Lord, how different it would have been to have those acts

rooted in love rather than wickedness. Was it possible, with the right man, that desire could be something pure and natural?

Tears rolled down Lottie's cheeks, evidence of her weakness. But tonight, after Elsa's questions, the memories were too strong to push away. The rides were closed. There was nowhere to escape to, no one to distract her, no way to avoid how she felt.

She slumped over the picnic table and cursed.

"Hey, doll? That you?" Rupert's voice broke through the sanctuary.

Lottie sniffled and wiped a hand across her nose, trying to hide the snot. The last thing she needed right now was Rupert's sticky-sweet mumblings. Or for him to realize something was wrong and use it against her. "Go away."

Instead, he approached, invading. "You aren't bawling are you?"

"I . . . I had a fight with Elsa. That's all." She took one final swipe at her face and turned toward Rupert, thankful for the darkness. "What are you doing still here?"

"Fixing a track on the coaster. Took me longer than I expected." He paused. "You ain't ever a gloomy Gus. The kid's got you down, huh?" He slung one leg up on the bench and leaned on his knee, readily accepting her story. More than she'd suspected he would.

She waved her hand, continuing the charade. "It's not important. Nothing I want to talk about. Time to forget about it and get over it."

"That's my Lottie. Always ready to put things behind her and move on." His infectious smile was evident, even in the dimness. That ready nonchalance of his had drawn her like a fly. She'd been so susceptible and she was pleased she was now able to resist him, to lead him, even. A tiny spark of pride glowed inside her, despite the events of the day.

"Yep, that's me," she said, playing along, curious to see where

Rupert was trying to lead her this time. "If the coaster was still open, I'd be on it."

He grinned. "I'd open it back up for you, doll, but I don't think the Longs would be too pleased."

Lottie stood and shrugged, feigning carefreeness. "Guess I'll have to read a book or something."

"A book? Doll, that don't sound like no fun." He drew her from the table, guiding her toward the cottage. "Tell you what, you go grab a wrap, and tell Mary you're going to town."

"To town?" She shook her head at the ludicrous suggestion. She was tempted. She'd made only casual acquaintances among the teenage help and it would be fun to spend time with someone her own age. Still, the last thing she wanted was to go to town with an oily snake like him. Unless . . . The germ of an idea sprouted. Rupert seemed to be in a malleable mood tonight. If she played it right, maybe she could get the information she needed about his father and be rid of the man for good. She'd follow his lead, wait for him to loosen up, and worm it out of him.

"You can hitch along with me and my buddy Charlie from the rooming house in his automobile. He's a good sort, works over at Manhattan Beach," he said, naming the small amusement park that competed with Elitch's. "Come on, doll. It'll be fun."

"I don't know, Rupert." She hedged, unsure.

"Come on, doll. Just a couple of friends out to have fun. I promise you, you won't think about your troubles for the rest of the night."

Her troubles. Even if the Longs agreed to let her broker rides, she still had to get rid of Rupert or her troubles would become a whole lot worse. She needed that information and tonight might just be her best chance of getting it. She'd be careful, she told herself.

139

★ ★ ★ ★ ★

Darkness had settled by the time Lottie arrived at Elitch's front gate. As Rupert had predicted, Mary had agreed to watch over Elsa. Still, Lottie had waited until Elsa was asleep before leaving the cottage.

She waited, leaning against the wooden gatehouse, questioning herself. If she wasn't careful, the sweet lure of distraction would run roughshod over caution. No matter how blue she was tonight, no matter how much she wanted to forget, she couldn't drift into her usual pattern. No matter how tempted she was to escape, she had responsibilities now. She had to pay attention if she was going to get Rupert loose enough to reveal the information she needed.

Despite Rupert having been a friend when she needed one, standing by her for years, protective and ready for a fun time, he was still a con man. She couldn't ignore that oily film in his salesmanship that she'd never before sensed.

The headlight lanterns on Charlie's sleek roadster glowed as the auto appeared out of the shadows. The engine clattered, and, despite herself, Lottie felt her heartbeat quicken in anticipation of her first automobile ride. The machine shuddered to a stop and sat, quaking, as Rupert jumped out of the passenger side and grinned at Lottie.

"Ready, doll?" he called over the din.

"Are you sure this is safe at night?" she asked, knowing she'd go even if it wasn't.

"Safe enough. Charlie knows the road and we'll take it slow." Rupert helped her into the rear seat, made introductions, and climbed aboard.

Lottie settled in, reassured by Charlie's ready grin and guileless smile. His face held an open welcome that steadied her nerves. He did, indeed, seem a good sort, a possible ally if she needed one. She might as well enjoy the ride. Once seated, excitement prickled, then leapt through her.

The roadster jumped forward and they were off, shimmying their way through the darkness. Lottie grasped the seat, feeling the air against her face, and hung on as the machine jiggled. The thundering engine stifled conversation, but she didn't care. She soaked in the thrill of the passing air, the unexpected bumps that tossed her up off the seat, and the sudden swerves she suspected Charlie made just for her benefit.

All too soon, they approached downtown Denver and navigated toward Blake Street. Billiard parlors and gaming houses lined the curbs like a row of plaintive cows at milking time. St. Elmo's Bar and the Scandinavian House Saloon battled for attention while would-be customers weighed their choices.

An octagonal structure on the corner drew Lottie's attention as they drove past.

"It's a drunk tank, doll," Rupert explained.

Lottie turned her head, looking back. The small wooden building was sized for one person and topped with a small turret.

"The cops round 'em up, lock 'em in, and they wait for the paddy wagon. No fuss, no muss, no bother."

Lottie laughed, imagining a cop trying to stuff an uncooperative drunk into the small structure. "Where are we headed?"

"We could drive over to Broadway, catch a vaudeville show," Charlie shouted over the din of the auto.

Rupert shook his head. "We're too late. Should we try St. Louis Hall?" He turned to Lottie. "They got a bowling alley."

"They only let women in on league nights." Charlie slowed the vehicle to a shuddering crawl. "Feel like dancing?"

"How about it, doll? Want to cut the rug?"

Dancing . . . it had been ages since she'd been dancing. She nodded, recalling the bright lights, excitement, and throngs of people at the Coney Island dance halls.

Charlie veered down a side street and pulled the car behind a well-lit building. The Rambler convulsed one last time, then quieted. The men jumped out of the vehicle, their footfalls thunderous in the sudden lack of clatter.

Lottie accepted Rupert's hand, her mind scrambling to form a more solid plan for persuading him to give her the information she needed. After dousing the headlamps, the trio made their way toward the rear entry of a boisterous building. A ragtime number poured from the dull gray structure, tempting Lottie with its catchy tune. They made their way through a propped open door, heat assaulting them.

Down the hallway, couples shot by, their feet flying. Lottie grinned.

"I'll find us a table," Charlie announced, pointing to the second floor balcony that overlooked the dance floor. He headed for a narrow set of stairs and disappeared.

Rupert pulled Lottie onto the dance floor as a lively two-step started. Her plain gray skirt swirled as she followed his lead. She caught sight of an overwhelming number of men lounging against the walls—so different from New York's female-packed establishments.

"Does Denver have a shortage of women?" she asked, hoping the conversation would help disguise her distrust of him.

Rupert gave her a lopsided grin. "It would seem the town's a bit behind the times."

Lottie took a minute to peer at the crowd, conscious of her reputation. She shivered under the stares of the men and her heartbeat quickened. Wanting to be sure Charlie hadn't led them into an illicit establishment, she glanced at the other women, trying to discern their character. Noting their modern attire, make-up free skin, and lack of predatory behavior, she breathed a sigh of relief.

The other girls weren't prostitutes. Though few in number,

they appeared wholesome, most of them in plain skirts and shirtwaists like her own.

In New York, factory girls impatient with the shortage of social club dances thronged to public dance halls. They came singly and in groups, with or without escort, ready to put the drudgery of their work days behind them. In recent years, the number of dance halls had exploded.

Here, the fad hadn't taken hold.

She slid into the music, letting it overtake her as her body swayed to the beat. The music changed and the catchy tune shifted into a waltz. Gliding across the floor, Lottie felt Rupert relax and caught his easy smile. A few couples, here and there, had forsaken traditional dance positions for the new fad of "rough dancing," holding each other more casually. Women circled their hands around their beaus' necks while the men placed both hands at the small of the women's backs. A few sets of hands crept lower as the couples circled to the rhythm without regard to proper waltz steps.

Lottie watched the other couples as she followed Rupert's lead. One of the men stroked his fingers over his gal's lower back, skimming her bottom as he drew her close, and the requisite space between them disappeared. Lottie imagined Caleb Hudson's well-toned arms pulling her flush against his hard body as they swayed to the music.

Too late, she realized it was Rupert who was embracing her. She took an abrupt step back and saw Rupert's surprised expression. "What's up doll?"

"Nothing. Just daydreaming."

"I was havin' some sweet dreams myself," he murmured, his smile lazy and suggestive.

Unsure whether she had drifted unwittingly toward Rupert or whether he had pulled her close, she stayed alert. While she did want to encourage his trust, tempting him was a thin line.

Nearby, a stiff-looking floor manager approached one of the more reckless couples and tapped the man on the shoulder. The men exchanged words and the couple moved apart.

The waltz wound down, and she pulled Rupert off the floor. "Let's find Charlie and have something to drink," she said. Maybe a few beers would loosen his tongue.

They sat out a few rounds, tipping beer with a group of Germans who claimed they'd been kicked out of the Zang Brewery on Larimer for rowdy behavior. With each sip, Lottie's troubles faded and Rupert became less guarded. Within an hour, she had danced with everyone at the table and more beer had appeared. By the end of the night, the entire crowd was singing along with the ragtime tunes. At two, as the dance hall closed, they stumbled out the back door together and mobbed the car.

Squeezed into the back, between Rupert and a fellow whose name she couldn't quite remember, Lottie leaned her head against Rupert's shoulder, drew a tired breath, and fought to keep her eyes open. She needed to talk to him about his uncle.

"Last stop, doll. C'mon, we're here," Rupert prompted, waking her. "What d'ya say?"

" 'Bout what?" she mumbled.

"You and me, making plans?"

She stirred and struggled to sit up, dizziness slamming her. "That's right," she murmured. "Plans. We gotta write your father."

Rupert laughed and eased her out of the automobile. Telling Charlie he'd walk back to the rooming house, Rupert propelled Lottie up the path to the cottage. As the car disappeared, darkness surrounded them, and Rupert settled his arm at Lottie's waist. "You did the right thing, bringing me here. You and me, together, taking 'em for all we can." Rupert pulled her tighter and kissed her cheek. "It's what we do best."

Lottie's stomach rolled as she stumbled forward. Her eyes

refused to focus. Damn the beer, anyway. She didn't remember having drunk that much. She drew a breath and willed the fresh air to fill her mind.

"How 'bout I write th' letter? I write th' best. Jus' get me an address and I'll whip it up."

"Ah, Lottie. You set things up good. But from here on out, you just turn it all over to me. Don't worry that pretty little head of yours. Trust me, doll. I got it all taken care of."

A long cold shiver crept up Lottie's spine, sobering her as she realized how mistaken she'd been to try to sucker Rupert. She'd bumbled it good, not only revealing her hand to him but offering herself in the process.

And she had a nauseating hunch that he was about to ask her to ante up—one way or the other.

CHAPTER NINE

Rupert ushered Lottie down the tree-lined path, plunging them deeper into the dark night. Within a few steps, the faint moonlight disappeared. Lottie's skin crawled.

She hedged to the side.

"Where you going?" Rupert muttered, pulling her flush against his side.

Lottie pushed at him, stumbled, felt him catch her. At the heaviness of his touch, old fears slithered through her. She lurched away. "I can make it from here," she insisted, louder than she'd intended.

"You're drunk, doll. You'll fall flat on your face and pass out on the path. Mary will have you shipped out of here faster than a mongoose chasing a snake. Let's sit down on the bench for a minute."

"I'm fine." Trying to project confidence, she took a step forward. Her balance was so uneven even she could feel it. No doubt about it—she was drunk, despite her best efforts to avoid it. How strong had that beer been? She took a second tottering step, overcorrected, and staggered.

"I don't think so." Rupert slung his arm back around her waist and hauled her off the path, pinning her against a tree. "Time to remember who's in charge."

Rupert's mouth jammed down on hers pushing rough bark into her back. Lottie struggled against his vice-like grip on her wrists. She tasted the stale beer on his breath, too much like

Uncle Edward's sour wheezing. She choked back bile and shoved at him.

"Get off me."

Rupert staggered backward, his hands still gripping Lottie's arms. Catching himself, he propelled her back against the tree. "Don't play the tease, Lottie. We both know you want it."

"No!" Not like this, not illicit, devoid of any love. She wrenched one hand loose and slapped his cheek.

He captured her wrist again and pushed into her. "You want to play rough?" He pressed her tighter against the tree, running his tongue across her face. She twisted her head. Sharp bark scratched at her and she jerked away. Rupert leered at her, then licked her again. Cold air struck the wet spittle on her cheek. She shivered. He reclaimed her mouth and ground his erection against her.

Silent panic screamed. She would not be coerced into this again. Never again.

She forced her body to slacken under the pressure and waited for him to release her wrists to slide his hands along her curves. The moment he did so, she twisted from his grasp, ran her nails across his cheek and sucked in a breath.

With lightning speed, Rupert cupped her chin in his hand, pinching her mouth into an "oh." "You don't want to scream, doll. One short telegram is all it would take to have your Uncle Edward hotfootin' it here for Elsa."

Cold dread filled her. She nodded, her mouth still in a pucker.

Rupert released her chin. "That's my girl," he whispered.

Fierce hatred poured through her at the words—Edward's words. She stared at Rupert with bitter contempt and spit into his face.

Rage filled Rupert's face as he stared back at her.

Footsteps sounded on the gravel pathway. In the space of a heartbeat, Caleb was on them. He wrenched Rupert away. With one fluid movement, he drew back his fist. A split second later, he smashed it into Rupert's jaw.

"You son of a bitch," Caleb shouted.

Dazed, Rupert staggered backward, then gained his footing. "What the—"

"You keep your hands off her."

"What's it to you, flower boy?"

"None of your business, grease monkey."

"Stay out of this," Rupert ground out, his words slurred. "Me an' Lottie are old friends." He glanced at Lottie, his lips drawing into a sneer.

Lottie stood, panting, tree bark still scoring into her back. She gulped air. The breath shuddered through her, relief and disgust registering as she trembled in aftershock.

"You stay away from her," Caleb threatened.

"And what if she don't want me to? Or didn't you notice the way she was begging for it?"

Lottie shook her head in denial. He couldn't really have thought that, could he?

"She might have been begging but it wasn't for you."

"I wouldn't bet on it. Lottie knows what's good for her. I'll wager she's reasoned out I'm it. Her and me, we got it made. She ain't gonna give that up."

She shivered, her mind seizing on what would have happened if Caleb hadn't appeared. Then, stunned disbelief gave way to white-hot fury.

Rupert was nothing but a lowdown schmuck. She might have flirted but she sure as hell hadn't given him reason to think he could do this. Heart pounding, she launched away from the tree and strode forward a few steps before stopping dead in her tracks.

Would Rupert really contact Uncle Edward?

In the second it took to formulate the thought, she knew.

Dread clenched her center. She'd given Rupert the one piece of information he needed to assure him of her cooperation. She had no doubt how he planned to use it.

If Edward knew where Elsa was, he'd come for her. He and Aunt Aggie had claimed Elsa as their own from the day of her birth, forging her birth certificate. Edward had told her Aggie had always wanted a baby to raise. Lottie had believed him but maybe he'd planned this for years, groomed Elsa, as he had Lottie. There were no other little girls in the neighborhood, but Edward wouldn't chance discovery with them, anyway, and Elsa had reached puberty. Young enough to be malleable but no longer physically a child. She was ten, for god's sake—he'd have at least three years before she matured beyond his tastes. He wouldn't give her up without a fight.

Ice-like fear crept up Lottie's spine as she made her decision. She'd do whatever Rupert wanted.

She moved forward, searching for an opening, a way to step between the men. "Stop it," she yelled. "That's enough. Stop."

Caleb's head jerked at Lottie's voice. The flinch was enough to allow Rupert's fist to contact. Blood burst from Caleb's lip. He drew back, shook his head, and sidestepped away, ducking.

Moments later, Tom and Mary emerged from the darkness. Grabbing Rupert's arms, Tom pulled him back. Rupert struggled, then grew limp in resignation.

Mary set down her lantern, rushed forward, and pulled Lottie into her arms. She drew her away, her gentle hands offering silent comfort.

"What's going on here?" Tom demanded.

"That greasy son of a bitch had his hands on Lottie."

"Is that true?" Mary asked.

Within Mary's soothing arms, Lottie was silent, her fear battling with righteous indignation. She raised her gaze to Rupert's. In the shadows of the lantern light, his scowl was piercing, full of threat. Thoughts of Edward, leering at Elsa, filled Lottie's head and she shivered.

"It was a misunderstanding," she said, choking back the bile. "Things got out of hand."

Caleb's eyes darkened. "Like hell."

"Lottie's right," Rupert sputtered. "We were a little tanked up. It went too far."

"You were groping her," Caleb said.

"That true, young man?" Tom asked.

Shame biting, Lottie moved away from Mary. "It was a kiss that got out of control," she said. "That's all."

Mary stared at Lottie with icy censure. "Drunk. What in heaven's name were you thinking, girl?"

"But you're all right? Do we need the police here?"

"I'm all right," she answered, avoiding Tom's second question. She felt Mary's disapproval and could see the questions burning in Caleb's eyes.

"That's all then. Caleb, go back to your cabin," Tom insisted.

Caleb stared at Rupert, then Lottie, his eyes somber. With one last look, he turned and strode into the darkness.

Tom released his hold on Rupert and glared at him. "I won't abide this kind of behavior from my employees. Intentional or not, you're the one who got her drunk. I don't care how good a mechanic you're reputed to be. Get whatever tools are yours and be on your way. You're fired."

Rupert's jaw dropped, and his eyes blazed but he held his tongue.

Mary frowned at Lottie. "You reek of beer. Go sleep it off. We'll discuss your behavior in the morning. I want you level-headed when we talk."

Heat crept up Lottie's face. "Yes, ma'am."

Tom picked up the lantern and led the way down the path as Mary grasped Lottie's arm and drew her along behind him.

Disapproving silence hung in the air.

"Ma'am?" Rupert called.

Mary stopped, turning.

Rupert bent and retrieved something from the ground. "Lottie forgot her purse." He trotted forward with it.

Lottie took a step toward him, numb, while Mary sighed.

He set the purse into her hands. Bending his mouth to her ear, he whispered. "Stay put and keep your mouth shut, or I'll send that telegram. And don't play me for a fool—I'll be watching you."

Lottie waited as he faded into the night, then turned away. He might not realize it, but she didn't plan on being his fool, either.

Caleb slammed the door of his cabin and muttered a curse. Visions of Lottie against that apple tree filled his head. Rage had filled him from the moment he realized Rupert had her pinned there, hot fury that his hands were on her, his fingers on the milky flesh of her thighs under her bunched up skirt, his mouth on hers, his body grinding against her.

Heat had pulsed through his veins, gut reaction driving him forward. Then, he'd seen the terror on her face and he'd wanted to kill the man. The anger was still sharp. He lit the lamp near the door and stood, panting, as light filled the room. Why was his heart beating so fast? It was righteous indignation, that was all—protectiveness. He'd have stepped in to defend any woman whose honor was being threatened.

But it wasn't all. He'd been incensed. Rupert Gennick had had his hands on Lottie. His Lottie.

Good lord. He crossed the room and sat on the bed, shucking off his work boots with a jerk. Hell, he didn't even like her. Did he? And he sure didn't trust her.

He dropped the second boot to the floor and padded to the

table. Glancing at his exacting plans for the park, he reminded himself that Lottie was the enemy. She'd come here to prey on the Longs, to reap a fortune selling them rides they didn't need. She'd brought Rupert in as a partner. The both of them were nothing but slick hucksters.

But he couldn't shake the nagging doubt in his mind that all was not as it seemed.

Despite Lottie's assertions that she'd been a willing participant in a situation that had gone too far, Caleb didn't buy it. He wanted to. It'd make it a whole lot easier to keep Lottie in the role he'd been so sure she fit. But something wasn't right.

Her assurances hadn't rung true. And this time, he was inclined to delve deeper. It was well past time to put his knee-jerk reactions on hold and learn what was really going on here. Just who was Lottie Chase, anyway?

First thing tomorrow, he'd start digging for the whole truth.

CHAPTER TEN

The kitchen door creaked open, and Lottie winced. She recognized Mary's brisk step. Her stomach threatening to heave itself up, Lottie turned and pushed a smile. She'd felt Mary's respect thin last night, and the loss weighed heavy.

Though she'd recognized how important Mary's good opinion was to her continued employment, she hadn't realized how much losing it would matter in other ways. She felt like she'd failed her own mother.

Lottie tried to ignore her pounding head. Somehow, she had to re-earn Mary's respect, for Elsa as much as for herself. Without it, she might as well give up. Mary would fire her today. There would be no job, let alone a chance to broker a ride sale or ask for employment through the winter. She and Elsa would be without a home, compelled to move on, give in to Rupert, or go home to New York. And she refused to roll over and let that happen, not without trying.

"Elsa is settled as assistant conductor on the miniature train," Mary said, crossing the kitchen.

"She'll like that."

"She will. And this is a conversation she doesn't need to witness." Mary turned to Lottie, her expression grim. "What in heaven's name were you thinking?"

Lottie swallowed at her harsh tone. "I wasn't."

Mary studied Lottie, considering. "Do you care for that man?"

"I . . ." Lottie looked down, her mouth dry. Lord, how she wanted to spill everything to Mary, to feel the support of her gentle arms and hear her soothing voice. To have Mary reassure her that it wasn't her fault. Except she knew it was. She'd lured Rupert just as she had Uncle Edward. Besides, she knew she had to tread with care. There was no way she could reveal all of the details, not without jeopardizing Elsa's safety. Rupert's threat was too real—she couldn't risk him contacting Uncle Edward.

"We've been friends for a long time," Lottie said, avoiding an outright lie. "He'd like it to be more than friendship."

"And last night? You led him on?" Mary's sharp gaze held a trace of disbelief.

Lottie's heart hammered. If she allowed Mary to believe Rupert had attacked her with no provocation, Mary would surely pursue the matter, maybe even involve the police. But if she let Mary think she'd encouraged Rupert's actions, Mary would never respect her again.

"Not on purpose," Lottie murmured.

Mary's gaze grew cold. "I will not condone drunkenness here. Nor will I tolerate promiscuity." Mary's brisk tone brooked no argument. It also told Lottie that Mary would never accept what she had done with Uncle Edward.

"Yes, ma'am."

"This is my home, Lottie. You should have been fired on the spot, as Mr. Gennick was." She sighed, her disapproval evident. "Tell me why I shouldn't do so this morning."

Lottie raised her gaze, grieving the chip in her relationship with Mary. She'd had no choice—she couldn't tell her the truth. Keeping Mary's professional confidence would have to be enough. She prayed she could project the self-assurance she needed to convey. Self-assurance she didn't feel right now.

"I'm good at my job," she said. "Good with the animals and

good with the bear show. Attendance has increased since I took it over." She paused. "What happened last night will never happen again. I promise."

"Do you?" Mary probed.

"Yes, ma'am."

"If you are going to be responsible for that child, you cannot endanger her with that kind of behavior. What if you'd been thrown in jail or if Rupert had put you in the hospital? Do you have any idea of what would happen to her if that man becomes part of your life?"

Lottie's chest tightened at the thought of how much danger Elsa was already in. One telegram and Edward would seize her. One false step and Elsa's life would be a living hell.

"The season ends next week," Mary continued. "I can keep you on two weeks past then. Since there will be no shows, your duties will include helping to winterize the equipment. I'll provide you a letter of reference and allow you time to look for a job in town if you're planning to stay in Denver."

"Yes, ma'am. I planned to enroll Elsa in school."

"A good idea."

Lottie's pulse pounded. This couldn't be it. Three weeks. It wasn't enough. She should have asked Mary a long time ago about continuing her job past the season. With all that had gone wrong, she'd put it off. Now, Rupert's threats made it impossible not to. More than ever, she suspected Rupert wanted to horn in on the equipment sale. While she might be able to broker the sale without being an employee, remaining at the park would appease Rupert as well as assuring her of steady employment, something she wouldn't otherwise bet on, not with her lack of skills.

She drew a breath. It was now or never.

"I was hoping you might need an animal tender in the off-season," she said, scuffing at the floor with the toe of her boot.

Mary pierced her with a sharp stare. "You've just received three weeks I shouldn't be giving you. Isn't it a little presumptuous to be asking to stay on longer?"

Lottie met and held Mary's gaze. "The animals need to be fed and tended all year. Old Man Farnum is no longer here to do it. And, I have the connections to help you build this park. Having me here would make that easier."

"I can purchase rides on my own. I'm not afraid to negotiate," Mary countered. "Tom and I can handle the animals. Caleb lives here year-round. He'll serve as caretaker while Tom and I are traveling."

"While all of that's true, I can get you a better price, Mary. If you work directly with an amusement company, they'll try to sell you the most expensive rides instead of those that will best suit your needs. They won't tell you about the less expensive models, and you don't have to have the top of the line on everything. I know which rides you can compromise on and which need to be top quality. I know which models have safety issues and which attract customers. And I can broker a much better deal because I have the connections and I know how much the profit margins are."

She softened her tone, hoping she was on the right track. "And, I can help Caleb. You've already told me you and Tom travel most of the off-season. Old Man Farnum was here to help before. Tending the animals and the grounds would be a lot for one person, more so with mechanical repairs added in. Caleb will need the help. Besides, we can keep one another company while you're gone." A pang of loss slid through her at the thought that she might have ruined any chance she'd ever had with him last night. "Most of all, I wouldn't need to uproot Elsa. She's grown to think of this as her home. And you've grown to think of her as family."

Mary cocked her head and pinned her with a penetrating

gaze. "You do know how to close a sale, don't you?"

"I don't see how any of us can lose."

"All right, Lottie. We'll give it a try. But know this—if you step out of line again, I won't hesitate to send you on your way." Mary's expression was stern. "I'm still not sure you've earned the right to stay. If you want to prove yourself the woman I thought you were, you keep that Gennick fellow away from here."

Lottie exited the top gate of the bear pit and locked the door behind her. The satisfied murmurs of the crowd still sounded around her, filling her with pride. The feeding, and the show she'd worked so hard on, had gone well. At least for this afternoon, Mary would be convinced Lottie deserved to keep her job.

At Mary's suggestion, Elsa was assisting as co-hostess of the last Children's Day of the season. Together, she and Mary were entertaining the dozens of kids who'd arrived at the park for the weekly admission-free day—something Elsa had not done while she was busy at the theatre with Tony Perry. Next week, Elsa would start school. Lottie hoped she'd meet some of her future classmates today, making the transition to school a bit easier.

Lottie headed for the storage shed. The empty fish and berry pails clanged together as she strode down the path. She should be light-hearted with relief that she and Elsa had a home for the off-season. Still, the loss of Mary's approval hurt, even knowing Mary's reprieve meant Elsa was safe. Their security was only an illusion, after all. Elsa was safe only if Lottie continued to play by Rupert's rules.

She exhaled a heavy breath. Though she'd hoped otherwise, it was now clear Rupert was no longer the man she had once trusted as a friend and confidant. The change in him left her few choices. If she didn't cooperate with Rupert, he would contact Edward. If she caved and became his puppet, he would steal any chance she had of independence. Worse, he would have the power to control her for years, just as Edward had. Her only chance of breaking free was to pretend to cooperate while preparing her escape.

Rupert already knew the Longs wanted to purchase a ride. If she kept the expansion ideas to herself, she could pretend to co-operate with him—even allow him to take the commission on the sale of the one ride he knew about. He might leave then, taking his threat with him. And if he didn't, maybe she'd have time to pocket enough savings to flee with Elsa. Once Mary calmed down, she might be willing to loan them money . . . or Lottie might be able to make connections with other companies for future sales. She'd need time, though, and that meant she had to placate Rupert for now.

"Daydreaming?" Caleb's voice jolted into her thoughts.

"Guess so," she said, heat rising to her face at the thought of what Caleb had seen the night before . . . what he was sure to be thinking of her. She glanced down at her suggestive woolen bathing costume and blushed. Mary had agreed to let her continue with the costume as long as she eliminated the provocative movements—now Lottie wished she hadn't.

"Are you all right?" he asked, concern in his voice. He took the empty pails from her and opened the shed door, then entered the tiny shack.

Lottie's pulse jumped as she registered his lack of judgment. She'd been so sure of his condemnation. His empathy chipped at the protective façade she'd created. Her eyes burned. "It wasn't what it looked like, last night."

"What do you think it looked like?" he asked from inside the shed.

"That I . . . that we. . . ." She paused, calming herself. There was no sense avoiding the truth—they both knew what he'd seen, and it was very important that she not lie to him. Not this time. He was being fair with her. As long as her answers didn't endanger Elsa, she'd be honest with him. Clinging to the shred of respect he was offering, she stepped into the shed and met his gaze. "I'm pretty sure it looked like two animals in heat."

Caleb's heart caught at her shamed expression. Though she was a woman who knew how to use her wiles on a man, what he'd witnessed last night was not a temptress and her quarry. Nor was it two people mutually attracted to one another. He'd discovered a predator with an unwilling victim. Her silent weeping confirmed it. He closed the shed door, shutting them away from prying eyes, then returned to Lottie. "It looked like he was forcing himself on you."

"I didn't mean to encourage him." She choked back a sob.

Good Lord, what had that man done to her? Caleb's gut clenched. There was such pain in her eyes. He pulled her into his arms. Her corset-free curves melded against him, and he fought the urge to run his hands over them. "Shhh," he whispered. "It didn't look like you asked for any of that."

"Yet there we were," she mumbled.

"That doesn't mean you encouraged him."

"But I went with him," she insisted. "I danced with him, flirted with him, let myself get drunk." Her shoulders shook as tears trailed her cheeks, wet against his neck.

Caleb stroked them away with his thumb. She felt natural in his arms. He wanted nothing more than to remain there, brushing away her cares. But he knew whatever threatened her wouldn't vanish as easily as her tears. Trouble was following Lottie, whether she encouraged it or not, and he couldn't ignore the situation. Not when it appeared much more complicated than he'd originally assumed.

Guilty that he'd allowed his hair-trigger doubts to cloud his earlier perceptions of her, he kissed her on the forehead and pulled back. This time, he needed to discover who she really was. And what was really happening.

Keeping his eyes on her face rather than her curvaceous body, he drew a breath, then exhaled, hoping his instincts were better this time. "What is he to you, Lottie? Why did you ask him here?"

"I didn't," she whispered.

"He seems to think you did."

She stepped back, then paced the small shed, refusing to meet Caleb's gaze. "I think I mentioned his father manufactures amusement rides. I intended to broker the purchase of Mary's rides so I could collect a sales commission." She turned to face him, as if bracing for his condemnation of her intentions. "I asked Rupert for a letter of introduction. Two weeks later, he showed up."

"And now he wants in on your deal?"

She nodded, sniffling.

Caleb willed himself to avoid irrational conclusions. He couldn't let his natural cynicism rule his reactions this time. Just because she hadn't looked him in the eyes, just because circumstances seemed too convenient, it didn't have to mean she'd arrived with ulterior motives—that she intended to scam Mary. His pulse pounded, but he kept his voice low. "Is that why you came here?"

This time she raised her gaze, her morning glory eyes meeting his as she drew a breath. "Elsa and I were traveling to San Francisco with Rupert. Denver was just a stop on the way. We had a disagreement, and Rupert went on alone."

Caleb nodded, relief washing over him. That information matched what Elsa had told him, the night she'd talked about their life in New York. Whatever had happened since, Lottie had not arrived here with malicious intentions. Still, he needed to hear the rest of the story. "He left you here?"

"Does it matter?" she asked, evasive.

Caleb fought a sigh. Lottie didn't spill information with ease; that was for sure. No wonder it was so damn hard to trust her. He checked his irritation and continued. "Of course it matters. I'm trying to understand what's going on."

"He stole my money and left us here." She spat the words out, her resentment clear. "Elsa and I were broke. Working amusement parks is the only employment I've ever known so we came to Elitch's." She slowed. "Selling rides to the Longs didn't occur to me until I was already here, and I saw the potential to make some money."

Money. Caleb recoiled. He brushed his hand through his hair and controlled his anger. "So, all the expansion ideas were about getting rich, then?"

Lottie stared at him, her jaw open. "Getting rich? Gads, Caleb. You don't get rich on amusement ride commissions."

"Don't you?" he ground out, old doubts rearing as he thought about all the plans she'd encouraged. An image of a treacherous spider stalking its prey filled his head. He couldn't stop thinking about how she'd pulled Mary into her web. "Not even when you propose over a dozen rides that aren't needed or wanted?"

"Maybe if you sell a dozen rides in a dozen cities like Rupert was planning. I was just hoping to make enough to survive."

"Survive? It seems to me it'd be a lot more than survival wages."

"Not if the season's about to end and you have no other marketable skills to support a ten-year-old through the winter."

Her statement brought him to an abrupt halt. Shame nipped at him. He'd forgotten about Elsa. My God, it wasn't about money. It was about security. He leaned his hips on the counter and plunked his head back against the cupboard doors.

"And that's why you concocted those grand plans?"

"The plans are solid. The Longs have huge potential here. I

didn't make any of that up."

"And Rupert's role in all this?"

"I only wanted him to send a letter of introduction. That's all. I've never met his father, and he'd told me the man is notorious for refusing to deal with strangers—women in particular. Unless Rupert paves the way, he'll ignore me. I didn't invite Rupert here and I would rather he went away." The moment the words were out of her mouth, she looked like she wanted to snatch them back. For a second, before she looked away, fear flashed in her eyes.

Caleb's hackles rose at the implication. Trouble had followed her, literally, it seemed. "So why not just tell him to go to hell?"

"I can't."

"Why not?"

"I just can't." Her voice trembled, deathly quiet. "Please, Caleb. I can't tell you any more about it."

He moved toward her, catching her arms in his hands, aching with her. "Then I'll tell him."

Lottie sucked in a breath, fear crawling through her. "No! Please, Caleb. Just let it be."

His hands slipped around her and he pulled her close. "I can't just let it be," he whispered, cradling her head against his shoulder. "The man attacked you. Send him on his way."

"Tom already did."

Caleb exhaled, his frustration evident. "You're scared to death. He's not going to pack up and leave Denver, is he? He wants something from you, and he's not going to stop trying to get it." He moved her head up until he caught her gaze. "Am I right?"

"I have it under control," she insisted.

"Do you?"

"Just trust me. I know what I'm doing."

He shook his head. "Let me help."

"I can't. I need to do this myself." She stared into his eyes, willing him to understand. The whiskey depths glowed. Lottie swallowed, drawn by the unspoken assurance she saw there. "If I can't, I'll come to you. I promise."

Rupert jostled his way through the growing crowds flocking toward Denver's cafes and saloons for their evening entertainment. He elbowed his way past a plump couple arguing about where to have dinner and scowled. From the looks of it, neither needed another meal.

He'd gotten sidetracked by Lottie Chase, and he'd been stewing about it all day. He'd come back to Denver so they could resume his original plans. Instead, he'd lost control. It galled him that his desire for her had reared, forcing him into bullying her. He'd prided himself on his finesse, and she'd destroyed it like he was just another of her marks. Rupert Gennick had never, ever, had to force himself on a woman before, and he resented that he'd given her that power. He was destined for better things than Lottie Chase.

He should have ignored her plea for a letter of introduction. He could have made the sales without her. But she'd pricked his pride, with her implication that she planned to break out on her own—in competition with him. He'd fooled himself, fallen prey to the very skills he planned to use to his advantage, and lost his "in" at Elitch's as well as the income that went with it.

He was stranded in the middle of nowhere, with no travel money, and no way to continue his plans except through Lottie. If he hadn't blown all his cash living high in San Francisco, he'd be fine. As it was, he needed the money from the sale she was setting up at Elitch's. A few more and he'd have the money to show his old man what was what.

But his mistakes in San Francisco meant he'd have to work harder. He'd hoped he could push things along by pretending there were failed parts on that old-fashioned balloon ride but the Longs hadn't even thought along those lines. But they seemed to trust Lottie. He'd need her to steer them into believing such rides needed to be replaced with modern ones.

Once the sale was brokered and he had the cash in hand, he'd dump her and be on his way. Future sales would be harder without her con skills but he had his doubts about how long he'd be able to keep her under his thumb—even with using the kid as a threat.

No bones about it, Lottie was smarter than she used to be. Given what he'd observed about her in the past few days, it wouldn't take her too long to work out a way around him. The sooner he earned his way out of Denver and got back to his original plan, the better. Until he did, he would continue to bank her fear. He stomped on a loose sidewalk board, grinding it down with his heel. Keeping Lottie afraid would be a lot more difficult from a distance.

Especially since he couldn't find a temporary job to keep his head above water while he did so.

Rupert slipped into the red brick building owned by Zang's Brewing Company and glanced around the dim taproom. Across the crowded barroom, he spied the group of Germans he'd been hunting and strode toward them. After spending the entire day job seeking in the backward hellhole everyone else was so intent on calling progressive, he craved a few beers and the input of a few natives—or at least what passed for natives in Denver—to guide him in the right direction. He needed a job and he didn't plan to spend another day like today.

The sting of having his application refused at Manhattan Beach this morning had stayed with him all day. It nettled him that the manager of the smaller of Denver's two amusement parks had declined to even interview him, claiming he'd already hired a mechanic for the off-season. Rupert bit back the bitter taste in his mouth and told himself not to take it personally. The park was beneath him anyway.

He neared the Germans, loosening his step so he appeared casual and sociable. "You boys are a tough crew to locate."

One of them, the red-faced, heavy-jowled fellow called Schmidty, lifted a beer stein in welcome. "Unless we're dancing, we're right where we usually are—halfway pickled."

Rupert slid onto the bench next to Schmidty and signaled the waitress. "I've been to a half-dozen saloons looking for you."

Schmidty's buddy, Hans, grinned from across the table, his smile filled with toothless gaps. "Unless we get kicked out for being disorderly, we're here more often than not."

"Considering the barkeep at the Tivoli knew every one of you by name, you must get kicked out fairly regular." Rupert offered his comrades-in-waiting an ingratiating smile.

The buxom waitress plunked a beer in front of Rupert, giving him a quick flash of the tops of her breasts straining to erupt from her tight bodice. She winked at Rupert and ribbed Schmidty with her elbow. "Only when the other customers complain. These fellows are a bit noisy when they get drunk."

"It's a German beer hall. Everybody in it is noisy."

Rupert's comment brought a round of lifted steins and rowdy cheers of agreement. The waitress rolled her eyes and sashayed away.

Hans grinned again. "That's why we drink here. Gives us plenty of room before we're considered outrageous enough to kick out."

Rupert laughed, then set down his beer. "I'm looking for the guy who was with you last night. The one I was talking to about roller coasters."

"Fritz?"

"Tall guy, skinny as a beanpole?"

"Ja, that's Fritz. Guy's nuts. Thinks he knows everything about every roller coaster there is."

"That's the one." Nuts or not, there was a slim chance that a guy who knew coasters might know locations of parks as well. That Rupert had been unaware of Denver's parks proved he might need to gain more knowledge about the smaller parks in this part of the country. If he was going to cut his losses with Lottie and move on to make it big, he'd need to learn all he could. "He around?"

"Saw him earlier, headed upstairs with Adolph Zang," Hans said.

"Zang? The guy who owns this place?"

"Used to own it. Stayed on as president but now he raises purebred horses. Does some bigwig investing."

Rupert nodded. Zang was a big name in town—even he knew that. The wealthy German had financed the opulent Oxford Hotel and had his hand—and money—in everything from mining and real estate to banking and politics. He wasn't the type to make time for a fleabag like Fritz. Rupert took another sip of beer and cocked his head in a casual move to encourage Hans' gossip. "So what's he doing with Fritz?"

"Zang wants to invest in a new amusement park. He heard Fritzy knew about coasters."

Rupert stared at Hans, his heart pounding. A new park, backed by Zang's money, was an opportunity beyond anything he might have hoped for. One he wasn't about to let pass him by.

He set down the beer, wiped his mouth, and turned to Hans. "Which way is Zang's office?"

CHAPTER ELEVEN

Lottie watched Elsa skip up the steps of the Glen Park School with her new friends. Intent on their animated chatter, Elsa gave Lottie no more than a quick wave before disappearing into the tiny brick building.

Lottie's heart swelled. Though she'd missed so much, tight hugs as her daughter faced the insecurity of her very first day of school as a five-year-old included, she was proud of the confidence Elsa had developed over the summer. She'd made friends straight off with the girls she'd met last week and showed no fear in her new surroundings. Indeed, she'd almost balked when Lottie had insisted on accompanying her the two miles to the one-room rural school.

Turning north, Lottie scanned the unfamiliar neighborhood. A chill crept down her spine as pride in Elsa shifted toward the ever-present fear that now crouched just beyond her awareness. Edward's haughty presence lurked in the recesses of her mind, his leers leaping into her awareness when she least expected them. Elsa's safety was paramount, and Lottie was scared to death that she didn't know how to assure it.

She'd thought they were free. But Rupert's threat had made it clear they weren't.

Fallen leaves from the trees near Sloan's Lake crunched underfoot as she mulled it over again in her head. Was trusting Caleb the right thing to do? She hadn't hit the nail on the head when it came to men so far. She didn't know if Rupert would make good on his threats or not, and while Caleb seemed genuinely concerned about her welfare, the last thing she needed was for him to stir up Rupert's illogical hostility by digging around for information.

Rupert seemed to have become so much like Uncle Edward that her skin crawled.

Clutching her shawl close around her shoulders, Lottie increased her pace. She wished she knew more about how things worked in the world. Aunt Aggie had insisted she quit school and remain cloistered indoors when it became obvious that she was gaining more than an "adolescent pudge." Sure, she had street smarts. But she didn't know how birth certificates worked and whether or not she was guilty of kidnapping Elsa. All she knew was what Aggie had told her—that Elsa was theirs, not hers, the only way to hide Lottie's shameful behavior. No one would believe otherwise because they'd "fixed things" on Elsa's birth certificate.

In truth, it wasn't so much the forged birth certificate as it was her deep certainty that Edward would move heaven and hell to get Elsa back. She knew Edward. He was cautious as well as possessive. He wasn't about to risk public scandal by preying on a neighbor child. Lottie had stolen his prize away. He wouldn't hesitate to come for her if he knew where she was.

For Elsa's sake, Lottie hoped she'd convinced Caleb to curb his curiosity as to why she remained under Rupert's thumb. If she hadn't, the situation was about to become much more complicated.

Caleb stepped off the trolley and crossed the street with a handful of fellow passengers. He passed under the wooden entryway to Elitch's Gardens gate and breathed in the fresh air. The scent of freshly mown grass was a relief after the stale odors of the trolley. He'd forgotten about the strong summer stench that lingered on public conveyances. Still, the trip had been worth it.

Though Lottie had asked him not to interfere, he couldn't resist the urge to protect her. Her eyes had been filled with too much pain and fear. There were things that she hadn't told him, that she'd refused to tell him. Aching to understand, he'd gathered as much information as he dared. It was knowledge he now needed to share with Tom and Mary.

He strode up the path. It was lunchtime, and he hoped to catch them both at home. As usual, Mary spotted him through the window before he had a chance to knock and waved him in.

The scent of ginger cookies hit him as soon as he entered. His mouth watering, Caleb sat down at the table and eyed the plate of small brown treats.

"Go ahead," Mary prompted as she cleared the table.

Caleb grinned and reached for a warm cookie. He bit into it, closing his eyes as he savored the combination of ginger and cinnamon.

"We don't generally see you at the cottage midday," Tom observed, a question in his eyes.

"I just came back from town, learned some information you two might be interested in."

"About?" Mary asked, handing Caleb a glass of milk.

"Rupert Gennick."

Tom leaned forward in his chair. "Somehow, that doesn't surprise me."

"I had him investigated." Caleb exhaled, suspecting he'd only scratched the surface of what there was to find about the con man.

Mary stopped, plates and silverware in her hands. "Investigated?"

"I couldn't get past feeling that something wasn't right about him." His instincts had jumped to high alert. "Call it a hunch if you want."

"Your hunches tend to be worth exploring, son," Tom said. "Sometimes I forget that until it kicks me in the face. What's going on?"

"Two things struck me as odd. First off, there's this whole commission thing Lottie's so intent on." He took a sip of milk. "When you bought the roller coaster, was it a complicated process?"

Mary frowned, set the dishes on the counter, and returned to the table. "There's a bit more to it than buying a new pair of shoes but all in all, it wasn't complicated. We talked to Fred Thompson, one of the park owners on Coney Island. He gave us the information on the coasters he had, then we contacted the companies. From there, it was a matter of looking through their catalogues, picking out what we wanted, and dickering on the price."

"You worked directly with the company?"

She nodded.

"Not a salesman or a broker?"

"The company sent someone out," Tom said, his brow furrowed.

"But he worked for the company." Caleb met Tom's gaze head on. "Why would a company pay a commission to someone else, someone like Lottie, to arrange a sale if they have their own salesmen?"

"Are you accusing Lottie of something?" Mary's expression was filled with censure. "I thought you were past that, Caleb." She shook her head. "Only the larger companies have salesmen. With the others, the purchaser negotiates. To me, Lottie's offer to act as a broker makes sense. Company salesmen try to keep the prices—and profits—high. She wouldn't have that allegiance because she'd be working for us."

"In essence, then, you'd be paying her commission, not the company."

Mary thought for a moment. "Not necessarily. If she's bringing a large amount of business their way, a payment of some sort wouldn't be out of order. It's a growing, and competitive, business."

"Even if a company offered some sort of bonus for bringing in a large sale, I doubt it's anywhere close to what she envisions."

Tom tented his fingers, tapping them against his lips for a few moments. "She does seem to have a special arrangement with the company the Gennick family owns," he said. "Maybe Rupert gets a share of the profits."

"That's the other thing bothering me—the part I wanted someone to check into."

"This sounds serious." Mary settled her attention on Caleb.

"I found out a few details about Gennick, things you should know about."

"Go on." Tom seemed to brace himself and a stab of regret poked at Caleb for having to deliver uncomfortable news. He'd let Rupert come far too close to harming the Longs.

"Gennick Amusements is a very small enterprise. Art Gennick makes roller coasters."

"Well, then it would be logical for Lottie and Rupert to negotiate the sale," Mary said.

"No. He makes roller coasters. Just roller coasters. That's it. None of the other fancy stuff Lottie's been talking about."

"Then what's going on?" Tom asked.

"I'm not sure. And there's more."

"What else?" Worry filled Mary's soft voice.

"Art Gennick has five daughters but no sons."

"What?"

"Rupert Gennick has no association with the company. None. For all anybody knows, his name isn't even Gennick."

Tom nodded, resigned. "So you think this is all a con?"

"Gennick's so oily he squeaks. I wouldn't trust him."

"And Lottie?" Mary asked. "Do you think she's part of it?"

Caleb exhaled, recognizing he felt none of the doubt pangs that usually troubled him. "Against all odds, I trust her. If she is in on the con, she's damn good. Deep down, though, I think Gennick's suckered her. I think she's a victim, too, and it's time someone told her he's lied to her about the way commissions work and about his relationship with the Gennick company."

As Tom and Mary nodded their agreement, Caleb clenched his fist under the table. He hadn't revealed how afraid Lottie was of the slimeball. In his gut, he suspected it had something to do with Elsa, something Lottie was scared of. Unsure of what Lottie had told Mary about their past, he thought it was information best kept to himself.

At least until he found out what Gennick really had on Lottie.

Rupert rocked on the back legs of the straight-backed wooden chair he'd been forced to occupy when Fritz had claimed the more comfortable, and important, one in front of Adolph Zang's desk. It was their second meeting and he expected Zang to offer them an employment contract. Pulling this con would make it a lot easier to pocket what he needed to open his own park and shove his success in Art Gennick's face.

He glanced at Fritz. Already he was tired of his superior attitude and inferior intelligence. Still, he needed the German. He'd learned in the middle of the first meeting that Zang himself was smart. Extremely smart. And he was the sort of person who didn't much abide with shady methods. That was the only reason Rupert hadn't gone around Fritz.

Fritz was his buffer, his insurance. His patsy.

As if on cue, Fritz turned and offered Rupert a cheesy grin. "So, you think we're in the money now, ja?"

Rupert settled the chair back on the floor and nodded

solemnly. If Zang hired them, they'd either be in the money or in the soup, one or the other. Fritz had bought Rupert's line about the ride companies just the way Lottie had. Just to be safe, though, he'd made a few modifications, taking the attention away from Art Gennick's company. His father's company wasn't large enough to supply a brand-new park. The son of a bitch hadn't earned the business anyway.

Rupert had set himself up as a key player, with inside connections to all the big companies. Zang was busy enough that he'd prefer to delegate purchase negotiations. Rupert would arrange the sales, pad costs, skim a bit here and there. Fritz could keep the books—he was dumb enough he'd never catch the small adjustments. If Zang investigated and things went wrong, Fritz would get the blame.

And if things went as planned, Rupert would leave town not only with a feather in his cap, but with enough cash to bankroll his own park and prove his worth once and for all.

The door behind the large polished desk opened and Adolph Zang strode into the office. He wore success like a tailor-made suit. Though his father had been an immigrant, Adolph had seized the American dream with both hands. He was one of the wealthiest men in Denver, with friends in high places and the kind of power Rupert envied. He was not the sort of person one crossed and survived.

Rupert masked the twinge of jealousy that heated his blood and offered Zang a respectful nod.

Zang returned it and claimed his leather chair. He folded his hands on the center of the ornate desk and smiled at Fritz. "Gentlemen," he said.

Fritz grinned, obviously feeling honored. "Sir," he said.

Rupert fought a groan. He needed Fritz to at least appear competent.

"Congratulations, gentlemen. Your references check out,"

Zang announced. "You brought the list?"

Fritz looked back at Rupert and snapped his fingers. "The list?"

Rupert stood and approached, subdued but not cowed. If Zang didn't have respect for them, the deal would never fly. "Right here, Mr. Zang." He laid a single sheet of paper on Zang's desk. "I've listed all the companies I have connections to, along with their specialties."

"What's to stop me from simply pocketing this and proceeding on my own?" Zang asked.

Fritz blanched.

Recognizing the game, Rupert played along. He adopted a comrade to comrade demeanor, leaned over the desk, and caught Zang's gaze. "Because you don't work that way, sir. You've asked us here because we have skills you need. You're a businessman, a mining industrialist, an investor. You are not an expert on amusement parks. Fritz and I can advise you on which rides will attract people to your park, which will best complement your space, and which will make you the most money. My knowledge will guarantee you a successful park. Once the park is designed, I have the connections to purchase the rides for you. Fritz has the skills to assure you will make a profit. We need each other. We've given you the list because we trust you to be fair."

Zang raised an eyebrow. "Straight talker, aren't you? I like that. Fritz, what do you have to say?"

Fritz swallowed. "I don't got so much spit and polish as this one does but what he says is the truth. We know our stuff. We work hard for you. This is what you want, ja?"

"Ja."

Fritz nodded, then looked up with a blank expression. "This was a test, no?"

"A test?" Zang sounded taken aback. "I'm not sure—"

Rupert interrupted, afraid Fritz's ill-formed questions were going to make Zang think they were a couple of yokels instead of intelligent businessmen. "I think Fritz means that you were looking for a gesture of good faith on our part to assure you we have the qualifications we represented at our last meeting. He wishes to know if we have satisfied your questions."

Zang nodded. "I think Fritz should rely on you for communicating in the future."

Rupert shook his head in false modesty. "I help Fritz out when the language barriers warrant and I know suppliers but he's the real businessman here. He knows how to maintain the bottom line."

"Then I suggest we proceed. I'll ask my secretary to bring in the employment contracts. In the meantime," Zang reached for a rolled paper and opened a map of the Denver area, "this is Lake Rhoda." He pointed to a location north and east of Elitch's Gardens. "I have one hundred sixty acres and seven hundred fifty thousand dollars. I want lots of rides and electric lights. Big, boys, big. I want a return on this. I don't invest just to make little kids happy. I intend to make money."

Rupert reached out to the map, his imagination stampeding at the opportunity of designing a park from scratch—making a reputation for himself while he raked money off the top.

"And boys? Once you start on this, you'd best succeed. I want a park that knocks the competition out of the running, and I want it soon, before anyone else has a chance to jump on this." Zang paused, his gaze boring into them. "If you waste my time, I'll bury you."

Halfway up the four-story roller coaster lift hill, Caleb straightened, stretching his aching back. He stared up the wooden slope. Looking at the twenty feet of chain yet to be inspected, he groaned. He wanted to be done with the task and away from the hated ride. His arms throbbed from the hours he'd already spent on the underside of the incline examining each of the safety "dogs" on the return channel.

"That looks too much like work," Lottie called from the bottom of the hill.

He glanced down at her laughing eyes and grinned. His thoughts had been on her all day. "How are the bears?"

"Missing the crowds, I think."

He wondered if Lottie missed them as well. With the season over, she no longer made a show of the bear feedings and had discarded her blue wool bathing costume for a plain gray work skirt. Within Caleb's imagination, though, he recalled each seductive sway of her derriere and those shapely legs below her bathing suit. It was enough to make him wish the season would continue forever.

"Do you want company?" she asked.

"If you like."

He was about to tell her to have a seat under the open-sided station where folks congregated as they waited to board the coaster, but she was already scrambling up the ladder-like incline. She moved with grace, comfortable as a monkey as she climbed up the two-and-a-half stories to his position. She turned and sat opposite him, the greasy chain and ratchet mechanism between them.

"Isn't it a glorious day?" Ignoring the grime of the chain drive next to her, she leaned back on the wooden hill, letting the sun wash her vibrant face. "I love these last warm days, don't you?"

He shook his head. "I've been sweating up here for half the day. Guess I'm not quite as enamored of the heat as you are."

Lottie laughed, the sound like wind chimes in the quiet air. She swept her hands under her neck, lifting the tendrils of hair that had managed to escape from her Gibson Girl hairdo.

His heart thrummed at the sight of her neck, the dewy sheen there, begging to be kissed. Reluctant, Caleb returned his attention to his task. Two stories up on a roller coaster incline was not the place to give rein to his lust, no matter how tempting she was.

Checking each link of the chain, he climbed up the hill. Lottie matched his progress, chatting about Sam's and Gertrude's antics. Funny, the sun seemed less intense in her company, the work less taxing. At the top, satisfied the chain, ratchets, and safety dogs were in good repair, he wiped his hands on a rag. The evening was ahead of them. Hoping to talk her into a quiet walk, he nodded to her.

"Done," he announced. "Ready to go down?"

"In a minute," she said. "I'd like to show you something, if it's all right."

He paused. "Show me what?"

"See that spot, over there by the theatre?" She pointed.

"That grassy spot by the fence?"

Lottie nodded, eagerness filling her bright blue eyes. "It's an empty space, right?"

He stared at her, wondering what she had up her sleeve. With Lottie, he could never quite be sure. "It's a great spot for some benches, maybe a quiet grotto."

"I was thinking it's the exact size and shape to put in a 'Helter Skelter.' "

"A ride." He should have known. Everything always came back to rides with her.

"Hold on. It's not really a ride—not in the way you're thinking. Before you get all stewed up, let me tell you about it. I think there may be a way to meld our visions. Will you hear me out?"

Caleb fought back his resistance and nodded. He wasn't sure he believed it possible, but if there was a way to merge their visions, it was long past time they explored it. He leaned back, ready to listen.

"The Helter Skelter is a simple non-mechanical slide with twists and turns. Less intimidating than roller coasters—tame, really. It doesn't take a huge amount of space. Since it's not as high as a coaster, the structure itself is less complicated. You could build a grotto around the base, with small nooks jutting underneath, between support beams. The plants would disguise the actual under-areas of the ride."

"A slide?" He tried to imagine it. "For kids?"

"For adults. Higher than a child's slide but not as tall as a roller coaster and not so spread out. It's less loud—there are no cars and no chains. Just lots of curves and turns."

"And screaming riders, no doubt." He fought back a frown and kept the scolding tone from his voice. "That wouldn't make a grotto very peaceful, would it? And what about the theatre? How would anyone hear the actors' lines?"

"That's just it." She sat up straighter, her enthusiasm evident. "The riders get thrills but they don't scream much—not loud screams anyway. Just lots of pleased laughter. Mostly, it's frequented by women who are too frightened to ride roller coasters. The slide seems tame but the unexpected turns make it exciting. They get to let loose without too much risk and they ride it again and again, their skirts flying."

Caleb pondered the idea, remembering how slides had attracted him as a boy. He'd loved the surprise of the speed and the rush of air. And Lottie was right, unless he'd forgotten about it, no one ever let out a bloodcurdling scream on the way down. A few whoops and hollers. Most had giggled and smiled, then circled around to climb the ladder again.

Giggles weren't what he'd thought about when he'd imagined a quiet grotto but maybe it wouldn't matter so much. Giggles were happy sounds. "I suppose you could put in enough foliage to buffer the sounds of so many people, make it less intrusive."

Lottie paused, her brow knit in thought. "You said something before—about not dealing well with screaming roller coaster riders. Is it the rides you hate or the screaming?"

Caleb shrugged, feigning nonchalance, unwilling to discuss the issue. "One and the same, really."

"Is it?"

"Seems like."

"That's not an answer."

Her probing touched too close, threatening to trigger memories he didn't want surfacing. The heat of the day felt too much like that muggy afternoon in the jungle. Already, images of bleeding soldiers filled his head. He pushed the impressions from his mind before they took root and ruined his time with Lottie. "I don't like the screams, all right?"

"All right." She paused and once again, he could almost see the wheels spinning in her pretty little head. Then she plunged on, prying further. "Why do the screams bother you?"

"I don't want to talk about it," he snapped, rising to a sitting position.

"Okay. What about the coaster itself—why do you hate it?"

He blew out a frustrated breath. "You have a coaster, you have screams."

"Caleb Hudson, have you ever ridden a roller coaster?"

"Hell, no."

She gazed at him, argument in her eyes. The moment stretched, the confrontational glare softening into something subtle and unexpected. "Then you can hardly condemn them, now can you?"

"I can and I will."

"What if the riders didn't scream?"

"What?" he stared at her, uncertain what she was getting at.

She circled her arms around her knees and leaned her head

on them, almost as if she didn't care. "Would you still hate roller coasters if the riders didn't scream?"

The gentleness of the question threw him further and his defensive irritation wavered. "That isn't going to happen."

"It could."

"Hah."

She glanced toward him. "Let's ride it right now. You and I. I promise not to scream."

"Why would I want to do that?" he asked, incredulous, his heart pounding.

"Because that is the only way you're going to understand what I'm talking about when I say the ride is thrilling. It's the only way you can see my perspective when I talk about the future of amusement parks."

"No thank you."

She raised her eyebrows. "So, you think it's fair that I try to see your side of things, but you can refuse to consider my views?"

"I can see your views just fine," he insisted, hating the tone his words took on.

"You don't have a clue about what I'm trying to say. You've never been on an amusement ride."

"I've ridden the miniature train, and I've ridden carousels."

"It's not the same."

He shook his head, hating what the screams did to him, hating that there was no way to tell her without revealing how he'd failed to protect those who had depended on him. "I refuse to get on this thing."

"Scared?"

His pride bristled. "Of course not."

"Then take a ride. One ride. No screaming passengers, just you and me. Then, if you don't understand the attraction of coasters, I'll accept your point of view. But until then, you don't know what you're talking about." She paused. "Do you?"

Caleb glanced away. She was right, he didn't know. He didn't know anything more about what she was saying than she knew about his fits. But what he did know was that if she didn't stop pushing at him, he might slide into one of them. He could feel the guilt welling up with every pressing question. "If I take one ride, you'll quit harping about it? No more pushing me about why I hate the damn thing? You'll let it be?"

"I'll quit harping at you. And, if you still hate it, I'll even promise to listen to your ideas about the park."

Caleb stood and glanced down from the four-story height. It was a bad idea. His heart was pounding and he could feel the cold sweat on his palms. One time, he told himself, that was all. He could handle one time as long as no one screamed if it meant she'd let it be. Spotting Tom below them, Caleb shouted, then waved him over.

"Come on, then," he muttered to Lottie. He tramped down the incline. Lottie followed, her footsteps loud on the bare wood.

By the time they made their way to the bottom, Tom was waiting. "What is it?" he asked.

"He's going to ride the coaster," Lottie announced, her voice full of victory.

Tom raised his eyebrows. "He is?"

"The woman won't quit nagging at me." The response was nonchalant, holding none of the anxiety filling every cell of his body. "Will you run the controls?"

Tom nodded, a grin threatening to spill across his face. He uncoupled the first wooden car from the pair behind it, and moved it into position at the base of the hill. "Front or rear?" he asked with a flourish of his arm.

"Front, of course," Lottie answered, jumping into the first seat. She scooted to the side, then patted the bright red seat. Caleb frowned, then slid in beside her. It was a bad idea and growing worse every second.

181

His thigh brushed hers and he heard her quiet intake of breath at the contact but she didn't pull away. Her leg, under the dark gray wool skirt, was hot against his, the pressure firm, intimate. He lifted his gaze, catching the slight blush on her cheeks before he looked away so he could make his mind blank.

In front of them, Tom's eyes twinkled as he locked the car into the first safety dog. "Ready?"

Caleb nodded, tensing.

Beside him, Lottie squirmed, her excitement palpable.

Tom moved the lever, and the chain engaged, pulling the car up the incline. The click of each ratchet announced its corresponding tug as the car moved upward, the sound reminding him of cocking guns. He drove the association from his mind, picturing the chain-drive instead. His gut clenched with each tug-tug-tug. He hoped like hell he didn't lose it when they crested the hill.

They neared the top. Beside Caleb, Lottie's animated face glowed, and she reached into his lap to clasp his shaking hand.

As they crested the summit, Caleb's chest tightened. There was no track in front of them.

Then, the car tipped over the peak, dropping with a jerk as it began its descent. His stomach still going uphill, Caleb braced his feet on the bottom of the car. They plunged, straight down, as if soaring on air. Wind rushed past and the car picked up speed as they raced toward the first curve. Caleb cursed the scream that leapt into his throat.

Not now. Not now. Don't scream.

They hit the curve, the force jarring the car as it slammed into the side friction rails. The whooping scream erupted, startling Caleb as the liberating release ricocheted through him.

Lottie turned, hugging him close. Her body jostled against him, her breasts pressing at his side. She grinned, eyes lit with excitement. Heat surged through him, fear, all thoughts of

Cuba, forgotten as the intensity of the experience caught hold.

Their laughter bubbled as the car bounced, dipping down, surging around corners. Each movement threw them against one another, their hair whipping. The clackety-clack of the wooden track countered the sway of the wooden structure as the car sped around the figure eight of the track. Then, they spilled around the final curve and into the station. At the side of the track, Tom pushed the brake lever and the parallel boards that served as friction brakes rose under the car, slowing it to a stop.

"You screamed," Lottie announced, beaming at him.

"I did not."

"Did too."

"I yelped."

"Well, whatever it was, you had fun, didn't you? For those few moments, you forgot every burden you have."

He stared at her, comprehension dawning, and he nodded. The scream had sprung from exhilaration rather than desperate fear and agonizing pain. Unlike anything he'd known before. Unlike anything he'd ever imagined possible.

"Wanna go again?" he asked, suddenly unsure of the reality he'd been clinging to so desperately.

Chapter Twelve

After Caleb exited, Lottie slid toward the edge of the coaster car. Her hands shook and goose bumps graced her skin but inside, warm exhilaration filled her. She brushed loose strands of her sagging pompadour from her face and glanced up at Caleb.

Her breath caught at the picture he made. Windblown hair and eyes full of abandon, he exuded delight. Then he smiled, the dawning awareness of his own joy stretching his mouth wide as a child's.

She placed her hand into his waiting clasp and stood, feeling his escalated energy in the fleeting touch. Hot appreciation jolted through her, and she stroked her fingertips against the heel of his palm.

"You two run along, get some lemonade." Tom's voice broke into her consciousness.

Cheeks burning, she drew back her hand. A glance at Caleb revealed a slight ruddiness on his face as well.

"Go on," Tom insisted. "I'll put the cars away. You can finish up with the maintenance in the morning."

"Thanks," Caleb said, his voice quiet. He slipped his hand back into Lottie's and squeezed. "Let's go to the greenhouse. I have a jar of sweet tea buried in the shade, keeping cool."

They set off toward the back of the park, silence embracing them. There didn't seem any need for words—the shared wonder of their experience connected them.

Lottie's fingers tingled, warmth coiling through her body with unhurried fervor, staggering her as the force of the sensations collided in her lower belly.

Stunned, she savored the feeling.

"Cold?" Caleb asked, his voice still holding traces of awe.

"Hmmm?"

"You shivered."

"I did?" She concentrated on the path, crunching the red and golden carpet of leaves, breathing in the musty scent of autumn. "Delayed excitement, I guess."

"I know what you mean."

"You had fun?"

A full throaty laugh erupted from him, the sound filling the pungent orchard, sifting through the rays of sun that pierced the trees. "I had no idea a roller coaster ride would make me feel so free."

She glanced at him, marveling at the wonder that danced in his whiskey eyes. Bliss lit his expression. This was a side of him she hadn't expected and seeing it warmed her heart more than she would have thought possible. A smile crept across her face.

"Are you going to make me eat my words?" he asked.

"About?"

"About rides being no fun. About people not wanting them. About it being a bad idea to add them." There was a sheepish admission within his banter.

"Are you saying you've reconsidered?"

"I'm saying I have a new perspective." They reached the glass door of the greenhouse and entered. The scent of turned earth hit her first, followed by the mingled floral aromas that lingered in the near-empty hothouse. They made their way down a narrow aisle and neared the tables at the rear. There, a riot of rust and yellow chrysanthemums exploded the corner with color as heady as their scent.

"I did try to tell you," Lottie teased, unwilling to surrender the new tone of their exchange.

"That you did." Shifting a few crates to the floor, Caleb cleared off a couple bales of straw. "Is the coaster always like that?" he asked, his timbre shifting.

Lottie nodded as she sat. "Pretty much."

"And the other rides?"

"Some are more exciting than others but those that provide thrills always pay off. They offer an escape that never fails."

Pulling a jar of tea from the damp flower bed, he wiped it clean with a bandana, and unscrewed the top. He handed it to her and settled on the other bale, next to her. "What dark woes do you have to seek so much escape?"

Lottie shrugged and took a drink from the jar, avoiding the question.

"Lottie?"

She struggled against the sharp pain of her memories, worthlessness and guilt threatening the exuberant mood they'd shared moments before. "I don't want to talk about it."

"I can see that."

She drew a breath, closed her eyes, and dammed up her emotions. "I didn't have a happy childhood. Let's just leave it at that."

His brows knit in thought. "Your uncle?"

Lottie's eyes flew open. "How did you—?"

"Elsa said he wasn't a nice person."

Lottie swallowed, unease knotting her stomach. "Elsa talked to you about Uncle Edward?"

"She said she knew Edward and Aggie weren't her parents, that Edward was too attentive. I told her she should talk to you." He paused, rubbing her arm with his thumb. "I guess what happened wasn't a good thing. Is that what you were running from?"

Exhaling, Lottie told herself to stay calm. Elsa hadn't told him everything, and he was the kind of guy who wouldn't probe any further—not unless she encouraged him to do so. "No . . . it wasn't good. I had to get away." She stared at him, willing him to leave it be.

Caleb's eyes darkened, his gaze dissecting her. "Did that son of a bitch touch you?"

She dropped her head, shame burning her skin. Memories of his touch flooded her, pressing in on her until she couldn't breathe. She gulped for air, thrusting the image from her mind. "I rode those roller coasters as many times as I could. I screamed and screamed and screamed until I was hoarse. To make up for every scream I choked back when he . . . until I felt free of it all."

"Damn the man, damn him." He set the tea on the ground and pulled her into his arms.

She sank into his strength, relief at having shared her burden washing over her. "Those rides were my salvation," she whispered. "When I rode, I was able to forget all the bad things in my life. I didn't have to be afraid or feel ashamed. I got rid of all my emotion in explosive, bloodcurdling screams."

He kissed the top of her head, his acceptance of her evident in the tender action. "And ever since Tom and Mary brought that roller coaster here, I've hated those blood-curdling screams for the emotions they bring to life."

Lottie sat back, sliding her hand into his until their fingers weaved together. "You said before, the day the balloon broke loose, that the screams brought back bad memories for you?"

He nodded.

"Want to talk about it?"

He sighed. "No, but I will. If I don't, it will keep rearing its head between us."

She knew she was prying but the need to know him, really

know him, nettled her. She suspected he had as many demons as she did and, for the first time in her life, hunger to share those hidden emotions with someone consumed her. She squeezed his hands in encouragement, glad that he trusted her enough to share his fears.

"I listened to men die, Lottie." His voice broke and, for a moment, she thought he would stop. Then he drew a breath. "In Cuba. For hours, I lay at the bottom of a god-damned hill and listened to two of the men I sent up its side lay there and die. I couldn't get to them. They screamed until they died."

The enormity of the words lay thick in the air. She recognized the guilt in his tone, and her heart squeezed tight, knowing there was nothing she could say that would ease it. "It was war, Caleb. Men die in war."

"I should have never sent them up that hill," his voice broke, "never left them there."

"You can't change what's already happened." Something deep within her clenched at the words. If only it were that simple.

Caleb expelled a heavy breath. "No, I can't. But I don't want it exploding in my head, either."

"I guess I understand that. I never realized why you hated the coaster—I thought it was the ride itself. The same ride that allows me to escape all the bad things in my mind."

"Strange, isn't it?" He offered a wavering smile. "I never thought about riding the coaster as a way to escape . . . for anyone."

"And I never thought of the screaming as anything but a release."

He thought a moment, then nodded. "It was, you know. A release. It felt great to let loose and yell like that. Even though listening to the screams has always been a bad experience for me, shouting my head off felt good."

"Not all screams are a sign of distress." She gave his hands another squeeze, then drew back.

"No, I guess they're not."

"So that's the reason you've resisted expansion?"

"Not the whole reason." He reached for the jar of tea, sipped, and passed it to her. "I like the peace of the gardens. For me, it's a place to forget . . . my escape. People need places like that."

"And here I am threatening to destroy them."

"Your plan has so many rides. There's no place of sanctuary. Nowhere to simply enjoy the cool breeze, the warm sun, the scent of nature. Your plan leaves no room for them."

"So what if we compromise?" She swallowed the last of the tea and set the empty jar under the bench.

"Design a plan that has both features? Two forms of escape?" Caleb mulled it over. Maybe it was time he looked at her ideas. Maybe there was a way to add more rides without sacrificing his vision. Had he been so intent on protecting Mary that he'd failed to see all that might be possible? "You know I grew up here?"

"In Denver?"

"At the park. Mary and John Elitch took me in when I was a kid. Just before they bought the place. It was a farm then, sixteen acres of orchards. I helped Mary plant gardens." Warmth seeped through him. "She mothered me like I'd never been mothered, even when my own ma was still alive. John was the father I had never had."

"They had the idea for an amusement park when they bought the farm?" Lottie leaned forward, interest bright in her blue eyes.

"Not at first. But when John told Mary the grounds reminded him of Woodland Gardens in San Francisco, they decided to make it a business. Mary was friends with P.T. Barnum. He'd given her a few of his circus animals, so they thought they'd include a zoo. They opened it to the public in eighteen-ninety with grand plans to include concerts, vaudeville, and theatre." He laughed, recalling how distant the place had been from Denver. "John had to hire carriages to bring people the last two miles because the streetcar line didn't reach this far. But it was a success. They sold their restaurant in town and moved forward with plans to expand the park."

"But it's Mary Long now. What happened to John?"

Caleb's memories shifted, his mood sliding with them. "That winter, he took his acting troupe on tour to raise money. He caught pneumonia and died."

"Oh, no." Lottie's hand went to her mouth.

"When he left on tour, he told me to watch over Mary. I was just fourteen but he trusted me. Then, later, when he was dying, he was so worried someone would take advantage of her soft-heartedness." He paused. "I promised him I'd protect her."

"That's a lot of responsibility for someone so young."

"When Tom first started courting her, I made his life pretty miserable."

"You didn't trust him?"

"With time, yes. I don't trust easily, Lottie." He shifted, uncomfortable with the admission. He'd never thought about it much until his reaction to Lottie, but the understanding that he'd felt a stronger-than-average need to protect Mary had begun to dawn on him. Still, he'd never before put it into words. "Until Mary, no one ever stood by me. I had to stand by her."

"And that's why you've mistrusted me?"

He nodded, a twinge of shame poking at him. "You're slick. You told me that first day that being a huckster was your biggest skill. Then you tried to sell her a bunch of rides. What was I supposed to think?"

Lottie nodded, understanding in her eyes. "Exactly what you did, I guess."

"She's my family."

They sat, surrounded by the pungent odor of the mums, as the new revelations settled into their minds.

"And now?" she asked. "Do you trust me now?"

He smiled at her. "I've discovered there's more to you than meets the eye."

"What changed your mind?"

He thought about how Lottie wanted to make the ride sales in order to support Elsa. Learning that was her motive had changed how he viewed her. She wasn't out to gouge the Longs, and she wasn't out to destroy the sanctuary of the gardens. She loved Elsa and was protective of her. But he knew that wasn't the whole reason. She was smart and sassy and didn't back down.

"Elsa. Seeing how you are with her. And seeing all the ways you aren't manipulative, how determined and full of life you are." He paused. "And the way you react to Rupert. Him I don't trust."

"Your instincts are right there. He used to be different. He was a friend. Now, I'm not sure what his intentions are. He's not the same person I used to know."

He leaned forward, tongue-tied. "I'd like to know you better . . . You're not what I expected when you walked through those gates. You intrigue me, Lottie Chase."

She laughed. "There's a lot more to you than meets the eye, too, Caleb Hudson."

"Let's start on the plans, see if we can manage to work together," he said. "Once we have a few ideas, we can take them to Tom and Mary." His eyes drifted to the new promise in her eyes. "But I'd like to start with this." He leaned toward her and took her face in his hands, conscious of all she'd revealed to him.

He kept the kiss gentle as their mouths touched, until her lips became warm and receptive. He felt, more than heard, the soft sigh escape her, and his body hardened in a primal response. The need to hold her filled him, and his arms surrounded her.

She slid into his embrace, soft and yielding. Her arms encircled his neck, fingers sliding through his hair as she pulled his head closer. Her tongue touched his lips, tentative, inviting.

He opened his mouth to her, his own tongue waltzing with hers, and her eyes drifted shut in silent pleasure. Those wispy lashes fluttered. Once. Twice. And he ached to feel their butterfly touch on his skin.

Pulling from the heat of her lips, he kissed her on each corner of her mouth. Once. Twice. An echo of her flickering lashes. An effort to let her know this was not simple lust. He kissed her eyelids. Once. Twice. Telling her she was cherished.

She shifted in his arms, her hands pulling him along as she lay back on the straw bale. She moved his mouth back to hers, bringing him close, telling him without words that she wanted him.

He kissed her again. This time with intensity.

She shivered and drew a shaky breath.

His hands drifted across her skin, past her shoulders, feeling the raised goose bumps on her upper arms. Goose bumps that had nothing to do with the humid air of the greenhouse. His gut tightened. And seconds later, as his thumb brushed the soft mound of her breast, Lottie moaned into his mouth.

He lowered his lips, letting them trace the path his hands were forging. She arched under him, and he nipped at her. She squirmed, her body rubbing against his, her breath sharp as she felt his arousal.

Across the greenhouse, the door opened, its glass rattling in the metal frame. "Lottie? Caleb? You in here?"

Lottie gasped, squirming as she recognized Elsa's voice. Her eyes widened.

Caleb caught her gaze, expecting fear or remorse as her awareness of their actions settled through her. But, instead, they were startled. Startled but still full of hungry desire.

That smoldering promise stayed with Caleb throughout the rest of the day. He wasn't sure how to proceed, given what Lottie had revealed, and such uncertainty was uncomfortable. Added to the mix were roiling anger, a need to comfort, and more questions than he knew what to do with. And, to be honest, more than a little fear that he'd do something wrong and hurt her worse.

He was treading on delicate ground.

What the hell did a man do with knowledge like that?

He stacked his mismatched supper dishes away on the open shelf and plopped down in the nearby wooden rocker that comprised his parlor. A lone late-blooming tea rose he'd nurtured in the greenhouse sat in a vase on an upturned crate, its vibrant yellow hue brightening the room.

Caleb cracked his thumbs and expelled a frustrated breath.

He had so many questions—about what had happened and when and how Lottie had managed to cope with it. He wanted to ask her about Elsa. He wanted to kiss Lottie, hold her, make love to her. Yet, he had no idea what the rules were or how to touch her so that he didn't churn up bitter memories. In the greenhouse, he'd held back, wanting to reassure her, waiting for her signal, trying to read each response. But the last thing he wanted to do was fuss over her, crowd her with too much tenderness. And he sure as hell didn't want her to mistake his caring for pity.

His gaze drifted back to the rose. The hybrid required careful nurturing and regulated temperatures. But his Lottie was no tea rose. She was much more akin to the blushing roses that grew wild, their delicate appearance belying their sturdiness.

Survivors. Wild roses needed only sun and soil. They didn't need pruning or special fertilizers or even protection from the elements. They made their own way, needing only the room to do so.

He reckoned that would be the way of it with Lottie, too. He'd need to let her shape the course of their relationship. She'd tell him the details when she was ready.

He would make sure she knew he was willing to listen.

Rupert set down his whiskey and looked across the elegant library of the Oxford Hotel, smug satisfaction filling him. Zang had sprung for rooms for both him and Fritz at the ritzy five-story hotel the tycoon had helped bankroll. Fritz sat across from him, puffing on a fat cigar the concierge had supplied.

Sitting in such plush surroundings almost made him feel he was in the money as much as Zang. Hell, if they could take Zang like he wanted, they would be. Not as flush as the beer-baron-cum-investor, but rich enough.

Rich enough that the world would be his for the taking.

Fritz caught his eye and grinned. Fancy digs or not, his partner still looked like a beanpole. At least he cleaned up good, looking enough like an accountant and businessman in his new brown serge suit. When he wasn't grinning, that was. But, then, looking stupid was Fritz's problem. Now that they'd been hired, all Rupert needed was some temporary semblance of skill. After that, if Zang realized the idiot was a fake, it was fine and dandy. The more Fritz attracted attention then, the less notice there'd be on Rupert.

For now, they needed to select rides and begin planning. The project presented a chance for Rupert, in more ways than one, and he was determined to create a design that would have folks talking about him. He'd set himself up good, that was for sure.

"Some fancy place, ja?" Fritz rubbed his foot on the marble

floor as if testing the shine.

Rupert rolled his eyes. "Stop it. We've got work to do."

Fritz rested the cigar on an amber-colored glass ashtray. "Should we sit at the table?"

"Ordinarily works best when folks want to look over paperwork together. Of course we should sit at the table, you Dummkopf."

Fritz just grinned more and ambled to the polished library table. "The saloon has a beer called the 'Fritz Imperial' so watch who you're calling a Dummkopf."

"Well, la-de-da."

Fritz shrugged. "I don't see Zang naming any beers after you."

"I hate to tell you this, Fritzy, but it ain't you he named it after."

"You don't know that. Not for a fact."

"Sure, Fritz. Whatever you say." Rupert followed him to the table, shaking his head. "Let's see what you have in mind."

Fritz rifled through the pages of paper he'd stacked on the table earlier, spreading them out on the gleaming surface. After their meeting with Zang, Fritz had offered to put together a list of rides for Rupert to consider for the park design. Fritz might look dumb, but the man knew his roller coasters better than Rupert did. He'd also been a bookkeeper—a skill Rupert intended to use to his full advantage. He planned to slip Fritz inflated numbers and let him take the fall if Zang ever examined them enough to notice.

"I did as you say. I put down all the coasters I know." He pointed to the one at the top of his list. "This one I think Zang will like, the Big Splash, ja? He wants big. This one is big and no park here has a water ride." Fritz went on to itemize the other coasters, supplying a host of details for each, nicely set into a columned table.

Rupert nodded, more than a little surprised at the beanpole's detail. He'd made Rupert's work easier by half. "Yeah, yeah. You know which companies supply each?" If he was lucky, they'd match up with the suppliers he already had an "in" with. His plan was to buy as cheaply as possible from his connections, doctoring receipts enough to make a tidy profit. It was an old trick but one that would likely work well. He'd already determined neither Zang nor Fritz knew squat about the amusement industry beyond what they liked. "Fritz?"

The skinny German looked up, his mind clearly somewhere else.

"The companies?"

"Ja, of course." Fritz pointed to the final column of his chart.

Rupert looked down, the organization this time giving him pause. His pulsed hitched, and he glanced at Fritz again, concern niggling him. "You know prices?"

"Prices? I know only the coasters. You told me you handle prices, ja? All I am is for the ideas and the bookkeeping. More than that, I do not know."

Rupert wiped his sweaty palms on his pants. "You're right, Fritz. I just wanted to make sure we didn't double up on the work."

"On the next page, I wrote down other rides, things I think people would like. You will figure out how to put it up?"

"Sure." He smiled at Fritz, surer than ever that he'd walk away from this with a big name to go with the wad of money in his pocket. "We make it like Coney Island. High towers, lots of electric lights, casinos. A park for grown-ups. I got lots of ideas."

"That's good. I don't think it would be a good thing to cross Adolph Zang."

Rupert expelled a breath. Fritz looked more than a little worried. "What do you mean?"

"Zang. I think he will make things very bad if we do not give him what he wants."

"A park design. Not hard to do, Fritzy. We can't fail. What're you shook up about?"

"Not just a design. Not just plans and good prices. He demands success. I think if we do only part of that, he will make it our fault."

"Our fault? We can't guarantee success—that's all on how he runs the place. Why would he hold us responsible?"

"Because he is that kind of man."

Rupert thought back to Zang's words the other day. What had he said? Something about burying them if they didn't deliver. He doubted that was going to happen. "So we'll create him a great park. Big, flashy, just like he wants."

"He wants more than that. You didn't read the paper we signed with him? Only after the park opens do we get all of our pay. If the park doesn't make money, we don't make money."

Rupert's heart pounded. "What? He can't do that. We'll be long gone by the time the park opens." Hell, he hadn't intended on staying, on giving Zang time to discover he'd been conned.

"He can. A man with that much power can do anything. It's right there in the contract. He doesn't trust us but how it is worded . . . if we build him a great park and no one comes, there's no money. Our park must be so good that all the people come to it and the Elitch park no longer has so many people."

"How the hell can we control that?" He stared at Fritz, unable to digest what he was hearing.

"If we don't do this, Zang will say it is our fault and we will not get other jobs. It must be so perfect that no one goes to the Elitch park anymore. Then Zang will be pleased."

"Well, shit. That should be easy." The blithe words rolled off Rupert's tongue as his mind scrambled. The design could be revolutionary and still the park might not turn a profit. Not for years. Not with two competing parks in town.

"Now who is a Dummkopf?" Fritz rose and stacked his list neatly, then handed it to Rupert. "Here is my work. When you make your deals, I will start the ledgers to show Zang how the money is spent. Make your plans, make your deals. But you better be as good as you bragged you were. If the Elitch park takes business from Zang, he won't be happy and an unhappy Adolph Zang is not an enemy anyone wants." His glare was hot enough to sizzle. "Make sure your plan is so good that no one wishes to go to the other parks. Ja?"

"Ja." Rupert muttered the word as if it were an oath, then watched Fritz exit the library. What the hell had he gotten himself into?

CHAPTER THIRTEEN

Elsa kicked at the kitchen chair, her face drawn into a frown as she studied the multiplication table in front of her. "I hate memorizing," she announced.

Lottie fought a smile. She wasn't much for it herself. "I know, sweetie. But you need to learn the times table. You'll need it as you live your life."

"For what?"

"To calculate out how much things will cost at the grocer and how much money to set back for the tram each month or even to factor how much it will take to ride the roller coaster seven times."

"Seven times? I'd only ride it twice. I can add for that."

"Elsa."

"Lottie."

"Study for ten more minutes. Then I'll quiz you. If you pass, you can be done for the night."

"All right." She drew the words out, letting her tone convey her dissatisfaction with the assignment. Her foot continued to swing against the chair leg.

Lottie lit the lamp and the sharp odor of kerosene filled the air, then floated away. She set the lamp on the table, preempting Elsa's standard complaint of not being able to study for lack of light, then returned to finish drying the dishes stacked in the drain board. The routine had been established over the past few evenings, and she enjoyed the quiet work time with Elsa.

Thoughts drifting to yesterday afternoon, Lottie felt a warm tingle spread through her. Had Elsa not come to the greenhouse, she suspected the encounter with Caleb would have progressed beyond what either of them expected. Her reaction still surprised her—not so much the longing but the lack of self-remorse. He was a handsome man and he stirred her. Granted, when she'd realized just how much, it had kicked her in the gut. But when Elsa had called out, there had been only a moment of alarm.

For the first time in her life, she hadn't felt guilt that she'd tempted a man to do something he hadn't intended to do. This time, she'd been drawn to every unspoken invitation offered her, to the gentle tender kisses that made her feel cherished. Desired, awakened. Like a dam had burst somewhere inside of her. If it hadn't been for Elsa's interruption, she might not have stopped Caleb's arousing touch.

But Elsa had broken the moment. They'd stayed silent, lying out of her sight line until she'd left, then straightening their clothes, Lottie blushing like a schoolgirl.

Caleb had walked her to the door, kissed her one last toe-curling time, and sent her on her way. She'd left him with hunger in his eyes, her own reluctance heavy. She touched her cheeks, noted their heat, and grinned.

The following morning, Caleb swiped his trowel across the cream-colored upper wall of the theatre lobby, spreading thick plaster into a hole left when an excited patron had knocked a vase of cut flowers from its pedestal. Overall, there had been fewer repairs this fall, perhaps an indication that the audiences were becoming more sedate. Or at least less clumsy.

The door swung open, letting in a strong gust of autumn wind along with Elsa. A curtain of blond hair flying every which way, she bounded into the theatre and closed the door on the blustery day. She bent to pick up the stray leaves that had blown in with her, tossing them into the waste can by the door. "Whew. I guess fall's here," she announced with no small amount of dramatic flair.

Caleb's mouth twitched. "No school, squirt?"

"It's Saturday, silly." She plopped onto a blue brocade settee, her blue play dress hiking up far enough to reveal its matching bloomers. "Whatcha doin'?"

"Fixing holes. Want to help?"

She scrambled across the settee and peered down at his assorted paint and plaster tools. "Not really." She glanced up at him and frowned. "I miss Tony."

"I'll bet you do. You two were fast friends. I have a hunch you livened things up pretty good in here." He took one last swipe with the trowel, grabbed the wood putty, and moved toward the door to the auditorium, where a small dent had developed from the doorknob striking the sky-blue wainscoting.

"We had fun. Even if Mr. Perry teased us, saying we were nothing but trouble."

Though not really worried about it, Caleb played along with her. "You two leave any spots that need repairing?"

She giggled, her mood brightening as he'd hoped. "Girls don't wreck things."

"How am I supposed to know? I'm not all that familiar with girls." He smoothed the putty over the dent, watching her from the corner of his eye. Funny he'd never realized how much he liked kids until Elsa had started tagging along with him. She had a way about her, that was for sure.

"Seems you ought to be. I've been here most of the summer."

"Too busy, I guess."

She made a dismissive swish with her hand, one he recognized as a habit of one of the summer's actresses. "I was busy and I noticed lots of things about you."

"Did you now?"

"I most certainly did." She puffed with pride. "I'm observant that way. Observant. That's one of my spelling words this week. O-B-S-E-R-V-A-N-T. Observant. That means I notice things."

"And what do you notice?"

"You used to be grouchy, when we first came. Now you're not. At least not most of the time."

Grouchy? He'd never figured himself for a grump but, then again, he couldn't much recall spending time in conversation before either. "Guess I've just gotten used to you. Maybe I thought I didn't like girls."

Elsa leaned toward him. "Maybe you thought you didn't like Lottie but now you do."

He straightened and stared at her. "Where'd you get that idea?"

" 'Cause it was her you used to grouch at." A triumphant smile stretched across her face. "Now you just look at her with puppy-dog eyes."

Caleb gulped. "Puppy-dog eyes?"

"You know . . . kind of like you can't wait to get petted."

"I'm not a puppy dog, Elsa."

"Nope. But you got that look, all the same. Lottie does, too."

He let the thought simmer a bit, rolling it about in his mind. He wouldn't have put it quite the same way, but there was no denying the attraction between them. He hadn't realized it was so obvious. Puppy-dog eyes, hmmm? "Maybe we just learned to like each other, finally."

"Nope. If Tony were here, she'd say the same thing as me. You're sweet on each other. That's what I think."

Uncomfortable exploring the topic further with a ten-year-old, he set his tools down and sat next to her. "What else have you observed?"

"That slimy Rupert fellow scares Lottie. Almost as much as Uncle Edward."

Caleb nodded. "I think she's right. To be scared. I don't trust the man at all."

"Me, neither."

"I'm glad he's gone."

"Yup. He's a bad actor, all right."

He rolled his eyes at the pun. "A bad actor?"

She looked around the theatre and giggled. "I used to think you got scared, too."

"Me?" He marveled at the natural discernment the youngster seemed to have. She was savvy beyond her years, this one.

"I thought you were scared of roller coasters, but Lottie says you aren't."

"What if I was?"

"I knew it."

"Except it wasn't the roller coaster. It was the people on it."

"You were scared of people?" She sounded incredulous.

"Not people. Screaming." He tried to find a way to explain it. "And not really scared. I just don't like screams."

"Sometimes, I don't either. It depends on what the scream sounds like."

He wasn't sure what she meant. "Screams sound different?"

"Of course. There's excited screams and scared screams and painful screams. You didn't know that?" She scrutinized him as if he'd grown horns or something.

It had never occurred to him to classify screams. Surprised at how simply she had explained the difference, he shrugged. "It makes sense but I never thought about it before."

"How come you don't like screaming?"

The image of two downed soldiers roiled in his head, then dissipated. "It reminds me of a bad memory."

"Every scream? How can every scream remind you of

something? They all sound different."

"Up until now, I thought they sounded the same."

"Now that's just silly. Nothing's ever the same. Every time something happens, it's different from the time before. You gotta open your ears."

The truth in her words slammed through him, jerking his reality like a roller coaster turn. Could it really be that simple? He shook his head. "Maybe I do."

"Know what I think? I think you just look at it the lazy way. You have to work at it to hear the difference. It's easier to assume. Assume. A-S-S-U-M-E. That was another spelling word."

Understanding kicked at him. He'd been working so hard to avoid the screams that he hadn't tried to see what was different about where he was now. By insisting on hearing things only one way, he'd plunged straight into the pain. "You're awfully wise for ten years old."

"Not really. I just like my glass half full instead of half empty. Maybe you need to listen to the screams the same way."

He reached across the settee and rumpled her head. He doubted it would be easy but the kid had a point. He needed to listen to the other emotions in those screams. Maybe it was time to ride that roller coaster again.

Lottie glanced across the kitchen as the door creaked. Caleb entered and her breath caught, then tumbled out of her as she met his gaze. His whiskey eyes darkened and a slow, easy smile rolled across his lips. She smiled back, her breath still uneven.

"Hey there. Am I early?"

"No, no. Right on time. I just tucked Elsa into bed. Tom and Mary are in the parlor . . . would you like to join them?"

"I'll just pop my head in and say hello. Why don't we work out here?" He lifted a roll of paper. "I've got some ideas I'd like you to look at before we talk to them."

"Okay. Let me just finish up here." She stacked the remainder of the freshly dried dishes into their proper places in the cupboards as Caleb greeted the Longs. Closing the last wooden door, she spun and caught Caleb staring at her, the same lazy grin on his face.

"You look good reaching up like that."

She glanced down, realizing where his gaze had settled, and blushed.

"Fresh," she teased in an effort to bounce back from her embarrassment.

"Just appreciative." He pulled out a kitchen chair, waiting. "Shall we?"

Lottie slid into the chair, and he pushed it tight behind her. She rather liked this new side of Caleb. Or, maybe it wasn't new. Chances were she'd been so busy finding fault that she'd never noticed the softer points of his personality before.

Caleb stood behind her, leaning over the table. He rolled out the paper, his arms brushing across her as he spread it flat and anchored the far corners with the salt and paper shakers.

"You've been busy," she noted.

"The ideas wouldn't settle. I thought I'd put them down on paper even if we hadn't discussed anything yet. It's easier for me to see the concept this way. I can make a new one once you chime in." He pointed to three main areas. "Here are the spots where we could combine amusement and garden features. There's space enough for both if we select rides that generate less noise. I can craft natural space around them."

Lottie skimmed the flawless drawing, noting the way Caleb had built garden areas under and around the rides. "Like the slide we discussed."

"Exactly." His hand shifted to another spot on the plan. "Right now, this area is fenced off from the park. It's nothing but a meadow on the other side of the orchard. There's a lot of land here. We could group several rides."

"Make it a specialized area?"

"Why not? I got to thinking about it. The cultural attractions are located together—the theatre and the orchestra pavilion. As are the animals. Why not add an amusement section and a garden section? Tie it all together with transition areas that include several features."

Intrigued, she nodded. "I can see it. It would give those who have strong preferences a goal while exposing them to other elements without them realizing it. I like it."

"Maybe if you pull out your old sketch, we can look for ideas about which amusements would work best." His enthusiasm was evident, along with new respect for her ideas.

Warmed by his response, Lottie voiced the opinion she'd been mulling. "We can use that, and I have a few other ideas, too. When I did the sketch, I was thinking that we would need to concentrate on rides that Rupert's father could supply. But I don't see any reason why I have to stick with that company."

Caleb's expression sobered. "It would be a little difficult, anyway."

Uneasiness ruffled her. "What do you mean?" she asked.

"I did a little investigating. Gennick Amusements makes coasters. Nothing else."

She swallowed. "Nothing else?"

"Nothing."

"That snake." Bitter resentment churned in her stomach as she realized he'd been playing her all along.

"I'm not sure what Gennick's game is but—"

"I do." She bit the words out, angry at both Rupert and herself. She hated it that she'd fallen victim to his manipulation. "He meant to keep me under his thumb, that's what. He told me he'd have to be the one to contact his father—that he wouldn't deal with people he didn't know, women above all.

That double-crossing sod was going to swindle me."

Kneeling beside her, Caleb stroked her arm. "There's more, too, sweetheart."

She closed her eyes and drew a breath, then faced him. "More?"

"Art Gennick doesn't have any sons."

"That lying piece of junk. How could I be so stupid?" She dropped her head forward and sighed. "I swallowed everything he told me. He must've taken me for quite a hillbilly, huh?"

Caleb rose, pulled out a chair, and sat. "You were thinking about Elsa, escaping from New York. Besides, you said yourself he was a con man. He played on your weaknesses. Dollars to donuts, he meant to gyp us all."

Still unable to believe she hadn't seen through Rupert's play, Lottie tried to reason it out. "As long as I thought we were buying from his dad, I wouldn't have reason to check prices anywhere else. I trusted him. I trusted the friendship we'd had. He'd have defrauded Mary and Tom and I'd never have known. Not to mention taking my share."

"Do you think there really is a share?"

The question gave her pause. "A commission?"

"Yeah. Wouldn't the companies have their own sales staff?"

A second wave of disbelief washed over her. Though less surprising, it still shook her. "I wouldn't be surprised," she said. "I took Rupert's word for it. It could very well be that there is no commission, that he simply planned to inflate prices. I don't know."

The implication settled through her. She'd pinned her future on that commission. Elsa's future. Dropping her head onto her arms, she kicked herself again.

Caleb's soft voice broke into her thoughts. "So if there's no commission, do you still want to do this?"

She lifted her head and looked at him. "Strangely enough,

yes. I wanted to support Elsa on what I would make but right now, I'm so mad at Rupert that I'd do it just as a way to spit in his face." She paused. "Plus, I believe Tom and Mary need to expand. They've done so much for me and Elsa. They trusted me. I'd help them even without a commission."

"How hard would it be to do without any connections?"

She thought about it, recalling names of Coney Island managers and supervisors who might assist. "I see no reason why I can't deal with ride manufacturers myself. We'll need to determine which companies sell what and how to contact them. I can get that information with little problem, now that it occurs to me to do it."

"And Rupert?"

Anger roiled again. "Rupert Gennick can go to hell."

Rupert drummed his fingers on the polished marble table in the ice cream parlor. At the jingle of the bell on the front door, he glared at the entrance. It wasn't her. He shoved his long-handled spoon into his ice cream sundae and cursed under his breath. She had some nerve to make him wait half the afternoon.

Things had worked so much more smoothly when he'd had her under his thumb. He had too many irons in the fire now that he was working the Zang angle in addition to trying to use Lottie to con the Longs. Not being at Elitch's Gardens meant it was harder to keep tabs on what the chit was doing. Not to mention that she was a lot easier to control when he was there to remind her of the stakes.

The bell rang again and Lottie stepped into the shop. She peered around, a big hat framing her pretty face. Her dress wasn't fancy and it hung on her frumpy-like instead of hugging a woman's curves like dresses used to. But the skirt swung when she moved, and he could make out the swell of her breasts under its blousy pouf.

His groin tight, he watched her sashay across the room. No matter how bothersome the woman was, she had a figure a man had to be blind not to appreciate. Under the sway of the skirt, he spotted her trim ankles—the only decent thing about modern fashion.

"What do you want?" she demanded as she stopped in front of the table.

"Well, hello to you, too, Lottie Girl." He kicked at the chair across from him, pushing it back from the table. "Have a seat."

Lottie flushed. A glance around the shop told her none of the few other patrons had noticed Rupert's insult. She eyed the chair, her stomach churning. She didn't want to sit and chat. She hadn't wanted to meet Rupert at all, given what Caleb had revealed about him. But the squirmy little rodent wouldn't let it lie. When he'd called to announce he was driving out to Elitch's, she'd said she had errands in town and would meet him instead. After Mary's warning that Rupert not be allowed back onto the property, there was no better option.

"Sit."

She ignored the steely gleam in his eyes, wanting the meeting to end as soon as possible. She wasn't sure what he wanted of her but she'd already decided she was through with him. Her anger over being used had allowed her to think past her fear. Rupert was a con man and the threat to contact Edward was part of the con. It was a bluff and she wasn't going to be his victim any longer. "I have nothing to say to you. Whatever you want to tell me, you can say quickly and be done with it."

"You seem to forget how difficult I can make your life. We have unfinished business. Like I said on the telephone yesterday, a few things need to be settled."

She swallowed, unease gripping her. He wasn't about to make severing their ties easy. She slid into a chair, ready for battle. "We could have done that on the telephone, Rupert."

"I don't talk business when the operator and half the town could be listening in. Person to person suits my purposes much better."

"And my purposes?"

"Your purposes?"

Hating his smug disdain, she raised one eyebrow.

Irritation flashed in his eyes. "Don't goad me, Lottie."

She exhaled, remembering he preferred women gushy and cooperative. She doubted he'd react well when she told him they were done. Maybe it would be better to not stir things further—to allow him to believe there was no sale. She'd play it meek and dumb, then, the way he liked and let him think she'd been unsuccessful. Getting rid of him was more important than the release of telling him off.

"We haven't talked since I left Elitch's," he continued. "I thought I'd contact my father, make arrangements for that ride. We can't be wasting time, not if you want to have the ride here for the summer opening."

"About that—"

"About what?" He glared at her. "I already told you Pops won't deal with you. Is it that difficult for you to have me be the go-between? Gads, Lottie, you're not as bright as I thought."

"I didn't make the sale." She dropped her head, hoping she interjected enough humility in her tone to convince him she'd failed.

"You what?" He fairly snarled the words.

Lottie shrank back, looking as contrite as possible. His irate tone was attracting notice, and she knew from experience with Uncle Edward that attention would only feed his anger. So would anything but subservience.

"The Longs won't buy. They've decided to stick with the way things are." She raised her gaze and let her jaw shake. "I'm so sorry. I should have told you sooner. I didn't want to ruin things.

I thought I could do it, I really did. I've tried to talk them into it and they still say they don't want to expand."

Rupert stared at her. "But they were all set."

"Mary was all set but Tom holds the purse strings. They contracted for a carousel when they bought the coaster. No more rides."

He shook his head, an incredulous expression filling his face. "You mean you've spent the past two months working on this and you've gotten nowhere?"

Drat it all. He didn't believe her. Maybe she still wasn't submissive enough to convince him he was in charge. She managed to snivel. "I thought I had. I really did."

"That's the only reason I came back here, kid." He shoved his ice cream glass away, the spoon clinking. "You said you had the deal made."

She drew a breath and faced him. "I'm sorry, Rupert. Truly I am."

He leaned forward, resentment knitting his brows. "That's twice I've done your bidding. Twice you've duped me."

Lottie swallowed. She hadn't expected this stubborn resistance. He should have bought the story of her failure already instead of seeing the events as a personal attack. "I tried. I guess I'm just not the salesman we thought I was."

"Funny how you had Mary sold but you couldn't sell Tom. Did you try cozying up to him? Using your wiles?" He reached across the table and stroked her hand. "That was the plan, wasn't it?"

She moved her hand away. "Tom didn't play along."

"Things don't seem to be working out too well for either of us. I don't like complications. Maybe it's time to cut our losses and move on to somewhere else." His tone was exploratory, as if he were weighing options.

Still, Lottie stared at him, bristling. "I don't think so."

Rupert's eyes flashed. "Whatsamatter, doll? Don't want to work with me anymore?" He sneered. "Did you get too good for me? Did you forget I own you?" His hand snaked out, grabbing at her arm. "You'll do what I say, Lottie, or I'll send word off to your uncle Ed. You and I are a team."

She jerked away from his hold, fury burning. "We are not partners, Rupert. I'm done with you, done being duped and conned and manipulated."

Shock crossed his face, filling it for an instant before it turned into a sneer.

"You'd best not be trying to dupe me, Lottie Girl, 'cause if you think there's a chance in hell that you're pulling one over on me, you have another think coming." He leaned in. "I'll be watching you. And if I even get a whiff that you're screwing with me, you'll be sorry, girl. Real sorry. Understand?"

Knowing what she needed to do, she caught his gaze and sneered back at him. She shoved back her chair and stood, leaning over the table as he backed away.

"I understand. But know this, you hurt what's mine and I'll hurt you." She paused. "Now, do you understand?"

CHAPTER FOURTEEN

Rupert slugged down his beer and swore to himself. Adolph Zang was waiting in his office above the barroom like an executioner atop a gallows. Rupert had been summoned, the directive abrupt, a deliberate insult, leaving him nervous as hell. Zang had offered no reason, just a clipped order to appear, delivered by messenger to Rupert's hotel room. That, in and of itself, had created a lead ball in Rupert's stomach that no amount of beer was dissolving.

Since Fritz had delivered the news about their contract, Rupert had done nothing but stew. Zang was sharper than he'd suspected and, for the first time in his life, Rupert was worried about his con. Until he turned the situation to his advantage, he had planned to lie low. This was the only game he had left and he couldn't afford to mess it up.

He wanted to go home and escape Zang's attention. Being caught by surprise was bad enough but being given a brusque command as part and parcel of the abrupt notice that he'd caught Zang's interest didn't bode well, at least in Rupert's experience. He didn't know what Zang wanted to discuss or why the man deemed it so important that he needed to order Rupert to the brewery but he doubted it was good.

Rupert drained the last of the beer, wiped his mouth with his hand, and rose from the table. The room teetered a bit, and he drew a heavy breath. Guess those three beers on top of the whiskey he'd had for breakfast were a mistake.

Measuring his stride, Rupert crossed the barroom and climbed the stairs, each step a careful placement of his feet. At the top of stairway, he paused to burp and dust off his worn clothing. Then, he made his way to Zang's office and rapped on the door.

"Come in," Zang's voice was authoritative, emphasizing the power he held.

Rupert pushed the door open, squinting as the brightness of the electric lights in Zang's office spilled into the dark hallway. "You wanted to see me?"

"Have a seat, Gennick."

Settling into one of the finely upholstered chairs in front of Zang's desk, Rupert fixed a smile on his face. He didn't want Zang to see how nervous he was. With feigned self-assurance, Rupert leaned forward. "Did you get my progress report?"

"I did. I must say, you have been busy. I didn't expect so many options. Cigar?" He opened a polished wooden box and waited while Rupert made the obligatory selection. Then he leaned back, struck a match, and lit his own cigar. He puffed, watching Rupert.

Rupert shifted in the chair, his own cigar clamped between his lips.

"Most designers I've worked with have been a bit more specific, offering recommendations."

Rupert lifted the cigar away. So that was what this circus was about—too many options. He could deal with that. A few well-placed words and he'd have things back under control. Apparently his goal of dazzling Zang with his wide range of knowledge had made him look inexperienced.

He searched for the right words to impress Zang. "I thought the best place to start was with a broad palette of choices, sir," he said, hoping he was projecting an air of bored confidence. "You were very general during our last discussion. This gives us a starting point—a place to begin discussing the type of design you want. Until you narrow things a bit, I wouldn't presume to select specific rides."

Zang raised his eyebrows and puffed on his cigar, as if weighing Rupert's words. He blew a smoke ring, and the aroma of aged tobacco wafted through the air in a thick cloud. "How do you like the cigar?"

Rupert sniffed at the tobacco, as he'd seen refined men do. "It smells excellent."

"Go ahead." Zang said. "Light up."

Rupert brushed his hand across the front pocket of his coat, patting for nonexistent matches. Knowing he looked like an idiot, he felt his trousers. Only then did he peer at Zang. "I seem to be out of matches."

"Pity."

Silence stretched. A burp rose up Rupert's throat, tasting of hops and barley. He swallowed it back down.

"Would you like a match?" Zang asked, his voice quiet yet full of power. He extended a smaller wooden box filled with matches.

Rupert took one, lit it, and puffed the flame until the cigar caught. He coughed, cursed himself, and leaned back. "Thank you, sir."

"I'll look over the report, make some notes, give you something more to work on. I expected you to be in touch, to ask a few questions, before you started on ideas. Guess you work differently."

"Again, sir, I didn't want to presume anything. A man like you calls meetings, not one like me."

Zang waved his hand, as if swatting away a bothersome insect. "You didn't strike me as a pussyfoot before. Is there a problem, boy? Something you're not telling me?"

Rupert coughed again. "A problem, sir?"

"A man in my position hears things."

The lead in Rupert's stomach got heavier. "What things?"

"Things like Tom Long looking for a loan." He leaned forward. "You do know who Tom Long is, don't you?"

"Who?"

Zang eased back into his chair. "His wife is Mary Elitch."

Rupert swallowed. "Oh, yes. Of course." He calmed himself and reached for the bored tone he'd used earlier. "Elitch's. Your future competitor."

Zang puffed on his cigar, drawing out his response. "Seems Long was asking about quite a bit of money."

"He was?" His surprise wasn't feigned. Had Lottie lied to him?

"Yes, he was. You know something about that?"

"I don't even know the man," Rupert lied. "How would I know anything about him asking for a loan?" Long had a solid business. There was no way he could be in trouble. He had to be thinking of expansion. And Zang knew it, too. Rupert's hand fisted. Lottie was playing him.

Zang met his gaze, compelled it. "I did a bit more investigating. Heard you worked for him for a few days."

Rupert swallowed, reigning in his anger, listening to what Zang was implying. "Temporary job. I fixed up a couple rides. Moved on once I was done." He stared Zang in the eye. "I didn't meet Tom Long. The wife hired me."

"Hmmmm. I've never known the Longs to hire temporary help before."

Rupert shrugged. "The old mechanic quit. They were in a spot, needed the work done. I wasn't interested in staying long term."

"How did they even know you were in Denver?"

"Girl I used to know works for them. She set it up." And set him up, too. Shit, if he wasn't careful, she'd mess up everything.

Zang's eyes widened as he nodded. He tapped his cigar into a glass ashtray on his desk, then leaned back in the chair again. "So you don't work for them?"

"No, sir. Just those few days." Rupert paused, knitting his brows together as if he hadn't just made a huge tactical error in revealing the relationship with Lottie Chase. Any con depended on the mark's perception of confidence. He had to concentrate. "What's that got to do with Long asking for a loan?"

"Seems Tom Long is thinking about expansion, buying a few more rides. He was inquiring about bank financing."

He knew it! Damn that lying bitch. How the hell was he going to turn this around? He had to cut his ties with her, throw all his effort into Zang's park.

Rupert scratched his head. "You think I'm involved?" he asked, letting insult fill his tone.

"Well, boy, that's what I'm wondering. You design parks, broker expansions."

"What are you implying?"

Zang leaned forward, deadly earnest. "Just making sure you aren't trying to double-cross me here. You work for me. That means you don't work for Tom Long. You don't make deals on his behalf and you don't take my ideas back to him."

"I don't work for Long." That much was true, anyway.

"Is Long expanding?"

"How the hell should I know?"

"Is Long expanding?"

"I don't know. He's not buying anything through me." Rupert slid the words out as if the subject were of no importance but his jaw clenched. Damn Lottie for double-crossing him. After everything he'd done for her, all he'd invested in her, she'd betrayed him. He'd be damned if he'd let her muck up his deal with Zang. She wasn't going to take him down, not if he could help it. Just as soon as he found out what she was planning, he'd make sure she paid.

"Well, here's how I see it. You're the only one in town touting himself as a park designer and ride broker. Either you're in Long's pocket or you're involved indirectly." Zang's gaze narrowed.

"If I find out you are, you are going to be one sorry son of a bitch. There's going to be one amusement park in Denver. My park. I'm not some greenhorn you can play with. Eyes are on you, boy." His finger tapped on the desk, emphasizing his words. "Don't jerk me around and don't cross me. You don't seem to realize how much power I have in this town. Consider this a test. If you're involved with Elitch's expansion, you'd better get uninvolved. Better yet, make sure it doesn't occur at all."

Outside the cottage, Lottie fidgeted, more nervous than she'd expected about presenting the revised plans to Tom and Mary. She wanted them to be as excited about the new ideas as she and Caleb were as well as being pleased that she and Caleb were able to work together.

She'd been able to spend most of her attention on the design, no longer fearful of Rupert's threats after standing up to him. His defeated expression had told her she was right in her assumption. It had all been intimidation—he had no reason to follow through with the threat. Now that she'd called his bluff, he had no weapon against her. For once, she felt she had taken control of her life. She'd gotten rid of the weasel, and she refused to have any regrets.

Beside her, Caleb grasped her hand and stroked it. "Settle down. You'll wear a hole in the porch."

She stilled her foot from its circular scraping and took a deep breath. "I'm ready."

Caleb smiled at her and knocked on the door.

A few seconds later, Mary pushed open the door and ushered

them inside. Her face was alight with welcoming warmth. "Come on in. It's chilly out there."

Caleb and Lottie entered the kitchen, Lottie chatting with Mary as Caleb spread out the papers on the table. The afternoon light was good, Elsa was at school, and they were as ready as they could be. Lottie's nerves eased as she slid out of her coat and accepted a cup of steaming cocoa.

At the stove, Tom poured himself a cup of coffee, its vapor filling the room with an aromatic scent. He settled into a chair, and beamed at the others. "Well, let's see what you have. We've been anticipating this for days."

Caleb took the lead, explaining to Tom and Mary how he and Lottie had combined their visions. "Here you can see how we've integrated small grottos into the niches below the giant slide, making quiet garden nooks out of space that would otherwise be wasted."

"That way, we were able to carve out small peaceful spaces throughout the park." Her nerves quieted, Lottie pointed to a defined area on the plan. "We have a part of the park dedicated to gardens. This way, we can satisfy those who want to escape the hustle and bustle." She smiled at Caleb, knowing how important that feature was to him.

He touched her arm, sending a wave of warmth through her, then continued the presentation. "We've made an effort to create special areas—for culture and theatre, for gardens, for animals, and for rides. But we've also tried to make sure there is a dash of culture, a bit of gardens, and a hint of fun everywhere."

"Like the main entrance area," Mary said. "I like it. It has a balanced feel."

Tom nodded. "I notice you left space for the new carousel in that area. I think that's important. We expect the ride to be impressive, and I'm glad your plan puts it center stage."

"As it should be," Lottie agreed.

As they discussed the further merits of the layout, Lottie offered explanations of the rides they had chosen, many of them for their ability to fit into the overall scheme. Caleb explained floral choices and uses of color. While there were a few alternatives debated and changes made, the Longs seemed pleased.

"Just so you are aware," Tom told them, "I stopped at the bank to get a feel for the plausibility of putting your plans into action. We weren't sure what you'd have for us but we were pretty convinced we'd like it, given the fact that you combined your enthusiasm this time around. I needed to see if any of this will be possible."

"And?" Lottie held her breath, as Caleb rerolled the papers.

"We're going to need to work in stages," Tom said as he cleared away cups and saucers. "I think the plan will lend itself well to doing so. Our profits this year were better than expected. The new coaster generated enough business to pay off the loan we used to purchase it. We took out a second loan when we ordered the carousel. If it brings in as much business as the coaster, we can plan to expand again the following year."

Mary glanced at her husband. "About the carousel . . ." she said.

Tom returned to Mary's side. "Mary and I have been watching the two of you this past week and had an idea. Based on what we saw this afternoon, you've confirmed our impressions. You two have become a team."

"And, you've found ways to combine the practical with the whimsical."

Lottie glanced at Caleb, saw the warm pride in his expression, and allowed herself to bask in the glow seeping through her.

"We're supposed to go to Pennsylvania next week, to meet with the Philadelphia Toboggan Company and discuss the finish work for the carousel."

"We'd like you to help us select the animals," Mary cut in.

Caleb's attention shifted to the Longs. "What?"

Mary beamed. "And the paintings."

"Oh, Mary . . . what an honor." Lottie's cheeks heated and she reached for Caleb's hand.

He grasped it, as his eyes sent a silent message of proud solidarity to Lottie. "I didn't know you could choose the animals."

"Well, the master carver does a variety of them as part of the stock supply," Tom explained. "Mary had in mind selecting those we have in the zoo here instead of letting him choose. And we'd like to talk with the artist, about colors and the paintings for the center of the carousel—around the machinery. I think he said there would be over forty of them."

"I'd be honored to help with the selections," Caleb said, squeezing Lottie's hand. "Lottie?"

She shivered at the tingle caused by the touch. "Of course. Should we make up a list together?"

"Actually," Mary interrupted, "that wasn't what we had in mind." A soft smile lit her eyes. "We don't want your help making a list. We'd like you to go to Pennsylvania on our behalf."

Rupert fumbled with the cap of his empty whiskey flask and drew back into the darkness of the trees. A dozen feet away, Lottie Chase was being soundly kissed by the Elitch's Gardens flower boy. If she wasn't careful, there would be dirty fingerprints all over the front of Lottie's starched blue sailor suit.

Rupert spit in distaste. The little tease seemed to be granting the gardener a lot more liberties than she had him.

A stab of resentment shot through him before he remembered to remind himself she wasn't worth the feeling. She was a double-crossing bitch that didn't know quality when she had it. He reached for the flask again, recalled he'd already finished it off, and swore under his breath.

This was the third night in a row Rupert had waited in the darkness spying on Lottie and Caleb. He had to find out what the Longs were planning for their park and Lottie was the key. But the scenario was always the same . . . slow walks, urgent kisses, petting, and low conversation he could hardly hear. He'd learned nothing whatsoever about specifics of the Longs' plans to expand and nothing to help him repair the damage Lottie had caused with Zang.

Rupert spit again, frustrated. Zang was watching him. In the brewery, Zang would pass through and frown at Rupert and his beer—almost as if disdaining the empty mugs that were bringing profit to his business. And if Rupert happened to choose another watering hole, one of the saps following him around went along to keep tabs on him.

He wondered if the same tails were stationed somewhere under the trees here, too.

Shit. He needed a drink.

He'd polished up his recommendations for Zang. With his own profits tied to Zang's success, he'd had to put more effort into the design, and the hours of work ground on him. At the entrance, he'd proposed a 150-foot-high tower housing a casino to attract the gambling crowd. For the cultured folk, he'd added a theatre. His major attraction, just inside the entrance, was a Big Splash roller coaster. He'd even added a German rathskeller, a bit of the old country for beer drinkers to order up Zang's specialties.

But the heart of his idea was his plan to paint all of the buildings a blinding white and illuminate them with 16,000 electric lights. White City, he called it. Garish, just like Coney Island. Where the money was. Exactly what Zang had in mind.

Still, none of it seemed enough to get Zang off his back.

He sure as hell wished he had a German tavern on hand

right now. Lord, he needed a beer. He hated being watched, like nothing he did met with approval. He'd never been good enough for Art Gennick to claim as his own. Zang's scrutiny stabbed him in his gut. He was just as worthy as anybody else. He'd prove them all wrong for their lack of faith, just wait and see.

Leaves rustled, and Rupert turned his attention back to Lottie and the gardener. He peered through the darkness, forcing his bleary eyes to focus. They were moving.

He held his breath as they neared and shrunk behind a fruit tree, stepping on a squishy rotted something-or-another. Apple, by the smell of it. A sweet, cloying stink rose up, and he gagged before his mind realized the fermented odor was similar to cider. The suppressed retch transformed itself into craving.

"Old Man Farnum agreed to stop by and feed the animals but he refused to stay," Caleb said as they drew within hearing distance. "What about Elsa, is she all set?"

"She'll go home with Becky Wilson after school on Wednesday. She thinks it's a grand adventure. I wish Tom and Mary's trip didn't overlap, though. I worry about Elsa staying with people I don't know well."

"The Wilsons are good folks." Caleb squeezed her close while Rupert sneered at the scene. It sounded like little miss Lottie and her dirt-covered sweetie pie had plans. "Tom and Mary have known them for a long time."

"But—"

"She'll be fine. If the Longs trust them, you don't need to worry."

"I can't help it."

Rupert sniveled at the sappy conversation. Fighting a yawn, he reached again for his flask, then fired off a silent curse that he wasn't already headed back to town for a refill.

"If Tom and Mary didn't need to negotiate next summer's contract with that Broadway actor before he leaves the country, you know they'd watch her themselves."

"I know. They offered to take her along, but I don't want her anywhere near New York."

"Are you nervous about traveling together?" Traveling? Rupert took his hand off the flask. Now, they were getting somewhere.

"No. It's a business trip."

"It's more than that, Lottie, and you know it. Tom and Mary knew there was something between us when we showed them the new plans, before they asked us to go. I wouldn't be surprised if Mary scheduled it this way on purpose to give us some time alone together. Even Elsa knows we're attracted to each other."

"Elsa knows?"

"She said we look at each other with puppy-dog eyes."

Plans. There were plans. Rupert's heart pounded. There it was, confirmation that she'd lied to him. He squeezed his eyes shut and smothered the urge to storm out of his hiding spot. That wasn't what he was here for. That conniving little slut might have double-crossed him but she'd been dumb enough to draw up plans. Now she just needed to reveal where they were.

"Caleb . . . I didn't mean for—"

"Shhh. Let's not pick it apart. I don't have any expectations of the trip, beyond choosing forty-six perfect animals. We'll leave it at that."

"That . . . that sounds good. Tomorrow will be here early. We should turn in."

"Let's get you back to the cottage, then."

Rupert watched them turn and disappear up the path. Bile rose in his throat and he turned to puke. Shit, he needed to stop drinking so much. He wiped at his sour mouth, the sweat on his forehead chilling him in the nippy air.

Adolph Zang had been right. All except for Rupert not being

involved. He doubted the ruthless German was going to believe that.

But the little double-crosser had left him a chance to redeem himself. He'd decide later whether it would serve him better to take the plans to Zang or simply use them to create a superior park and steal all their business away. Whether Zang paid him for the espionage or they worked together to build the best damn park this side of New York, he'd soon be back on top.

Rupert grinned. All he needed to do was get ahold of the Elitch plans.

CHAPTER FIFTEEN

Caleb slid sideways as the train rounded a sharp bend. Opening his eyes, he found Lottie smirking at him. An easy comfort stretched between them and his mouth curved into a smile. Overhead, the elaborate Pintsch gas lights cast a warm glow throughout the near-empty Pullman car, setting a cozy mood.

"You look a little startled," she teased.

Caleb stretched in the cramped space. "Guess I fell asleep again. The motion seems to lull me. I can move to the other seat if you want." He nodded to the plush facing bench in their section.

"No. Stay." She slid her hand into his. "I like having you next to me."

Warmth filled him. He'd enjoyed the hours beside her, too. But he'd wasted too many of them dozing in a half-awake state. He'd intended to spend these days learning more about her—exploring the past she'd hinted at last week, then said no more about. They would be in Philadelphia tomorrow and he still didn't know the details of what had happened to her at Uncle Edward's hands.

If he was blunt with himself, Caleb recognized he wanted to touch her, to run his fingers over those curves, hear her moan under his hands. But, given her past, he didn't know if he dared.

"Caleb?"

"Hmmm?"

"Sleeping again?"

He shook off his thoughts. "Sorry. Where are we?"

"I'm not sure. Before it got dark, there was more farmland. Trees with no leaves. Snow on the ground here and there."

"The berth's down," he noted, glancing upward at the curved mahogany panel that had been lowered during his nap. "Did I sleep through dinner again?"

Lottie nodded toward several paper-wrapped packets on the opposite bench. "I got a couple sandwiches for you, when the porter came past to make up the berths. I didn't have the heart to wake you."

He stretched. "I didn't think I'd been out that long."

"Over an hour." She shifted, drew a breath. "Are you all right?"

"Fine," he answered, puzzled at her tone. "Why?"

"I wasn't sure . . . you've been sleeping a lot. I thought maybe riding the train bothers you." Her voice was tentative.

"Bothers me?"

"Like . . . like the roller coaster."

He shook his head, confused. "Nobody screams on a train."

She blushed, looking out into the darkness for a few moments before turning back to him. "Mary worried the trip might bring back some memories. I thought maybe you were sleeping to avoid them."

That explained it. Though trains had never bothered him, it was like Mary to fret about the possibilities. "Mary worries too much. The motion puts me to sleep."

"She was afraid the trip would remind you of the ride to Florida, before you shipped to Cuba."

He shook his head. Unlike some of the other soldiers he'd heard about, recollections of traveling to war weren't among the situations that set him off. "Those memories aren't the ones that cause the problems. It was a train trip. Not significant one way or the other." Except for those missing on the journey home.

"Then why are you grouching at me?" Lottie's expression had shifted into a pout. One he very much wanted to kiss away.

"I'm not grouching."

"You are." The pout softened but the worry remained in her luminous eyes.

He drew a breath. The last thing he wanted to do was bark at her. Not over this.

"Okay. There are some memories," he admitted. He stroked her hand, trying to reassure her he didn't begrudge her concern. "I expected them. I prepared for them. I can deal with them. Even with the loss and the pain that came with them." He drew a breath, not wanting to talk about it, but she needed answers, explanations beyond their previous discussions. She could read him too well now.

"What I'm feeling now are duller memories. Thoughts of men I knew. They happen, then they fade and they're not too often bothersome because I've learned to anticipate them." Sweat formed on his brow but he continued, needing to tell her as much as he suspected she needed to hear. "It's the all-of-a-sudden visions in my mind that are so intense. If I remain alert, avoid becoming too involved in the memories, I'm fine. But the sudden screams, when I'm immersed in thoughts of the past, plunge me into reliving it all. My mind is tricked into thinking I'm still there." He released the rest of his breath in a whoosh and waited for his pounding heart to settle.

"Why did you enlist?" she asked, her voice soft, sincere.

His pulse raced again. "What?"

"Why did you leave Mary and go to war?"

"Aw, hell. I don't know," he answered. He hated talking about this.

"I know you well enough to be sure you had a reason.

Especially after promising John you would take care of Mary."

He sat in the flickering lamplight, swaying with the car as the train rocked eastward. Her hand wrapped around his, stilling his tapping thumb, her silence giving him the time to decide, to ready himself.

Moments dragged by before he was ready to continue. "We'd read about the atrocities in Cuba for months. Everybody was worried. Mary cried when she read the stories. Nobody realized how sensationalized it all was. In the end, I guess I got caught up in the patriotic fever. I felt I needed to do my duty. Tom was here by then and I'd come to trust him. He was a good manager and I didn't think the war would last too long."

Caleb swallowed, then plunged forward, putting the worst of the memories into words. "I was promoted, reassigned to a unit shipping out to Cuba. When we got to San Juan Heights, I had to order my men up that hill. Then I listened to them die." Though he'd told her that much before, he was surprised at how much easier it had been this time.

She exhaled, squeezed his hand. "Caleb, listen to me. You didn't give the order. Someone higher up the chain of command did. You relayed the order. There's a difference."

He closed his eyes, hearing what she'd said but unable to accept it. "Not when I hear them screaming." His voice cracked and he fought a flinch.

"You weren't responsible."

"I feel responsible." He stared at her, waiting for her condemnation.

Instead, acceptance filled her eyes. "You can't be responsible for something you had no control over. What were you going to do? Defy your orders?"

"I should have gone up there after them." His voice trembled. "I should have tried harder."

"Tried harder? Mary told me you'd been shot, too. You seem

229

to have forgotten that."

"Don't you see? I shouldn't have left them up there. It was my job to take care of them."

"Sometimes, there are things that we simply cannot change. No matter how much you want to or how responsible you are. Sometimes, you can't control things." Reassurance filled her gentle words. She lifted his chin with her finger and turned his head until he met her gaze. "There are things you feel bad about but no matter how much guilt you feel, you know, deep down, that you did all you could. It's in the past. You cannot do anything to change how the situation turns out. It simply is."

Mary and Tom had told him the same thing, over and over. But, their words hadn't held the ring of forgiveness that Lottie's did. He stared at her, realizing why.

She knew. She knew what he felt because she felt it, too. And, like him, she couldn't make the truth fit around her circumstances. But, together? His heart pounded. Maybe they could fight their pasts together.

"Does that apply to you, too?" he asked.

"Me?" Her eyes widened, alarmed.

"You know you couldn't change what happened, either, don't you?"

"What do you mean?" She looked away, glancing out the window.

He turned her face back, as she'd done with him moments before. "I'm talking about your uncle."

"That's different," she insisted.

"Is it?"

"Of course."

"What makes it different?"

Lottie shifted, gazed furtively around the sleeper car, seeking out other passengers. She lowered her voice. "I wasn't under anyone's orders. I wasn't pinned down by gunfire. I wasn't injured."

A wave of tenderness engulfed him as he considered how badly they'd both been haunted. "Not in so many words, no." This time, he stroked her hand, easing open her fist, which had tightened on the seat between them. He searched for words. "You were just a kid."

"So?"

"So Elsa's just a kid. Do you think she had any control over your uncle's actions?"

"Of course not." She sighed. "It wasn't the same with me."

Ah, Lottie. He squeezed her hand. "What makes you different? What makes you responsible for what happened to you?"

"I just am."

Caleb ached to pull her into his arms, hated the uncertainty that swamped him. "Did someone tell you that?"

"I made him want to do it. I tempted him and he lost control." Her voice wobbled.

Giving in to what he felt she needed, what they both needed, he pulled her close, and prayed she wouldn't push him away. "Did he tell you that?"

She nodded.

"Oh, honey. Don't you realize that was his way of avoiding responsibility for his own actions?"

"But if I hadn't—"

"Shhh." He stroked her, held her, wondering how he could make her understand. "A woman doesn't have to do a damn thing for a man to feel tempted. Nature makes us that way. Sure, a particular woman might catch our attention. But we get lustful all on our own." He pushed her back, looked into her eyes. "You were a kid, for Pete's sake. You couldn't have done anything to encourage a grown man. He isn't normal. If he was, he wouldn't lust after young girls, let alone act on what he felt."

"But I didn't turn him away."

"Did you even know what was happening?"

She shook her head, comprehending at least that small piece of the situation.

"Then how could you have been responsible?"

She gulped, her breathing slowing.

"It was beyond your control," he told her, echoing her words to him, believing them for the first time. "Sometimes, you feel bad about things, guilty even. But, it's in the past."

Peace filled him and he tightened his arms around her, feeling her surrender, too, as she relaxed within them. He held her, accepting the release of her guilt despite the fact that he still wasn't sure about its exact nature.

Lottie clung to Caleb, drawing strength from the knowledge that he understood. For the first time, she felt her guilt ease a bit. Her heart clattered in her chest because she'd not told him the whole story. Would he still hold her blameless once he found out everything she'd done with Uncle Edward?

She needed to tell him the rest. Tonight. Before she lost courage.

She was just so exhausted. Her head lay on his shoulder, her face buried in his chest. She didn't want to move.

"Lottie? The porter is here. He wants to make up the bottom berth. We're the last ones."

She shook her head.

"Go on down to the washroom, sweetheart," Caleb told her, easing her up from the seat. He turned her, placed her valise into her hands, and gave her a gentle push. She took a few mechanical steps, regaining awareness as she made her way down the quiet aisle. The modern Pullman car contained twelve sections, each of which converted to curtained berths. Most of the seats Lottie passed remained in place, only the last few being occupied. Closed draperies shrouded them and loud snores told her the occupants had already settled in for the night. She and Caleb were the only ones still awake.

Inside the washroom, she changed into her nightclothes, brushed out her hair, and cleaned her teeth. Fatigue filled her drained body. She peered into the mirror, frowning at her puffy eyes. She exhaled, covered her face with a warm cloth, and leaned against the washstand for a few moments. When the cloth cooled, she donned her robe and returned to their section.

Caleb sat on the bottom berth; the bench seats were folded down to form a bed. He was clad in his undershirt and worn dungarees. His feet were bare.

Lottie stared at his toes, and her cheeks grew warm. Caleb wiggled them and the flush crept its way over her body.

"Why don't you take the bottom berth tonight? It's more stable." He stood, held back the curtain, and motioned for her to lie down.

"Sit with me a little while," she whispered as she slipped off the wrapper.

"I'll sit on the edge. Let's get you tucked in. You'll get cold in just that." His gaze traveled over her white cotton empire nightgown, from her own bare toes peeking out from under its hem to her breasts. Her nipples puckered, hardening under his scrutiny.

Caleb swallowed. Then he pulled back the blankets and waited for her to climb in.

She slid her bare feet under the crisp white sheet and lay down.

"Are you all right?" Caleb asked. "You're awfully quiet."

"I feel like I've been through the wringer."

"Me, too." He kissed her on the forehead. "But I also feel like a cloud of peace is surrounding me. Does that make sense?"

"Mm-hmm. It does."

"I should turn in. You're tempting, lying there like an angel. Your hair looks like a halo."

She shook her head, knowing the truth. "I'm no angel."

"You are to me." He stood.

Panicked, Lottie grasped at his hand. She needed to tell him now. Or she never would. "I'm not," she said. "There are things I haven't told you."

"You've told me all you need to."

"He didn't just look at me, like he did Elsa. There was more." She closed her eyes, wanting to escape the memory, realizing that this time, she had to face it instead.

"Shhh. You don't need to talk about it." His hand brushed her brow.

"But I do. For the first time in my life, I need to." She opened her eyes to his warm whiskey gaze and trembled. "Hold me?"

Caleb stretched beside her, shifting one arm under her neck, and pulled her tight. "I'm here."

She lay, nestled in his embrace, and drew a breath. "When I was ten, he started coming into my room. At first, it was just to sit beside me. He'd stroke my hair and tell me I was a good girl, that he was proud of me. Then he started coming in earlier, as I got ready for bed. He'd sit there, telling me I was pretty, that he was so pleased at how grown up I was becoming." She swallowed, closing her eyes. "I liked it. After how cold Aunt Aggie always was to me, I was glad that someone finally loved me. He'd kiss me goodnight and I liked it."

"Of course you did. All kids want to be loved. He knew that. He preyed on it."

She bit her lip. "After a while, it felt like bugs creeping over my body—the way he stared. He'd touch my hair and I wanted to cringe. Once, when I did, he scolded me for not letting him love me. He told me it made him feel bad that I was rejecting his love.

"He said he'd wanted a little girl like me for so long, that he'd been waiting for me to grow up, so I could share secrets with him—something babies couldn't be trusted to do. I cried, promised to be a good girl, to love him back." She swallowed. "Then he ran his hands over my body."

"Aw, Lottie." Caleb tucked her closer, and she nestled her face against his chest. "He manipulated you. You know that, don't you?"

Lottie pondered the words. As a child, it had not occurred to her to doubt Uncle Edward. Then, she'd pushed all thought of that time from her mind, continuing to believe what she'd been told, all these years. Her body shook. Oh, God. Caleb was right.

As an adult, she'd never pulled out those memories. Never refuted the lies she'd been told. She shuddered, knowing she needed to face the rest of it.

"It got worse, after that. He started touching me under my nightgown, mostly after . . . after my breasts started to develop. There were always explanations, if I resisted. Warming me up, working the kinks out of my muscles. He kept telling me how much he loved me, how this was our special time—just between us, how grown up I was to be his special girl and not a baby anymore. And if I pulled away, he'd say I didn't love him, that I hurt his feelings, that I wasn't as grown up as he had thought.

"Then, one night, he said his back hurt and asked me to rub it for him. After that, he'd ask me to touch him other places. He'd praise me and tell me how proud he was. It felt wrong but I didn't know why. I only knew if I thought about it, it was unbearable. So I didn't. Even when he put his fingers inside me and made me stroke him."

Caleb whispered words of reassurance, his breath warm against her ear, absolving her.

Tempted to melt into his arms, to let his acceptance lull her to sleep, Lottie squirmed until she could see his face better.

"I couldn't stand being in the house. So I took some of the money Uncle Edward gave me for being such a good girl and went to Coney Island. I went again and again until I almost never was home. That way, I didn't have to see him looking at me all the time. I could have fun for a while and forget about the things he did at night."

"Did your aunt know?"

Lottie shrugged, unsure.

"Hell, Lottie. What kind of woman lets something like that happen?" Rage filled Caleb's voice. He shook his head.

Lottie breathed in, then exhaled. She turned in Caleb's arms, until he spooned her, unable to face him for the rest of the story.

"The touching wasn't enough. One night, he put himself into me. It hurt so bad. I felt like I was being torn apart. Afterward, he cried and said he was sorry, that he hadn't wanted to, that I lured him to it. He wouldn't have hurt me if I hadn't made him lust so much that he couldn't hold it back. I was a whore for doing that to him. He promised me he loved me anyway and he'd never hurt me again. But he did. And every time, he told me it was my fault." She sighed, finished, and waited for Caleb to push her away, to tell her she was a whore.

"But you know it wasn't. Not ever." He pulled her close against him and held her.

"But—"

"But nothing. None of this was your fault. You are good and pure and perfect."

"No . . ."

"Yes."

She lay, Caleb's strength filling her as her pillow grew wet and her nose stuffy and dripping. She had no words.

"Lottie?"

"Hmmm?"

"Elsa is your daughter, isn't she?"

Brittle panic slammed through her and she tensed.

"Shhh . . . it's all right. You don't have to tell me."

She lay there, silent, waiting for the panic to subside. What had she suspected would happen when she told him? That he wouldn't put two and two together? She sighed and turned to face him.

"I didn't know what was happening until Aggie told me there was a baby growing inside me, a punishment for being a whore. But it wasn't a punishment because Edward left me alone." She sniffled and he handed her a handkerchief. She sat up, blew her nose, then met his gaze again.

"When Elsa was born, they took her from me. Aggie told me Elsa would be their little girl, my cousin, and that I could hold her only if I stuck to the lie. They didn't want any shame brought on the family. They would be Elsa's parents. I could keep living with them only if I paid my way. So I found work at Coney Island. Once, when I threatened to take Elsa and run away, Edward told me Elsa belonged to them, that her birth certificate listed them as parents, not me. If I ran with her, they would report it as a kidnapping. In the end, I stayed, because that was the only way I could be part of her life. I stayed until Rupert gave me a way out."

Her voice hardened. "If Edward finds us, I'll go to jail. And Elsa will go back to him and he'll do to her what he did to me."

"Does Rupert know?"

She nodded. "He thought she was my cousin, just like everyone else did, until I lost my temper and blurted out the truth. But it's of no import to him, not anymore. Once I stood up to him, the threat was useless. He most likely moved on and forgot all about us."

Caleb nodded back and opened his arms for her. She lay back down, taking comfort from his silent strength. He held her close, stroking her, reassuring her. She drifted toward sleep, fatigue at last claiming her as a small unwanted voice protested inside of her.

Caleb knows.

Can I trust him?

Rupert stood inside the gate of Elitch's Gardens. The darkness hid a strange quietness that seemed eerie in a place usually filled with laughter and shouting. He stumbled away from the wall of the gate and tried to focus his eyes.

It was later than he'd intended, no thanks to the damn trolley driver who'd tossed him off two miles before the Elitch's stop, claiming he didn't tolerate drunks. Rupert wiped his mouth and took a wobbling step. Drunk? Hell, he'd had a few beers was all. Maybe a bottle of whiskey. He wasn't sure anymore.

All he really remembered was that he needed to uncover what was going on here, what that double-crossing Lottie had hatched up. He'd find the plans and put them to shame, he would, and if he fixed that cheap hussy in the process, so much the better. Once Zang started raking in the money, he'd regret having put Rupert on the shit list.

Making his way down the empty pathway, he approached the cottage where the Longs lived. Staring at the gray and white bungalow, he swayed on his feet and debated the merits of forcing his way into the house. He picked his way up the stoop and tried the door.

Locked. Just as he'd thought.

He slid down, plopping on the small porch, and leaned against the railing. Where would a chit like Lottie hide the plans?

He needed a damn drink.

Rupert patted his jacket, found the pint bottle he'd nestled there earlier, and pulled it out. Unscrewing the lid, he tipped the liquid into his mouth and swallowed. The sharp scent of bourbon filled the air. The flow slowed, then stopped. He stared at the empty bottle, then threw it into the bushes beside the door.

He tugged at his pant leg and fumbled for the half-pint he'd tucked into his boot. It was rot-gut gin but it'd do the trick. He drew a long sip, then closed the bottle and grasped the railing as fire filled his throat.

Shit. He shook his head. He needed to find those plans. He could drink later, celebrate. He breathed in and tried to clear his thoughts.

He needed to find the gardener's shack. That was it. He'd seen the way Lottie and Caleb had been sniffing around each other. She'd hide the plans with him.

Rupert lurched through the trees, glad they framed the pathway. It was too damn dark to see where to place his feet, otherwise. He stopped once, took another drink, and winced at the lingering bitterness of the cheap liquor. Then, he trod on until he arrived at the picnic tables. Moving through them, he neared Caleb's cabin at the back of the park, behind the greenhouse.

It, too, was locked.

Rupert bent, wobbled as a wave of dizziness rose, and swallowed the fire rising in his throat. He clutched the rock he'd been eying, straightened, and lobbed it through the window of the wooden door. The glass broke, long shards flying inward after the rock. He loosened the shattered glass, reached in and turned the lock, then opened the door.

Crunching over the glass, he stepped into the room. His hand moved along the wall, looking for a light switch. Instead, he found a lantern, hanging from a hook, and a tin box of matches. He lit the lamp and pulled the bottle of gin from his pocket. Staring at it a moment, he sighed and tucked the bottle away.

The room was dim but Rupert spotted the plan with no

problem. Right there on the table, open for all the world to see. His pulse pounded. He would roll it up and take it with him. It wouldn't be too tough to revise his own design to top anything Lottie and a gardener could throw together.

Rupert steadied his wobbling feet and searched the stacks of notes on the table, scattering pages as he rifled through them. He grabbed at one of them, recognizing Lottie's handwriting. A list. He brought it to his eyes, and waited for the swimming words to still.

The names of ride companies and respective sales contacts.

His heart hammered. Elitch's couldn't be planning that much expansion. Maybe it was just a list.

Peering at the plan itself, Rupert tried to make out the details, seeing symbols he was too drunk to interpret in the dim light. But he wasn't too far gone to realize what they represented. Rides. A hell of a lot of them. More than he'd imagined for Zang's park.

He reached for the lantern, stumbling back to the table with it, trying to see what they had planned. He leaned over and brought the lantern close.

Heat surged through him as he recognized what they had in mind. He snatched up the drawings, crumpling them into a ball as he seethed with anger. His hands shook, the papers quivering as he tried to puzzle out his next move. Seething with anger, he tossed the plans back onto the table and plunged his aching head into his hands. He was screwed.

Crackling pops and the acrid scent of burning paper brought him out of his stupor.

The plans were on fire.

Rupert seized the flaming papers and rushed to the sink. Cursing, he scanned the counter. Where the hell was the pump? What the hell was a gardener doing with a sink with no damn pump? Flames gobbled at the papers. Rupert slapped at them, recoiling as the searing heat burned his hands. Charred black pieces crumbled under his fingers as he tried to choke the cursed fire. He dropped the papers and sank to his knees as the last of the plans burned to ashes.

He sat there, too stunned to move, as realization crept through him. The plans were gone. He'd have to work from his hazy, intoxicated memory if he was going to best what they'd drawn. Hell, they could have more than one set of the damn plans. Reaching into his pocket, he pulled out his bottle, and drained the last of the gin, hatred churning him as roughly as the gin itself.

When he regained his feet, he staggered out of the cabin, pitching his way through the park, so angry at Lottie that he could barely think. The need for revenge pushing him, he stumbled toward one of the small toolsheds, yanked open the door, and looked around the dark interior until he found what he wanted.

Grabbing the sledgehammer, he swayed out the door, dragging the tool behind him. He floundered to the pit where he'd seen Lottie showing off with the bears. Bracing himself, he swung the hammer at the top railing of the pen. The force knocked him off his feet and he reeled. Stumbling, he landed on his butt.

He stood and swung the hammer, again and again, until he was unable to lift it for another blow. Satisfied the railing would fall with the slightest push, he dragged the tool back to the shed and dropped it on the floor.

Then he hobbled out of the park. He had a telegram to send. If the bears failed to kill her, her Uncle Edward would.

CHAPTER SIXTEEN

The scent of fresh-cut wood filled Lottie's senses as she and Caleb entered the Philadelphia Toboggan Company's first floor carving shop. A menagerie of half-constructed wooden animals lined the back of the room. Lottie's eyes widened with each step, and she reached for Caleb's hand, imagining the finished animals, bright with paint, encircling the carousel at Elitch's.

It felt good to have her hand in his. They'd woken uncomfortable with each other. A different relationship had risen from their shared secrets but it fit like a new shoe, a little in need of stretching. Like well-made footwear, it held the promise of comfort guaranteed by good leather and a gifted cobbler. They would examine the fit later. But for now, all she wanted to do was wiggle her toes a bit and forget the tightness. Today, she wanted to feel the magic of their task. She offered him a smile and he squeezed her hand, almost as if letting her know he felt the same.

"Well, come on in," a male voice welcomed. "Best keep the heat inside." In a small workroom, a man was hunched over the back of a prancing wooden horse. He was intent on his work, not taking his eyes from it.

"Mr. Leopald?" Caleb asked.

"Yep."

"We're from Elitch's Gardens. Tom and Mary Long sent us—"

"Caleb and Lottie. To pick out the animals and the paintings.

242

I'll be right with you." Leopald continued to sand the horse with measured strokes. Poplar dust covered the floor below the animals, stirring with each shuffle of Leopald's feet.

Lottie smiled at his brisk tone. A hint of German accent laced his clipped words. No nonsense. She suspected that was one of the reasons Mary liked the carver so much.

"Have a look around. We'll take a look upstairs at the paint shop as soon as I finish this neck. The finished animals are up there."

Caleb joined Lottie, drawing her attention to the head of a stately lion, its flowing mane so intricate that no one would suspect it was made of wood. Sharp teeth and a lifelike tongue were nestled inside its open mouth, beneath nostrils that almost appeared to flare with feline prowess.

Drawn by an irresistible force, Lottie crossed to the lion and reached out. Her palm touched the smooth wood. She stroked the texture of the mane and her fingers glided over the head to its nose.

Caleb's footfalls sounded behind her and she jumped. Shivering, she folded into his sheltering arm. "It's so real. I expected to feel the fur."

"Mary said Leopald was good, but I never suspected this."

"They're made of basswood and poplar," the carver said, behind them.

"They're amazing," Lottie told the man as they turned to him.

"The bodies are hollow boxes?" Caleb asked.

Leopald's eyes twinkled. "They are. Two by twos, laid just so, to form the basic shape. I attach the head and neck, sculpt them so the animal appears, then do the more intricate carving." The man beamed. "You are fortunate. We will make only three more carousels with full menageries. Then, horses only."

"But why? The animals are gorgeous."

"So many different animals take time. I can do only a few carousels per year. We shift to horses only and my journeymen can do much of the work before I add finishing touches. That way, we keep up with the increasing orders." He guided them toward the stairs. "Come, we'll walk up to the paint shop."

As they neared the second floor, the cloying odors of paint and varnish permeated the room. Leopald opened the door and a blast of cool air hit them. "Ventilation," he explained. "Even in the winter, we must leave some of the windows open."

Leopald stepped to the side, allowing Lottie and Caleb to enter first.

Lottie gasped. Bright animals filled the room, workers hand-painting nearly a dozen of them with vivid colors.

"Gustav Weiss." Leopald pointed to an older man at the center of the group.

Weiss looked up at the mention of his name, and Leopald made introductions.

Weiss offered a quick smile, then waved his hand around the room. "Welcome to the paint shop." He pointed into the cluster of animals. "Horses are here, exotics there, and so on. Have a look."

"Oh, my." Lottie's breath stalled as she and Caleb drew closer to the animals. Proud medieval horses wore bright silver armor. She saw Appaloosas and Pintos, fine Thoroughbreds and noble Arabians. They pranced, galloped, and trotted, wearing an assortment of saddles. A spirited Indian pony stood next to a whimsical creature with the upper body of a horse and the tail of a fish.

Laughing, Lottie caught Caleb's hand back into hers. "Look at them all." Excitement filled her as she imagined the animals circling. She could see the entranced children, their gleeful faces as they went round and round, Mary, full of pride as she shared their pleasure. She envisioned Elsa beaming and awe-struck.

Across the room, there were zebras and giraffes, llamas and camels, lions and tigers. Even a dog.

"How do we begin?" Caleb whispered. He pulled her close, their arms touching. Even through their coats, she could feel the tingle of his excitement. "They're all fascinating."

"If you will allow me?" Weiss said. "I will show you what the standard collection is for Carousel Six. Then, if you wish to make changes, we can do so."

Caleb nodded. "That sounds like a good place to start."

"First, let me show you a model of the carousel, so you will see how everything fits together." Weiss and Leopald led them to a side office. Inside, a beautifully crafted model sat atop a table. Leopald approached it and lifted the top off.

Lottie examined the scale carousel, her mouth agape.

"It is beautiful, is it not?" Weiss beamed at her.

Leopald motioned at the model. "The completed carousel will be forty-five feet in diameter with room for forty-six animals and four chariots. You can see the outside animals are bigger. You will need sixteen of them. Fourteen for the middle row and sixteen small ones for the inside. There will be two large chariots and two smaller ones."

"You can see on the inside, around the drive machinery, there are painted muslin panels," Weiss added. "I paint landscapes and portraits. You will tell me if there are special requests. Otherwise, it is my choice. There will be forty-five."

"Now, let me show you the animals we had in mind." Leopald led them back into the menagerie, pointing out a giraffe with a snake twined around its neck, a zebra with a tiny spear-laden gnome hidden behind its saddle, and a lion with tiny cupids seeming to float at its side. Each animal had intricate detail from real antlers to horseshoes to glass eyes.

"Do you have ostriches?" Caleb asked.

Lottie giggled and elbowed him in the side as Leopald shook his head.

In the end, Caleb and Lottie accepted most of the factory choices for the Longs' carousel but replaced several with other selections from the stock on hand. They offered a number of ideas to Weiss for colors and painting subjects. They continued the day with a brief tour of the remainder of the factory where the carousel platforms, mechanical drives, and various structural parts were produced. The last stop was at the factory showroom, where an assembled carousel awaited.

Lottie stepped onto the platform, her eyes drawn to the gilded scrollwork under the canopy. The rich gold lent a regal aura, taking the rider into a world far away from the everyday. Around her, the fantastic animals, with their pageantry, intricate carvings, and bright colors, brought joy to life.

She selected a magnificent prancing pony and stroked the shiny varnish, noting the varying shades of brown paint Weiss had selected. The carved mane seemed to bounce in the air and a real horsehair tail flowed out behind the horse. Its tongue even lolled from the side of its mouth. She was entranced.

Caleb assisted her up, his hand lingering on her bottom for a moment. He grinned, childlike enchantment mingling with desire in his whiskey eyes. Then, he mounted his own horse.

Lottie shivered, watching him, and a warm sense of promise filled her.

The ride began with a slow circle, speed increasing to a breathtaking twelve miles per hour. The Orchestrion belted out a dreamy waltz, simulating a full orchestra as the carousel circled around it. Dizziness swamped her by the time the ride ended and she dismounted. Beside her, Caleb staggered before gaining his footing and she smothered a giggle.

They left the factory hand in hand, Lottie effused with delight.

"You had a good day?" Caleb asked.

"Wonderful."

"There's something I've been thinking about . . . something that I hope will make it even better."

"Must be something pretty good."

"I sent a telegram from the train station while you were freshening up. I wired an attorney in Denver about getting Elsa's birth certificate corrected."

Lottie stopped, staring at Caleb as her heart pounded. Didn't he understand? If an attorney started snooping around, Uncle Edward would find out where they were. Elsa would be gone.

"What in God's name have you done?" she whispered.

Caleb watched Lottie storm into the hotel, the magic of the day fleeing with her. Narrowly missing the door she'd swung shut on him, he dodged a patron exiting from the opposite door. Ahead, Lottie strode to the central staircase and hurried up to the second floor, her sexy derriere sassing him with each twitch. She hadn't said another word to him but he felt her anger as surely as if she'd given him a full dressing down.

He'd expected her to be pleased, to appreciate his actions. Instead, she'd raised her hackles like an alley cat and stalked away. Didn't she know he wouldn't do anything to hurt her? He meant to spend the rest of his life with her, for Pete's sake.

The realization walloped him and he stopped in his tracks.

The rest of his life? Lord in heaven, somewhere along the line, he'd fallen in love with Lottie. Lottie and Elsa and all that came with them. Including the mess he was in right now.

It was time for her to sheathe her claws and tell him what was wrong.

Expelling a heavy breath, Caleb rushed up the stairs, cresting them in time to see Lottie paused before her room. Her shoulders heaved. She inserted the key into the lock and turned toward him as he neared.

"Are you all right?" he asked, though it wasn't at all what he wanted to say.

"Yes. No. I don't know."

"Can we talk about this? I don't understand why you're so upset."

She looked at him, the hot anger fading from her eyes. Then she nodded and stepped into the room, holding the door open for him to enter behind her. He closed the door and turned the electrical switch. The wall light flickered on. Lottie stood at the bureau, placing her purse on the polished wood top.

"Sit," she told him.

He drew the single ladder-back chair away from its place under the window and moved it closer to the bed where Lottie had perched. Though she was calmer, her jaw was still tight.

"I don't know what I did."

"You got a lawyer involved. If someone starts poking around, Edward will find out." The words came out in a tremor.

"Aw, honey—" He reached for her hands. They felt like ice.

"He'll know where we are." Panic filled her voice.

Caleb's pulse jumped. He hadn't meant to cause her distress. He'd only wanted to make the situation better, to take the first steps in freeing Lottie from Uncle Edward. "All I did was ask him to look into how we can get the birth certificate," he tried to explain.

"Uncle Edward has the birth certificate."

He paused, trying to find the words to calm her. In the end, he settled for logic rather than platitudes. "If a certificate exists, there should be one filed with the county or maybe the state. You could get a copy of it. All the attorney is doing right now is getting details on where they're filed. That's all." He whirled his thumbs across the tops of her hands. "Then, if you want to order it, it should be a matter of simply giving your names to somebody in a government office."

"My name isn't listed on it." Weary desperation laced her words.

Caleb's heart clenched and he dug deep, searching for a way to convey the strength she needed. "Do you know that or is that what Aggie and Edward told you?" he asked with care. "Have you seen it?"

"N . . . no."

He squeezed her fingers in his until she looked up. "Then how do you know it's true?"

"Because it's something they would do." Tears filled her eyes. "Elsa was born at home. Edward said he listed Aggie as the mother; no one else was there. Who would know otherwise?"

"There's no way to know the truth unless we look into it."

"What if Edward finds out we're checking?"

"What if he doesn't? What if Aggie isn't listed?" Lottie's chin jerked up and he paused. "If your name is on that certificate, you have the legal right to keep Elsa away from him."

Her eyes widened. "And if it isn't?"

"Then you fight to have it changed. There must be people who knew you were expecting. And that Aggie wasn't."

"In whatever case, he'd still be listed as her father."

"Then we deal with that." Though he knew her refusal to accept rational alternatives was borne from years of fear, he tried to make her realize there could be other outcomes. "He wouldn't stand a chance of getting custody, not given the circumstances."

"And if he paid someone off in the government office, someone who would alert him? Edward has connections." Her words rushed out in breathy spurts.

"Lottie, listen to yourself. You're inventing excuses."

"But—"

He kept his voice calm, to counter the rising panic in hers. "Take it a step at a time. Find out the procedure for ordering a certificate. Then you can decide whether to send for it. You'll either be listed as Elsa's mother or you won't. If not, you can file to have it changed."

"If I try to change the record, he'll have every right to take Elsa back until I can prove I'm her mother." Her chin trembled. "I can't take that risk."

"We won't let that happen. I'll be with you every step of the way, Lottie, whatever it takes. I won't let that son of a bitch take her back. Ever."

She stilled, her breath no longer hitching, and clutched his fingers in a death grip. "I'm scared."

"I know, sweetheart. But you won't know until you check into it. What if he lied? You'll never be free from him until you find out."

She sniffled and drew her hands away. Standing, she pulled a handkerchief from her pocket and blew her nose. The sound filled the quiet of the room like an irritated goose announcing itself, and Caleb held back a chuckle as he repositioned the chair against the wall. When he turned, Lottie offered a wavering smile from beneath the white cotton hanky.

"I must look a mess."

"You look beautiful."

"I'm all puffy."

"There's nothing wrong with honest tears, Lottie," he said, touching her arm in reassurance. From all she'd told him, she'd allowed herself far too few tears in her lifetime.

She smoothed her dress, then tucked the handkerchief away with awkward movements that underscored her discomfort with the display of emotion. With a final sniff, she caught his gaze. "What you said? Did you mean it?"

"That I won't let him take her back?"

"That, and that you'll be there."

"With all my heart."

She slid into his arms, laying her head against his chest. "No one's ever been there for me. Not that way. Ever."

"I'm here now."

"Yes, you are."

Her head tipped, her lips reaching for his. He kissed her, keeping it soft and full of reassurance. Tough as she wanted the world to believe she was, he saw her vulnerability.

But her mouth was greedy, urging his response, inflaming his body. His kiss deepened, and when her tongue flicked at his, he was lost.

Her hands encircled his neck, clutching his head closer. Pulling her into his embrace, he let his tongue meet hers, following her pace but no longer holding back. God, she tasted sweet.

He splayed his hands across her back, stroking her with increasing pressure, circles of reassurance. Reminding himself not to overwhelm her, he slowed himself until his thumbs edged toward her breasts. His breath grew ragged. God, he wanted her.

He waited, allowing her time.

"Touch me, Caleb." She shifted and then she was there, under his hand. "Touch me, please."

His hand cupped her breast, teasing it with gentle touches, whispers of movement, until her nipple hardened and she gasped.

Surprise flooded Lottie. No man's touch had ever prompted such a response. Molten desire coursed through her, from her nipple to the center of her being, and back again. Sweet Lord. This wasn't a touch, it was a caress. And this wasn't any man.

This was Caleb, and she wanted him.

Panting, she moved her hand to his chest, her fingers greedy at his buttons. As they gave way, she slid her hand to his skin, brushing his chest. For a moment, panic bubbled and she stiffened.

"Lottie?"

"Caleb." Speaking his name reassured her. She stroked him, discovering the sparse hairs on his chest, her fingers sweeping over the heat of his skin until his nipple pebbled and he groaned.

Emboldened, she opened his shirt further and slid it from his shoulders. He was magnificent. Hardened muscle rippled beneath his skin as she ran her hands over him. Hot need, unlike anything she'd ever known, filled her.

He waited, his eyes dark and intense, craving. "What do you want me to do, Lottie?"

His surrender of control melted her. She turned, wordlessly offering him her back. He slid open the few buttons under the blousing, parting her shirtwaist. Then his lips were on her neck, hot, moist. He trailed kisses down her back to the edge of her chemise. Then, he removed her hairpins, one by one, until her hair tumbled down. He buried his face in it and drew a breath.

"Your hair smells like gardenias," he whispered, "and your skin like roses. My own flower garden."

A smile lifted her lips at his appreciation of her efforts. His deft fingers pushed the shirtwaist from her shoulders. As it fell to the floor, she turned and untied her chemise, opening it until her breasts were bared to him.

He stood before her, panting. For a moment, doubt threatened her, clawing at her as old memories swam through her mind. His gaze caressed her but again he waited. For her. He lifted his eyes. Need, desire, *love* filled them. Nowhere was there the greedy domination she'd been subject to before. *This* was Caleb. She shivered, the uncertainty gone.

"I never knew . . ." she whispered, reaching for his hands. She placed them on her body and nodded.

He removed her chemise as she fumbled with the button at the back of her skirt. The skirt pooled at her feet. "I want you," she told him, sureness flooding her. Her heart pounded. Her breath grew ragged, mirroring his, and she reached for the buttons of his trousers.

He stalled her hands. With gentle movements, he divested her of the last of her undergarments, then sat her on the bed. He raised each leg, nimble fingers slid her shoes from her feet, then rolled her stockings down her legs. His lips trailed soft kisses from the top of each thigh to the tips of her toes. Then, he raised her legs higher, one at a time, and bent to touch his tongue across the back of each knee until goose bumps rose across her skin.

Panting, she watched him shed the rest of his clothing. Lean, hard muscles graced his legs and his hot, hard desire held her attention. She swallowed.

"Lottie?"

"Yes, Caleb. Yes."

He moved to her and she pulled him down. She touched him, amazed at the hot velvet ridges beneath her fingers, the incredible softness of the taut skin. Each touch brought a current of electricity rushing to her core. Then his hand moved to her center, finding the center of her aching desire, fondling it until she trembled. Need swamped her. "Please."

Shifting his finger, he stroked her inside, each movement taking her farther upward until she tightened around him, shuddering as a kaleidoscope of pleasure overtook her.

He entered her then, stroking her with slow sureness. She climbed with him, the steady drive of anticipation building, urging her to match his movements. She fought for breath, her heart pounding as he thrust harder, driving her upward until she shattered, screaming as she clenched him. She crested again and again, riding a roller coaster unlike any she'd ever imagined, until she lay wet and dazed and panting.

Sated, they settled together, their heart rates slowing. As she sank into lethargy, she realized she'd screamed. And Caleb had shouted as he came with her. Her lips turned in a smile, and unexpected warmth cocooned her, puzzling at first, until her mind grasped the unfamiliar sensation of being safe.

Chapter Seventeen

Rupert staggered out of the cheap hotel he'd had to move into, squinting against the glaring afternoon sun. Sweat covered him and he could swear his skin was pulsing under his temple. It felt like there was something in there, hammering its way out with one hand while it thrust needle-like daggers with the other. Sobriety, even in its smallest form, was hell after a thirty-six-hour binge. Time to down a little hair of the dog to clear his head and figure out how to handle the mess he was in.

He entered the first saloon he came to. His stomach roiled at the lingering smell of stale hops. Rupert choked it down and picked his way across the stickiness on the floor. Sidling up to the bar, he ordered a beer before changing his mind and barking out a command for whiskey instead. He downed it in one swift gulp and slammed the glass onto the counter. His stomach lurched, then settled.

"Troubles?"

He sneered at the nosy barkeep. "Damn right."

"I can leave the bottle. Might save some time keeping that glass filled."

Nosy but not stupid. "Might as well."

After he'd knocked back a couple more shots, the pieces began to fall together, dredging up a vague recollection of stumbling into the telegraph office. Rupert slid a hand through his hair, wincing as he recognized the oily feel of days-old pomade. Had he really sent that telegram? He wasn't sure if it was a memory or something he'd imagined.

He set down the glass as the rest of the details filled in. He recalled the plans in the gardener's cabin, dropping them onto the lantern, watching in disbelief as they burned away in the dry sink.

Shit. He poured another glass of whiskey but let it sit on the bar. Staring at it, he remembered raging against Lottie, taking a hammer to the bear pit. And then, he'd returned to town and sent the telegram to Edward Chase.

Revenge against Lottie but a fat lot of good it was going to do him.

His clouded mind retained little of the detailed drawing he'd found on Caleb's table. There was no way in hell he was going to be able to improve his own designs to compete with plans he couldn't remember. Damn. He grabbed the glass and poured the whiskey down his throat.

Elitch's Gardens was going to expand, bigger and better than the park he'd envisioned for Zang—even after the Longs sunk in the money to fix the bear pit. Hell, he doubted he'd done much damage to it anyway, not as drunk as he'd been.

White City, as he'd been calling Zang's park in his mind, would draw people, but not the crowds they'd need to make a profit. Not with all the money Zang would need to sink into the place to build it from scratch. It'd be years before he saw any return on his work. Years before he could move on and make his mark on the world.

Tipping back another shot, Rupert weighed his options. His gaze drifted to the dirty front window of the bar. Outside, a woman dragged a petulant kid down the sidewalk. Reminded him of Lottie's brat.

Gee whiz . . . the brat.

He didn't remember much about sending the telegram to Chase but he sure as hell knew Lottie was convinced the man wanted the kid. Might even want her enough to pay for the information if he could figure out how to play it. He swallowed another shot, smugness warming him as much as the whiskey.

"You gonna need another?" the bartender asked as he passed.

Rupert glanced at the bottle, noting the remaining liquid. He thought about holding back, nursing what was there. "I guess," he said.

The barkeep shuffled his way down the bar, wiping haphazardly at sticky spots with his rag and dishing out advice to anyone who happened to look up at him. Rupert drained the last swig from his bottle, dispensing with the glass, and waited for the bartender to return. He'd stalled a few feet away, consoling another customer.

Rupert eyed the bottle in his hand and signaled.

The barkeep had the good grace to look apologetic as he approached. "Sorry," he said as he plunked down the whiskey. "Guy just lost his job. Mining accident. Company went bankrupt and had to close."

Rupert nodded, knowing what it was like to be left high and dry. "Pour him a drink," he said. He watched the barkeep deliver the offering and caught the nod of appreciation from the miner. Poor sap.

If only Elitch's would close. That'd solve everything.

He stared at the miner, his head spinning. Shit, it *would* solve everything.

He grabbed the bottle and tossed it back. The whiskey burned. Then he set the bottle down, lay his head on his arm, and began to puzzle it out.

People wouldn't go there if they didn't believe they were safe. They wouldn't go if they were afraid. All he had to do is start a few rumors and Elitch's would be driven out of business. He was good at weaving tales. A few well-placed stories and all his worries would disappear.

Rupert grinned as his face slid off his arm and onto the sticky table.

Caleb held Lottie's hand as the trolley neared Elitch's. He lifted it to his lips and kissed her knuckles, remembering her naked in his arms. She shivered and edged him a smile.

The past few days had been a glorious reprieve from their cares. They'd spent hours in bed, exploring each other's bodies as he learned all the different ways Lottie could scream. He was hard just thinking about it, about pouring into her again and again. Screams would never affect him the same way they had in the past—that was for sure.

Lottie had softened as well, learning to wallow in her emotions for a change. She was so vibrant, so alive. And now that they'd returned, he meant to keep both her and Elsa safe.

"You all right?" he asked, squeezing her hand.

"Purring like a well-fed cat."

"Mm-hmm. I can see that." He winked and she blushed. The trip home had been long, the trains offering no privacy. Caleb hadn't stopped touching her or whispering innuendos that she claimed left her giddy with desire. He was imagining goose bumps spreading up her back when the trolley jerked to a stop outside Elitch's and brought him back to reality.

Disembarking, they stood for a moment, taking in one another.

"You're okay with this?" she asked him.

"I gave you my word. We take this one step at a time with Elsa. When she's ready for us to be a family, we move forward. Until then, we keep our relationship private." He'd promised they'd visit the lawyer and begin the process of securing Elsa's custody. In the meantime, they had plans to discuss with Elsa. Plans for a future that would include all three of them.

"We'll talk to her soon," Lottie promised. "As soon as we talk to the lawyer. I want to make sure we don't do anything to jeopardize getting legal control of her."

Caleb chuckled. "I'm not worried. I don't think she's going to be surprised, or opposed."

"Me either."

He pulled Lottie into a quick hug, letting loose just as Elsa stormed out of the Elitch's gate.

"Lottie!" Elsa burst across the street and wrapped her arms around Lottie.

Caleb's heart caught, watching them. Lottie seemed more than ready to shift gears, to mother Elsa, to make a family with him.

"You're home!" Elsa announced. "I've been waiting all day for you. The kittens are so huge you won't believe it; they're hardly even kittens anymore. Tom and Mary came home yesterday. And me. And you know what? I had such a good time at the Wilson's I almost forgot to miss you, but I did anyway. Miss you, I mean." She stopped to draw a breath and looked at Caleb. "You, too."

"And I missed you, too, squirt."

They made their way up the path, nearing the cottage. The scent of fresh-baked oatmeal cookies greeted them. Tom met them at the door. "Thought I heard the trolley. Elsa's met every one of them since lunch. Come on in, have some cookies and warm up, tell us about the carousel."

They entered, set down their bags, and shed wraps as Lottie described the factory and its assorted employees. Her face glowed as she told them of the animals, with their intricacy, carved details, and bright paint.

Finally tearing his eyes from her animated features, Caleb pulled the drawings from his bag and showed Mary their selections.

Mary's face lit with satisfaction, Elsa's with anticipation. "I can't wait," Elsa said.

"The children are going to be so happy," Mary said. "It's going to be a good year, I think. Did you get to take a ride?"

"We did. It was incredible. I've never ridden a carousel that went so fast. I'd say it's going to be a great year." Eyes sparkling, she told them about their stop to visit a ride manufacturer in Chicago and the bids they'd secured for several new amusements.

Mary clapped her hands together, beaming. "Let's fire up the roller coaster and take a celebratory spin. After all, what good is living at an amusement park if you can't enjoy an off-season ride now and again?"

As the ladies gathered coats and mittens, Tom drew Caleb aside. "Not everything was peachy while we were gone," he said.

"What happened?" His skin tingled as he remembered Lottie's concerns about Uncle Edward. "Elsa?"

"She's fine. Vandals, it looks like."

The tingles failed to subside. "They damage much?"

Across the room, Lottie's gaze met his. She left Elsa with Mary and neared them. "What's wrong?" she asked, her face growing pale.

"Someone took a sledgehammer to the bear pit railing, dented it pretty good. We'll need to pound out the damage and give it a coat of paint." Tom's eyes narrowed. "I also found some empty booze bottles in the bushes and somebody smashed the glass in the door of Caleb's cabin."

Lottie exhaled, her color returning as quickly as it had left.

But Caleb's mind whirled. He'd left the plans on the table. "Did they damage anything else?"

Tom shrugged. "We're not sure. Lots of glass on the floor, papers scattered about but no other damage that I noticed right off. I left things how they were there. Thought you'd want to see it."

"Maybe I ought to go take a look." He looked at Lottie and offered her a smile of reassurance. No sense worrying her about anything further until he knew whether or not the plans were gone.

"Go on," he said. "Celebrate. I'll catch up later."

It wasn't as if they didn't have a future full of rides together.

Rupert sat in the Scandinavian House Saloon nursing a beer. He shifted in the dark wooden booth, fighting his thirsty urges. His hand twitched and edged toward the beer. He stilled it and reminded himself what was at stake. Edward Chase was due any minute, and Rupert would be damned if he'd leave here with anything less than the fortune he planned to milk from Chase in return for information about the kid.

Chase had wired him yesterday of his impending arrival and Rupert had spent the remainder of the day sobering up. He'd even poured half a bottle of gin down the sink. Too much was riding on today's meeting.

For the third time since taking his seat, Rupert glanced at the clock. Chase's train should have arrived thirty minutes ago. The saloon was two short blocks away. The man would be here any minute. Rupert straightened his worn wool jacket and spiffed back his hair. Then he watched the door, drumming his fingers on the table.

A distinguished middle-aged man with a pronounced limp entered. His quality clothes were travel-rumpled, and he carried a satchel. Heavy jowls framed the annoyance within his features, and a prominent gray mustache twitched beneath his Roman nose.

Rupert swallowed and waved his hand.

The man neared, disdain filling his eyes. His gaze moved over

261

Rupert, reminding him how tattered his clothes had become. Full of himself, just like Art Gennick always was. No wonder Lottie had wanted out from under his thumb.

"Edward Chase?"

"You Gennick?"

"Guess I am." Figuring that sounded pretty stupid, he added, "Have a seat."

Chase frowned at the booth, then exhaled and tucked his towering frame in opposite of Rupert. "You sent me a telegram? About Lottie and Elsa?"

Rupert nodded. So much for pleasantries. The old fart got right down to business. "I did. Thought you might want to know where they're at."

Chase eyed him again. "Well, I guess I have to say you're pretty much the type I'd expect her to run off with."

Silence stretched as they glared at each other. The old coot was nothing more than a bully. Rupert's hand crept toward the beer. "I'm a working man, Mr. Chase. Nothing more, nothing less."

"You're a bum."

Rupert flinched, then grabbed the glass and took a long draw. Damned superior old goat. "Can I order you a beer? Maybe a whiskey?"

"Save your empty hospitality, Gennick. I didn't come here to share drinks."

"Some lunch, then?" Cripes, the man made it hard to keep a friendly tone. He raised his hand and waved for a waiter. "An early dinner?"

"Look, you lazy turd, I'm not interested in chitchat. Take me to my girls."

"Not just yet, Chase. I think we have some business to discuss first."

A trim man in a white apron approached and Rupert ordered whiskeys.

"Scotch," Chase corrected. "Decent scotch."

Rupert winced. In other words, expensive scotch. He drained the last of the beer and reminded himself again what he was there for.

They sat, staring at each other, until the waiter returned. He set the glasses down and scuttled away.

"You're a man of good taste, I see." Rupert waved toward the scotch.

Chase scowled and sampled the drink. "Good taste, little patience."

So much for a smooth con. If that's the way Chase wanted to play it, he'd get right to the point. "I thought we might bargain a little." Rupert tossed back the whiskey. "You want your girls. I know where they are. I'd hoped you might extend a reward to me for sharing that knowledge."

Chase's face reddened and his jowls twitched. "You think I'm going to pay you for information?"

"You've traveled all the way out here. Seems to me that's a pretty good indication they're worth at least something to you."

"Elsa is worth a great deal."

"Then why not let me take you to her?"

"Why not, indeed? Shall we go?"

They slid from the booth, Rupert's nerves on alert. He hadn't closed the deal and the knot in his stomach told him all was not well. Damn, he needed another drink. "About that . . . I'm sure you'll be overwhelmed with excitement once we get there. I wouldn't want to burden you with business details at a time like that. Perhaps you'd like to dispense with the payment now?"

Chase's hands shot out, seized Rupert's collar, and jerked him forward. "Look you little shit," he said, drawing out the last word. "You can take me there or not but I'm sure as hell not going to pay you. Push me any further and I'll rip you to shreds with my bare hands."

His breath was hot on Rupert's face, hot and sure and full of threat. Rupert's bladder squeezed in dazed response and he fought to keep from pissing his pants.

Chase glanced back at the room, then threw a solid jab into Rupert's stomach.

Hot bile rushed up Rupert's gullet.

"You puke on me and it'll be the last thing you do."

Rupert choked down the vomit and straightened. "Find her yourself," he choked out.

Chase shook his head. "You think I can't? You're filth, Gennick. Filth I don't need. I planned on doing this the easy way but I'm through here. I'll find her myself. Lottie's predictable. How many amusement parks can there be in this town?"

CHAPTER EIGHTEEN

Caleb rushed through the door of his cabin, his feet crunching on the scattered glass. He paused and looked at the table.

The plans were gone.

Lottie's lists remained, strewn across the floor. The lantern from beside the door sat on the table, a lone soldier guarding nothing.

He made his way into the room, scanning it for other disruptions. Aside from what he'd already noted, nothing seemed disturbed. Grabbing a match, he turned the wick of the lantern and touched it with the match. Nothing. The lantern had burned empty.

Moving through the dim room, he found his notes on hybrid rose experiments complete and all his personal files intact. But as he approached the kitchen area, a faint smell of charred paper met his nose. Ashes filled the dry sink. A few unburned scraps told him their plans had met their end there.

Caleb drew a breath. The plans seemed to have been the target but the culprit had burned them rather than stealing them. A competitor? He doubted any of the owners or managers at Manhattan Beach would stoop to this. They'd coexisted for some time, each finding a special niche.

What was going on? First, suspicions about disrepair, now burned plans, and damage to the bear pit. It didn't make sense.

But it *was* getting progressively worse. Caleb sank onto a chair, his pulse racing.

None of this had started until after Lottie—no, after Rupert—had arrived. It was a con, wasn't it? Or could Rupert have worked his way up to sabotaging Elitch's?

Caleb's chest tightened, throbbed.

Holy cats, they were going to ride the roller coaster. He stood, the chair falling with the briskness of his movement.

He didn't know how, he didn't know why, but somehow he knew they were in danger. And he doubted he had much time.

Rupert stumbled out of the bar, bottle in hand, stunned at how the game had turned on him. He'd thought Chase would be an easy mark, that he'd pay up, pleased to have Rupert's assistance. Instead the old pisser had brushed him off like he was worthless trash.

Just like Art Gennick had done.

How long would it take Chase to learn Lottie was at Elitch's? Given that there were only two amusement parks in Denver, he doubted it would be long. Once Chase had the kid, that route to income would be gone as well. Rupert stared at the bottle, then took another swig.

Maybe, if he could get to the kid first, Chase would pay a ransom. Information was one thing but if he wanted the kid, he'd pay up to get her, wouldn't he?

Rupert staggered up the street to Charlie's favorite bar and spotted his roadster out front. Charlie wouldn't care if he borrowed it. He cranked up the car, climbed in, and sped northwest, whiskey sloshing with each bounce. Chase, he figured, would get stuck riding the trolley.

Five bone-jarring miles later, he'd sobered up a bit. He stopped the vehicle and jumped out. Grabbing the side to steady his footing, he opted to leave the bottle where it was, and careened down the path into the park.

He wasn't sure how he intended to convince Elsa to go with

him but he'd decide once he got there. Voices drew him up the path, toward the coaster. He moved forward, trying to sort out a plan. The sight before him stopped him dead in his tracks.

Lottie was tucking Elsa into the first car of the coaster. Mary Long was seated behind them.

He couldn't let the ride take off. He needed Elsa. Now. Before Edward found her. Enraged, he raced down the path.

"No! No! Get out!"

Shock registered on their faces.

Confused, he stumbled, looking around in a daze as they sprung out of the ride, before realizing the voice hadn't been his.

His gaze landed on Elsa, standing a few feet in front of the others, and he plunged forward, his last-chance plan to extort money from Chase solidifying as he reached her.

"Your uncle's here," he whispered. "I'll get you out, but you have to come. Now."

After yelling a warning, Caleb burst from the trees. Deafening quiet filled the clearing. Scratches from the branches burned his face as he skidded to a halt, his eyes on the coaster.

They were safe.

Caleb's gaze sought Lottie, needing reassurance she was all right.

She stood, staring at Rupert Gennick and Elsa. Elsa squirmed in Rupert's arms as he backed away from the others.

"Noooooo!" Lottie screamed. She raced toward Rupert.

Caleb sped forward, leaping a tidy row of shrubs. He was there only a second after Lottie but she was already clawing at Rupert's face.

Rupert's hands flew up in self-defense, and Elsa rushed away from him. He turned, reaching for her as Lottie pulled her away.

Caleb dove in with a front jab, sending Rupert backward, clutching his stomach. Satisfaction spread through Caleb and he drew back for another swing and punched Rupert again and again until Rupert collapsed to his knees.

Unable to catch his breath from the flurry of punches, he toppled forward, face down onto the ground.

Tom raced to Caleb and held him back. "He's done, son."

Mary drew out a handkerchief and dabbed at the scratches on Caleb's face. He could hear Rupert's sobs, babbled nonsense about ruined plans, losing everything, and Edward Chase. Caleb knelt beside him and tried to make sense of the whiny words.

Ed Chase.

Caleb stood, unable to breathe as he looked for Lottie and Elsa.

They were gone.

CHAPTER NINETEEN

Lottie drew Elsa away from the fight, holding her close as she guided her down the path. Elsa didn't need to see any more violence. Already, she was shaking, her eyes haunted.

"L . . . Lottie?"

"Shh, sweetie. Everything's going to be all right. Caleb has Rupert—he can't hurt you."

"N . . . no." Elsa's voice trembled. "It's Uncle Edward. Rupert said Uncle Edward's here."

Lottie's breath rushed out in a gush. "What?"

"He said Uncle Edward is here."

"No. That can't be." She pulled Elsa off the path, into the trees, and knelt in front of her, peering into the wooded area that surrounded them. "Here in Denver or here at Elitch's?"

"I don't know."

"Criminy. How'd he find us?"

A twig snapped, the small sound echoing through the park. Lottie put her fingers to her lips. Footsteps sounded on the gravel path. Uneven footsteps she'd heard creeping toward her room a thousand times. Panic stabbed at her as she pulled off her brown coat and threw it over Elsa. Crouching beside her, she squirmed under the coat, too, and prayed Edward would pass by without noticing them.

His footfalls faded, and Lottie rose. "We have to run," she told Elsa. Pulling Elsa with her, Lottie dodged trees, crashed through frozen flower beds, trying to follow a route opposite that which Edward had taken. Her chest hurt, the cold air fill-ing her lungs as she ran. Passing the lion cages, they emerged near the shed behind the bear pit.

She stalled, her chest heaving. Beside her, Elsa panted, her eyes wide.

Was this, then, the life they'd always have? Running away, trying to escape Edward forever? Hurting people she loved because she was too afraid to face him and fight?

Her breath came in hot spurts.

She didn't want to do this anymore. She wanted to trust. She wanted to love. She wanted what was hers.

Drawing Elsa with her, she moved toward the shed, opened it, and searched for a weapon.

This time, there would be no escape. It was time to fight.

She closed the door, turned, and felt his presence.

Caleb crashed through the trees, his footfalls heavy on the frozen ground. He could hear movement ahead of him, at once rushed, frantic, and determined. Then silence. He surged toward the animal area.

As the trees thinned, he could see Lottie near the bear pit, a bloody gash across her cheek. An immense mustached man stood across from her, Elsa struggling in one arm while he brandished a knife in his other hand.

Uncle Edward. It had to be.

Caleb's gut clenched, and he ducked behind a shed, willing himself to remain motionless as he sorted out what to do. Mary had run to telephone the police but it would take time for them to arrive. He didn't think Edward had seen him. If he could circle around, behind his line of sight, he might be able to take him by surprise.

With light footfalls, Caleb inched around the shed. As he crossed between buildings, he caught glimpses of Edward lurching up the path beside the pit, yanking Elsa along with him.

Nearly stumbling over a pail of paint, Edward kicked at it and paused to clutch the girl closer. "Get out of my way, Lottie. It didn't take much to take that knife away and slash you. I can cut our little Elsa here just the same as I did you." His words rang out, clear in the winter air.

"You won't do that. You aren't going to mar her."

"Back away and she'll be safe. All the way to the trees. I'm even willing to forget that you kidnapped her."

His gaze on Lottie, Edward limped forward, his knife dangerously close to Elsa's face. "Move aside, you kidnapping whore."

Caleb's heart hammered, he was using the words that stung Lottie the deepest, raising the threat she most feared. True or not, it would rattle her.

"I didn't kidnap her. I swear I didn't." Lottie's voice was plaintive, almost whiny and Caleb hated Edward for reducing her to such a state. "Didn't you get the note? Rupert said he left a note."

"That bum? That worthless pile of shit's the one who squealed on you."

Caleb crept behind the low wall of another enclosure and peered around it. Lottie stood in front of Edward, her face red with tears, but her eyes confident. Her submissiveness held Edward's attention. Caleb drew a breath, understanding. Edward's eyes remained on Lottie until Elsa squirmed in his arms. Edward shook her with a jerk and mumbled something. Elsa stilled.

Lottie took an awkward step and lowered her head. "He said we were going to Niagara Falls. To be married. Instead he brought us here and dumped us without a dime. I didn't even have money to wire you."

Edward's head swung up. "Elope? With you? What kind of idiot would believe a fool thing like that?" His voice dripped contempt. Caleb held himself steady, fighting the urge to rush to Lottie's defense. She was playing the son of a bitch and Edward was stepping right into it. He needed to trust her.

"He wouldn't let me come home. I'm sorry. Me and Elsa wanted to come home so bad but he wouldn't let us."

"Are you brainless, girl?"

"He wouldn't let Elsa go." Lottie was sobbing now, all shades of adult confidence gone. Realizing her intent, Caleb listened as she became more and more childlike in tone. "I'm so . . . sorry, I didn't know what to do."

"You worthless whore."

Caleb moved around the last cage, emerging behind Edward. Elsa stood, limp in his arms. Edward's hold on her was loose, his concentration on Lottie.

Sinking to her knees, Lottie seemed to grovel before the man. "Take us home . . . Please. I'm sorry. I won't be any problem. I'll do whatever you say. Please."

"No, Lottie. You've been a bad girl. I'm done with you and all your trouble. I'm taking Elsa back home where she belongs. With her parents."

Lottie sobbed, her cries mingling with Elsa's. Edward wavered, his attention divided, and his knife hand shifted away from Elsa. Caleb moved forward. He was within yards of Edward as the man leaned to whisper at Elsa. "Hush, little girl, Papa's here."

"You're not my papa!" Elsa screamed, kicking at Edward's bad leg, then shoving him as she leapt away from him.

Caleb sprang the last few feet.

Edward teetered, his bum leg unsteady as the force of Elsa's shove sent him stumbling over Tom's toolbox and the paint can. He cursed and flailed his arms, searching for balance. His tall frame hit the railing, momentum pitching him over it as the knife clattered to the ground.

CHAPTER TWENTY

Lottie watched Edward tumble into the bear pit, his hands frantically clutching at the railing. Relief flooded her as she rose to her feet and rushed to Elsa. Caleb reached the sobbing girl first, scooped her into his arms, and moved her away from danger. Lottie knelt as Caleb released Elsa into her arms. She pulled her daughter into a hug. Their two hearts pounded as Elsa gulped frantic mouthfuls of air. "Shhh, Elsa, I'm here."

"I w . . . was so sc . . . cared. Is he gone, Mama? Is he gone?"

Lottie tore her eyes away from her daughter. Caleb was at the edge of the pit, yelling at the bears. "Stay still," he called to Edward. "Curl up in a ball and lay still."

"Like hell." Though strained, Edward's tone was hateful, accusatory.

Caleb turned, caught Lottie's gaze. His eyes were full of pain. "Sam's already taken a swipe at him. He'll kill him if he keeps lashing out." Concern filled his voice.

"Let him," Lottie said, wincing at her bitterness.

Caleb swallowed, then rushed toward the nearest shed.

Lottie clutched Elsa, reason surfacing through the fog of enmity and resentment that squeezed her heart. Could she face Elsa if she allowed Sam to kill Edward? If she did nothing, let it happen? She sighed, her heart tight. If she let him die, she would be no better than him.

"Run to Mary," she told Elsa. "Tell her Edward's in the pit."

As Elsa darted away, Lottie turned toward the pit. She called to the bears, drawing Sam's attention away from Edward, then raced for the gate. As she neared it, Caleb emerged from the shed, several buckets in hand. Seeing her intent, he dashed to her side.

"I'll go in. You take a bucket and distract Sam from up here."

She shook her head. "Sam knows me, I know him. I have a better chance of distracting him. Trust me." She grabbed the keys from him along with one of the pails.

Caleb nodded, worry etching his brow. "I don't like it but you're right. I love you, Lottie. I'll be there as soon as I can."

As she unlocked the gate and hurried down the steps, she heard Caleb calling out, instructing Edward to play dead, creating a diversion with berries and fish. She opened the bottom gate and stepped into the pit, adrenaline powering her.

Edward lay to one side, twitching in pain, cursing at the bears. He lay, one leg twisted, blood pooling beneath his head. Gashes through his clothing bore evidence of Sam's claws.

Lottie shifted her attention to the bears. Ever placid Gertrude was already nosing after several piles of treats Caleb had tossed down on the opposite side of the pit. Sam lurched from one foot to another, untempted, his eyes on Edward. Lottie edged closer. "Hey, Sam," she singsonged.

Edward thrashed in pain. "Get . . . me . . . out of here."

Sam raised unto his hind legs and Lottie's attention remained on the bear, watching Sam's every movement. "If you want to live, shut up and listen. Your tone and your movement anger him. Be quiet and lay still." She hissed out the advice, then returned to coaxing Sam. She tossed the bear a fish, grinning in triumph as his nose twitched at the scent and he lowered to all fours. He lumbered to the offering, taking it into his mouth.

"Can you move?" she asked Edward.

"I'm here. I'll get him," Caleb's soft voice sounded behind her.

Lottie stole a glance toward Gertrude, who had waddled to another pile of goodies. Assured, she edged closer to Sam's side of the pit, waving another fish in his direction. Again, his nose caught the scent and he lurched closer. She tossed the fish to him. Behind her, she heard Edward's stifled grunts and shuffling movement.

Sam swallowed the fish and turned back to Lottie. He waddled forward, sniffing.

"We're out," Caleb called.

Lottie moved the pail from side to side, letting the smell drift into the air. Sam stilled. She tossed the remaining fish to him and backed away, to the safety of the gate.

She stepped into the stairway and closed the gate, locking it behind her. She emerged from the top gate and stepped into Caleb's waiting arms. Exhaustion filled her as the adrenalin rush evaporated. Tremors shook her body as her breath rushed out on a great, heaving sigh.

"Breathe. Just breathe." Caleb's strong arms circled her, holding her tight, reassuring. His lips distributed desperate kisses across her brow as his hands clutched her head.

She sank into his embrace, pressing hard against his chest. Her arms circled him, clenching him until she felt his heart beating against hers. She lifted her mouth to his and kissed him.

"Lottie?" Tom's voice broke into the moment.

Becoming mindful of her surroundings, she noted Mary at the edge of the animal area, sheltering Elsa in her arms. Rupert sat on a bench, scowling, his hands bound. Tom knelt over Edward. "He's slipping, Lottie."

Caleb guided her forward, her own awareness still fuzzy. Tom bussed her on the forehead, then stepped away.

Edward lay, still, at her feet. His eyes were blank and unfocused. "Lottie?"

She swallowed and sank down beside him.

His hand floundered in the air above his chest. "Lottie?"

"I'm here," she whispered.

"Couldn't help . . . never meant to hurt. . . ." his words were mumbled. He'd said the same thing. So many, many times. Desperation yanked at her senses, urging her to flee. Repulsed, she willed herself to look at him instead. He was dying. If she didn't face him now, she would never escape the memories.

His facial muscles twitched as his fingers clutched at empty air. "El . . . sa?"

"She's safe, Edward. That's all you need to know." Lottie glanced at her daughter and offered her a wavering smile of assurance. "We both are."

"Elsa?" he gasped.

"No more, Edward."

"Didn't mean. . . ." The words were barely audible.

Lottie's heart pounded. Even dying, he was trying to manipulate her. She knew he wanted forgiveness, that he believed it would free him. That was his right, she knew, but Lottie wasn't fooled. She would never be fooled by someone like him again.

She sighed, unable to give him the absolution he craved. Instead, she offered him a small wavering smile, knowing it was over, and a small piece of the bitterness she'd held so long escaped from her heart.

"Birth . . . cert . . ." he paused, panting. "Ne . . . ver . . . filed." Edward's hand fell and landed with a dull thud on his stomach. He was gone.

Lottie didn't know how long she sat there before she felt Caleb's arms engulf them. "It's all right," he said. "I'm here. I love you."

She stilled, drawing strength from him as she accepted

Edward was dead.

She was free.

EPILOGUE

Opening day at Elitch's Gardens dawned bright and sunny. Lottie's heart swelled. She could hear excited voices outside the gate before she neared the gatehouse. She rounded the bend and stalled. Her pulse raced. Gads, how many people were there in that line?

This morning's edition of *The Rocky Mountain News* had featured an interview with Mary about the new carousel, predicting thousands would turn out to see the new features and foliage. A good portion of them had to be waiting out there right now!

Lottie neared the carousel, stunned anew by the fantastic carvings. A grand pavilion stood over the ride, protection against the elements, with a freshly painted white fence surrounding it. Three wide steps up to the entrance where the bright, painted animals and intricate gold trim beckoned.

Elsa jumped down the steps and bounded toward Lottie. "Did you see 'em, Mama? Holy cats! There must be a million of 'em."

"Not a million, sweetie. But hundreds for sure." She ruffled Elsa's unruly hair, wondering how she'd already managed to loosen her neat braids. "Papa's got a spot fixed for you." Elsa grabbed Lottie's hand and led her to the carousel. A padded wicker chair sat in the shade near the entrance steps.

Lottie's mouth stretched into a smile as Elsa scampered up the stairs and onto the merry-go-round. As usual, Caleb had thought of her comfort—the large chair would be ideal as her girth grew wider over the summer. She settled into the chair, wriggling until she found a comfy spot.

Her pregnancy had meant a lot of changes, but she suspected she'd enjoy the music, laughter, and animated faces more than enough to compensate for giving up her role as animal-tender. The bears had adjusted to the new trainer, even if he did refuse to wear a bathing costume. Her eyes misted over as she thought about Sam. She loved the grouchy old bear—maybe not as much as Mary, but enough to be glad they'd not had to put him down for killing someone.

"All set?" Caleb asked, appearing at the top of the steps. He descended and moved toward her.

A slow tingle crept up her back. His chambray shirt stretched across his wide chest. Under the torn-off sleeves, his rock-hard muscles glistened with beads of sweat, reminding her of their time together earlier that morning.

"Hello, handsome."

"Hello, baby," Caleb said and bestowed a kiss on Lottie's stomach.

"You should see the crowd! The paper ran a story this morning. It's going to be a busy day."

"I suspect so. Opening day always is. This year, there's even more reason for excitement."

Lottie nodded. All around, it was going to be a great season. The past months had been filled with tension . . . shipping Uncle Edward's body back to New York, detailed safety inspections, waiting for Elsa's birth certificate. Rupert had been promptly fired by an outraged Adolph Zang and, when no evidence of sabotage was found, he was allowed to depart Denver in disgrace. Over time, Lottie had managed to come to terms with Edward, to let loose of all those years of guilt as well as her lack of sorrow over his death. She drew a breath and offered Caleb a smile. It was over, they were free.

"It's going to be a wonderful summer." She thought about the months to come, the construction of Caleb's new greenhouse, the new rides they planned to order, the little house they'd soon be moving into, the new baby. She stretched her toes as warmth filled her.

Elsa popped out from behind a carousel horse and raced over. "Is it time? Should I go tell Mary?"

Caleb chuckled. "She's wound up tighter than a spring."

Lottie grinned up at him. "That she is. What do you think? Are we ready?"

He smiled down at her and drew a finger along her cheek. "I think we're more than ready, sweetheart. I love you."

"And I love you."

Elsa whooped and tore down the path, shouting for Mary to open the gate.

Caleb shook his head as they watched her disappear. "Get ready, Lottie. There's no escape now."

"I wouldn't want it any other way," she murmured and melted into his kiss.

ABOUT THE AUTHOR

Pamela Nowak's debut novel, *Chances,* was awarded the HOLT Medallion for Best First Book, was a WILLA Finalist, and was named one of the "Top Ten Romance Novels of 2008" by *Booklist.* Her second novel, *Choices,* received a HOLT Finalist Award. *Changes* received the 2014 Colorado Book Award in genre fiction and the HOLT Award of Merit in historical romance. Pam has been in love with history and rich characters for most of her life. She has a B.A. in history, taught prison inmates, served as project manager for the Fort Yuma National Historic Site, and ran a homeless shelter. She was named the Rocky Mountain Fiction Writers' *Writer of the Year* in 2010. Pam and her partner, Ken, live in Denver. Their blended family includes six daughters, multiple grandchildren, a dog, and a cat. Please visit/contact her at www.pamelanowak.com or on Facebook.